"Just a minute," Paris said, holding back when Randy would have run on

"You know, you've completely lost your cardio momentum," he said, jogging in place.

"And you've lost your mind. Why did you tell your friends I was coming to the picnic when you haven't mentioned it to me?"

"Because if I go with a woman, they won't spend all afternoon trying to fix me up. Please, Paris. Help me out here."

Paris gave him a dirty look and jogged off. She hated to admit that there was something delicious about the ground flying under her feet, the sweet air filling her lungs and a strong man beside her, looking wonderful in his T-shirt and shorts.

"I'll get you for this," she threatened so that he wouldn't see her pleasure in the moment.

He cast her a glance, his expression curious. "I think you've already got me."

Dear Reader,

As a nondriver, I take cabs a lot and have found cabdrivers to be the most interesting people. One of our local companies is owned by a woman who employs her daughter and another woman I know. I love riding with them. Not that male drivers aren't also interesting, but it's always nice to have a woman-to-woman conversation while watching the scenery go by.

When I was looking for a way to extend our MEN OF MAPLE HILL series, I remembered that I'd made casual mention in a previous book of two sisters who came home after their dreams were short-circuited and now owned a cab company. I had intended that little tidbit to simply give texture to that moment, but now appreciated that it held story potential. So many of our paths in life are taken because other carefully made plans fall through and we're forced to search for a new direction. What better way to do that than with other people on a journey, sitting in the back seat of your cab?

Hope you enjoy riding with Paris and Prue.

Sincerely,

Muriel

Man in a Million
Muriel Jensen

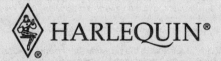

TORONTO • NEW YORK • LONDON
AMSTERDAM • PARIS • SYDNEY • HAMBURG
STOCKHOLM • ATHENS • TOKYO • MILAN • MADRID
PRAGUE • WARSAW • BUDAPEST • AUCKLAND

ISBN 0-373-71172-7

MAN IN A MILLION

Copyright © 2003 by Muriel Jensen.

All rights reserved. Except for use in any review, the reproduction or
utilization of this work in whole or in part in any form by any electronic,
mechanical or other means, now known or hereafter invented, including
xerography, photocopying and recording, or in any information storage
or retrieval system, is forbidden without the written permission of the
publisher, Harlequin Enterprises Limited, 225 Duncan Mill Road,
Don Mills, Ontario M3B 3K9, Canada.

All characters in this book have no existence outside the imagination of
the author and have no relation whatsoever to anyone bearing the same
name or names. They are not even distantly inspired by any individual
known or unknown to the author, and all incidents are pure invention.

This edition published by arrangement with Harlequin Books S.A.

® and TM are trademarks of the publisher. Trademarks indicated with
® are registered in the United States Patent and Trademark Office, the
Canadian Trade Marks Office and in other countries.

Visit us at www.eHarlequin.com

Printed in U.S.A.

To Paul and Tiana and the gang at the Urban Cafe.
Thanks for the wonderful food and the even better company.

Books by Muriel Jensen

HARLEQUIN SUPERROMANCE
422—TRUST A HERO
468—BRIDGE TO YESTERDAY
512—IN GOOD TIME
589—CANDY KISSES
683—HUSBAND IN A HURRY
751—THE FRAUDULENT FIANCÉE
764—THE LITTLE MATCHMAKER
825—FIRST BORN SON
842—SECOND TO NONE
880—THE THIRD WISE MAN
1000—"HOME, HEARTH AND HAYLEY"
        (a story in the anthology ALL SUMMER LONG)
1033—MAN WITH A MISSION*
1056—MAN WITH A MESSAGE*
1093—MAN WITH A MIRACLE*

*Men of Maple Hill

Don't miss any of our special offers. Write to us at the
following address for information on our newest releases.

Harlequin Reader Service
U.S.: 3010 Walden Ave., P.O. Box 1325, Buffalo, NY 14269
Canadian: P.O. Box 609, Fort Erie, Ont. L2A 5X3

CHAPTER ONE

PARIS O'HARA WAS SERIOUSLY tempted to run in the other direction. This was not about being rude, she told herself. This was about taking charge of her life, clearing the decks, pulling it together. If Randy Sanford's feelings were hurt in the process, she wasn't to be blamed. She had to let him know where she stood.

It was all Addy Whitcomb's fault. If she wasn't so determined to turn every unattached man working for Whitcomb's Wonders—her son's formidable collective—and every single woman in Maple Hill, Massachusetts, into one half of a happy relationship, Paris wouldn't be hiding behind her cab and mustering her courage.

She'd peeked around the corner just a moment ago and seen Randy Sanford in the driveway of the fire station, washing down the red-and-white ambulance in which he and his partner responded to emergencies.

Paris's friend, Mariah Trent, had pointed him out at a school fund-raiser. He was short and portly and clearly the life of the party. Everyone around him had been laughing.

Had it been a year ago, and had Randy Sanford been more serious, Paris might have caved in to

Addy's insistence that they meet. But it wasn't. It was now. And nothing in her life was funny.

Paris peeked around the corner again.

The timing was perfect. One of the fire trucks was being serviced, and the other was being used to conduct a demonstration on fire safety at the elementary school. Except for a skeleton crew of firemen shooting hoops on the other side of the building, her quarry was alone.

Russell Watson's voice blared from inside the ambulance and Randy lip-synched ''Va Pensiero'' as Paris squared her shoulders, marched around the corner and stopped beside him. ''Randy Sanford?'' she asked.

He opened his mouth to reply, then raised his index finger in a ''just-a-minute'' gesture as he crossed the driveway and turned off the water. She followed him.

The moment he straightened away from the faucet, she offered her hand and what she hoped was a warm smile. ''Hi, I'm Paris O'Hara,'' she shouted over the music. ''That's my favorite CD, too. We've never been formally introduced, but Addy Whitcomb's been trying to get us together for months. I apologize on her behalf for putting you through that. She means well, of course, but she's so convinced that man can't live without woman and vice versa, that she doesn't understand 'no' when she hears it, and I've certainly said it to her enough times.''

As he studied her closely, apparently waiting for her to get to the point, she noticed that he had very nice brown eyes and a very sweet face. She wasn't much for buzz cuts, but it seemed to suit him. She followed him back to the ambulance as he ran around the vehicle, reached through the open window and turned off the music.

He came back to her and opened his mouth again to speak, but she forestalled him, remembering that the last words she'd spoken had not been very complimentary. She was afraid he'd misinterpret the point she was trying to make.

"Not that I have anything against you, personally. I mean, I gather you've been resisting her efforts to bring us together, too, because there was that one time when I'd driven the fourth-grade class to Boston because the usual bus driver was sick, and I came home so exhausted, I couldn't think of a ready excuse to turn her down when she said you were coming to her house for dinner that night. But, then, she called me a half hour later and told me *you'd* backed out." She winked at him. "I think you even volunteered to take over someone else's shift so you could avoid me." She laughed.

When he continued to look dismayed, she cleared her throat. "Look, the truth is it's clear you don't want to date me any more than I want to date you."

He blinked and folded his arms and she added quickly, "Not that you're not perfectly…appealing and…and… But I'm just not relationship material, you know what I mean? It's hard to…to…want to get to know someone else, particularly a man, when you're not even sure who you are." Then, wishing she hadn't even let that fact surface, she tried to cover it up. "Oh, I'm Paris O'Hara, of course. We both know that. But I mean—know myself in a Zen sort of way. Do you understand?"

He looked as though she'd fried his brain. She shifted uncomfortably, hating that the strong, secure woman she'd always been turned into a chatty idiot when trying to explain herself. And she'd done that a lot lately because she really *didn't* know who she was—in a Zen sort of way or any other way.

She put a hand on his arm, desperately trying to make a friend of him rather than an enemy.

"Randy, I'm sorry. I seem to be…" She stopped abruptly when she noticed something she hadn't seen at all until this moment. Until she'd finally focused on him instead of her garbled explanation, which had seemed like such a good idea this morning when she'd been determined to get control of her life, but now seemed ill-advised and pitiful.

He was wearing a wedding ring.

She looked into those nice brown eyes. "You're married?" she asked in disbelief. What was Addy thinking?

Then she caught a glimpse of amusement that moved from his eyes to tug at the corner of his mouth. "Yes, I am," he replied. "But I'm not Randy Sanford."

RANDY HAD BEEN LISTENING since he'd heard his name early in the conversation. Taking inventory in the back of the rig, he'd remained undetected, his attention captured by Paris O'Hara's long, shapely legs and trim but nicely rounded backside clad in brown cords as she paced by the open back doors. Pale blond hair was tucked into a messy knot on top of her head, long strands like spider webbing brushed the shoulder of a rose-colored shirt.

So, this was Paris O'Hara. He listened in amusement as poor Chilly stared at her, clearly confused. Randy couldn't imagine how this misunderstanding had occurred, but he had to admit that he was enjoying it—fully appreciating how Neanderthal that was.

Curiously, he could relate to everything she was saying. He hadn't wanted to meet her, either, had also said a loud, clear "no" to Addy's eager invitations. Including that one time when Evan's wife had accepted a dinner date for him and he'd had to call and decline. That must have been the day Paris had driven the schoolkids to Boston.

He'd felt guilty about it. He never deliberately hurt anyone—physically or emotionally. But he knew in his heart there'd never be another Jenny Brewster. Even almost two years after her death and his move to Maple Hill, she was often on his mind. So, while he usually accepted Addy's invitations, and showed her candidates a good time, he never called them again.

And Paris O'Hara looked too much like Jenny for comfort. At least at a distance. Evan Braga had pointed her out one day when they'd gone to the Breakfast Barn for lunch and she'd stopped in to get a coffee to go. Randy wasn't dealing well with the loss of his fiancée, and anything that brought back thoughts of her—like long, blond hair—was unwelcome. Though now that he was able to inspect her more closely, he saw that she was several inches taller than Jenny, more slender, except for a nice flare to her hips. Her hair was almost platinum, not the gold Jenny's had been.

He would have remained hidden, happy to let Chilly handle the misunderstanding, but then she noticed his partner's wedding ring. Now Chill was stammering, trying to explain.

Randy stepped out, determined to react in a gentlemanly manner to her mistake, agree with her dismissal of the possibility of any relationship between them, then laugh it all off with Chilly when she walked away.

Until he saw her face.

Jenny had had a softly round, cute sort of face in which every sweet and lively quality she possessed shone like a candle. It had made him feel happy and loved.

Paris O'Hara's face should have been pretty but wasn't. She had a small, nicely shaped nose and a wide mouth with even teeth. Her perfect oval of a face glowed with a peaches-and-cream complexion. But beauty was in the eyes, and though hers were mossy green and thickly lashed, they were worried, as if she anticipated trouble. She didn't seem afraid of it precisely, just uncertain about it.

She had doubts about herself, he guessed, and took no pains to hide it behind wiles or makeup. So the face that should have been stunning was simply interesting instead. He was surprised by how much that attracted him.

And—he was sure he wasn't imagining this—a glimpse of sexual interest disturbed that worried look as she stared at him.

She seemed to consider him a moment before a grim sort of dismissal came into her eyes even as Randy prepared to introduce himself.

"This—" Chilly began.

"You're Randy Sanford," she said, sticking out her hand. He liked the way she refused to be embarrassed. He caught a whiff of jasmine.

"Yes," he said, taking her long, slender fingers in his. They were cool and her grip was firm. He liked that, too.

"I was just explaining to—"

"Chilly," he supplied for her. "Percival Childress. You can see why we call him Chilly."

Chilly, who hated his pretentious first name, rolled his eyes.

She cast him a gentle smile. "I knew it had nothing to do with his personality."

Chilly nodded modest acceptance of the compliment.

"I was starting to explain that he was pointed out to me at the spaghetti feed at the school," she said.

He remembered the event. He and Chilly had gone together after a day of painting Chilly's garage.

"We were sitting side by side," Randy said, realizing what had caused her confusion.

Apparently she did, too. "When my friend pointed, I thought she was pointing to Chilly. My mistake."

"No harm done. But even though you thought he has a warm personality," he taunted gently, "you didn't want to date him."

He watched her blink, fascinated. "He's married."

"But before you knew that, you were giving him this big long story about—"

"I was explaining that I'm busy." A little flicker of annoyance had appeared in her eyes and her voice. Her interest in him was definitely waning.

"No." He didn't know why he was taking issue with her claim. A moment ago, he'd have been grateful for the easy escape from Addy's manipulations. Something about her was having an unusual effect on him. He didn't know what, but it was pushing him— and there was nowhere to go but toward her. "That's not what you said. You said you didn't know yourself. In a Zen sort of way, whatever that means."

She was absolutely still. He felt sure that was an indication of true annoyance.

"It's intuition arrived at through meditation," she said stiffly.

"Oh, I know what it is," he replied. "I just wonder about the wisdom of meditating over one's self. You'd miss everything going on around you."

She expelled a breath—some safety-valve thing, he was sure. "You don't know how to react to what's around you," she said with forced calm, "without self-knowledge."

"Aren't women supposed to have intuition without needing meditation?"

"I believe Zen implies a certain enlightenment."

"But don't you look for that to come from outside rather than inside?"

She dropped her arms impatiently. He felt the air stir around him. "You don't know anything about me!" she snapped at him, as though his argument had been an accusation.

Quite accidentally, though, the argument seemed to have gotten him where he wanted to go.

"And I never will, will I, if you don't want to go out with me."

She stared at him. Even Chilly looked at him in surprise.

All the times he'd ever said he wanted nothing to do with women on a permanent basis echoed in his ears. Well, he didn't want anything to do with her on a permanent basis. But he didn't appreciate being dismissed so easily, and wondered what was going on inside her that made her look so troubled. And why it interested him.

It was scientific, he decided finally. That was it. Women were all so cool and contained these days, except for this one, who looked as though a tempest spun inside her.

He smiled. "I think you should reconsider."

PARIS FELT NAKED. He was absolutely right; she'd told herself the same thing over and over. She was thinking this to death. She'd been focused completely on herself since she'd discovered that she wasn't who she thought she was and retired home to Maple Hill. She knew that wasn't healthy, but everyone had the right to the details of their parentage. How was one expected to march into the future without understanding where one came from?

And how had Randy Sanford guessed within sixty seconds of looking into her face that she was on a long personal search?

She looked into dark brown eyes in an angular face, nicely shaped eyebrows raised in question, waiting for her answer. He was tall, square-shouldered and flat-stomached in the dark pants and white shirt that were the EMTs' uniform. His sleeves were rolled up, revealing nicely shaped arms.

For an instant, she was distracted by the impression he made of strength and solidity. He looked as though a truck could hit him and would bounce back with its hood dented, leaving him uninjured. For a woman who felt exhausted by the vagaries of life and the strain of business, the temptation to lean in his direction and test that strength was hard to resist.

But she did. She tossed her hair and smiled flatly. It didn't matter how solid he was, her foundation was completely gone. And she suspected that all she'd done was hurt his male pride. This wasn't serious interest, just a knee-jerk reaction to rejection.

"I don't think I'll reconsider," she replied good-naturedly, then stuck out her hand. "No hard feelings?"

He considered her a moment, then took her hand. "Of course not," he said. "Nice to finally meet you."

"You, too." She waved at Chilly, who'd walked away to give them privacy.

Chilly waved back. "Sorry," he said. "If I wasn't married, I'd make you change your mind. And if I was Randy Sanford."

"Can't be done," she said.

She started to walk away, but Randy caught her arm. Certain he intended to try to charm her into going out with him, she tried to draw away. Then she noticed that his eyes were focused on hers and frowning. There was a professional air in his touch as he put a hand to her chin and turned it right, then left.

"Are you getting enough rest?" he asked.

She was surprised by the question. She worked long hours and never slept well. But she'd pinched her cheeks and carefully brushed her hair today before coming to see him. Perversely, though she didn't want to date him or anyone, she wanted to look her best while telling him so.

She found herself fumbling for an answer. "I...I put in a twelve-hour day."

"No time for fun?"

"No," she said, hoping to put an end to the conversation.

His thumb rubbed gently under her left eye. "You should make time. You're too young for dark circles."

His touch was cool, and she was momentarily paralyzed by it. Solid. *And* tender. No time for that, either.

She caught his muscular wrist and yanked it away from her. "You have no idea how old I am," she said, shocked by the annoyance she felt. Probably because she'd looked in the mirror that very morning and thought she looked matronly.

"You're twenty-six," he said. "You live at home with your mom and your sister, and you own the Berkshire Cab company."

She knew she looked astonished.

"Addy told me." He grinned. "Why? Did you think I'd hired detectives or done an Internet search on you?"

While she continued to stare, wondering why Addy hadn't told her such details about him, he went on. "You left Maple Hill for law school about four years ago, then changed your mind and came home last year. But she didn't tell me why." He seemed to rethink that information, then asked with sharpened interest, "Does that have anything to do with why you're on this soul search?"

She noticed two things simultaneously. She was still holding his wrist, which he was allowing her to do with no resistance. And she could feel his pulse under her thumb. Curiously, it seemed to be causing hers to race.

She dropped his wrist and said with all the cool hauteur she could muster, "That's not your concern. I have to go."

"Don't fall asleep behind the wheel," he cautioned, following her to the station wagon with its magnetic sign bearing the name of her company in bright yellow letters.

She gave him a dismissing look as she pulled open the door. "I'm more responsible than that."

He held the door open for her as she slipped behind the wheel. "Exhaustion can sneak up on you," he warned. "A dark patch of road, the hum of the motor, the warmth of—"

"Thank you," she said, and pulled the door closed. Without hesitation, she turned the key in the ignition and drove away.

She groaned aloud, the sound filling the confined space inside her car. "You can't get some men to give a darn that you've got a problem!" she grumbled. "And others come off all pompous and superior because they think they can read your mind and know what's bothering you on five minutes' acquaintance." Equally annoying. She was going to have to talk to Addy about the amount of information she dispensed about her. In fact, she was going to have to get tough with her about this whole blind-date thing.

Now that she'd seen Randy Sanford, she definitely didn't want to date him. Her life was too much of a mess already to add another untidy element. Because she was sure that despite his well-groomed good looks, there was nothing relaxed and easy about him.

"INTERESTING WOMAN." Chilly came to stand beside Randy as he watched her car disappear down the highway.

"Yeah," Randy agreed, trapped in the vivid memory of her standing in front of him, pale and cool and smelling of jasmine.

"*You're* interested?"

Randy forced himself back to reality. He'd loved Jenny and lost her to one of life's dirty tricks. They'd been young and hopeful, with a lifetime of plans in front of them, then she was gone within four months of a brutal diagnosis. He'd been interning at a county hospital, full of new knowledge and proud of all modern medicine had to offer. But it hadn't been enough to help Jenny.

"No," he said to Chilly, heading back into the ambulance bay. The shadows, he hoped, would hide the hopelessness that always overwhelmed him when he thought of her.

"You looked interested," Chilly persisted. "And—you know—it's time."

"It's never going to be time." He went through the bay to the office, aware that their afternoon break was overdue. He needed caffeine. Badly. "And if I look interested, it's only…scientific, you know? What gave her that troubled look coupled with that cool exterior?"

Chilly followed him. "You told her she was too young for dark circles," he reminded him. "That sounds pretty personal. I say you're too young to give up on marriage and family."

"I haven't given up," he said, grinning at Kitty Morton, who answered the phones and did most of their paperwork. She was in her early thirties, had two little boys and an ex-husband who hadn't paid child support since he'd walked out on her. She was blond and pretty and he was always surprised by her optimism.

"Then, why'd you let her get away?"

He turned the grin on his friend. "Because she expected me to try to stop her. You never get anywhere with a woman doing what she expects."

Kitty looked at him with a frown. "Who told you that? That's totally false. Particularly if she's expecting chocolates and diamonds and stuff like that. Who are we talking about, anyway?"

"Paris, um…" Chilly began, groping for her last name.

"O'Hara," Randy provided. "We're going for coffee, Kitty. Want us to bring you back something?"

Kitty was still focused on the woman under discussion. Her eyes widened and she leaned toward them, her arms folded on her desk. "The cabbie? She's something, isn't she? Everybody wonders why she came home from school and started the cab company. She was so set on being a lawyer. Her mom was a model, you know, then an actress. She's on a shoot in Africa right now for some new line of designer clothes for older women. And her sister was married to some senator, or something, and she found him fooling around and came back about the same time Paris did. Those women remind me of the Gabors. They're so beautiful, and they live in that wonderful old Craftsman bungalow on this side of the lake. Well, Paris isn't beautiful, but I think she's mysterious and fascinating.''

Randy studied her. ''How do you know all this stuff?'' Kitty knew everything about everyone.

''I'm in Addy Whitcomb's quilting group. What she doesn't know, she finds out.''

Randy rolled his eyes. ''Of course. I understand even CNN goes to Addy when they want to confirm information. You want coffee? A doughnut, or something?''

Kitty shook her head. ''Thanks. I've got a date tonight and I have to fit into my leather skirt.''

Randy and Chilly, headed for the door, stopped. ''I thought we had clearance rights on all your dates,'' Chilly said. ''Who is this guy, and how come we don't know about him?''

''He's Mike Miller, the new guy on nights,'' she supplied, her cheeks becoming a little pink. ''And he works his days off for Whitcomb's Wonders, just like you two. That makes him sort of preapproved.''

Hank Whitcomb, Addy's son, had begun a sort of temp agency for craftsmen several years ago that now provided a broad variety of services for the homeowner or businessman. Whitcomb's Wonders provided plumbing, electrical work, carpentry, gardening, furnace maintenance and a variety of other services. Randy worked with the janitorial crew on his days off. Chilly was on the gardening team. The simple work was a welcome relief from the life-and-death pressure of being a paramedic.

It was a boon for all of them to work part-time

while going to school, raising children or living other dreams.

"What's he do?" Randy asked.

"Carpentry," she replied. "Jackie Whitcomb assures me he's a gentleman. He redid the cabinets in their kitchen."

Jackie was Hank's wife and the mayor of Maple Hill. Her judgment could be trusted.

"Okay, then," Chilly said. "But we want a full report tomorrow."

"We'll see." The telephone rang and she picked it up. They waited to see if they were needed. She put a hand over the receiver. "It's Mark and Charlie. They're finished at the school and on their way back. Go have your coffee."

Randy and Chilly loped across the lawn, headed for the bakery a block away. Randy glanced back in the direction of the driveway, absently wondering if the newly washed ambulance left sufficient room for the vehicle returning from the school, when he noticed a dark object on the pavement. He veered toward it and saw that it was black leather and shaped like an envelope. A light chain attached to it had a broken link on one end.

"What is that?" Chilly asked as Randy bent to pick it up. "Looks like a trucker's wallet."

Randy turned it over in his hand and, seeing no identification, unsnapped it and looked inside.

There were quite a few bills in it, some of small denomination, but a few twenties, and a lot of change.

Glued to the inside of the flap was a business card with the Berkshire Cab telephone numbers on it.

"Ah," Chilly said, looking over his shoulder. "It belongs to the lovely Miss O'Hara. What's that?" He pointed to something tucked behind the bills.

Randy pulled out a foil wrapper that had been folded over. It was half of a chocolate bar. "Seems the lady has a chocolate habit."

"Is that the first of your scientific observations?" Chilly asked with a grin.

Randy snapped the leather envelope closed. "I'll take it back to Kitty. I'm sure the first time the lady tries to make change this afternoon, she'll notice her missing wallet and call."

Chilly snickered and followed as Randy hurried back to the office door, ran inside with the wallet and explained briefly to Kitty what had happened. "I don't know," he said when Randy reemerged. "It was weird. She stared at you as though she couldn't believe you were real, yet she couldn't wait to get away from you."

"There's money involved—she'll call." Randy started off again for the bakery. "And I do have this sort of mesmerizing effect on women. They can't help but stare at me."

Chilly responded to his teasingly conceited claim with the same matter-of-factness. "You have a similar effect on men, actually. We all thought evolution had filtered out the ugly and stupid, and yet, here you are. It makes one stare."

"That's it," Randy replied. "Coffee's on you."

CHAPTER TWO

PARIS HAD NOTICED HER wallet was missing when she dropped off old Mr. Kubik at the senior center. He paid his fare with exact change and gave her a quarter tip—a routine he'd followed every week for eight months. She had a standing order to pick him up every Tuesday afternoon. She went to slip the money in the wallet always tucked under her right leg on the seat, but it wasn't there.

She felt a moment's panic. It had been a good day. She'd had that trip to Springfield, the generous Shriners on a tour of New England after their conference in Boston, and a lot of short hops from the nursing home that helped her make up in volume what the seniors couldn't pay in tips.

She struggled to remember where she'd been, then concluded she had to have lost it at the fire station. She'd changed a twenty for Starla McAffrey and she'd had it then. Her next stop had been the fire station. Then she'd picked up Mr. Kubik.

Well. She wasn't going back there. Prue, who drove whenever Paris needed a break, had promised to drive a few hours for her tonight while she made some phone calls. When her sister, Prue, had first returned home, she'd driven a full shift, but business was slow at night, and she'd taken a job at a dress shop instead. Paris would charm her into stopping to pick up the wallet.

Paris then remembered she was supposed to pick up her sister at the library in—she glanced at her watch—ten minutes. She would have to brace herself as she always did to deal with the misnamed Prudence. It was easier when their mother was home. Prudence took after Camille Malone with her bright beauty and her mercurial personality. They always had a lot to talk about, which left the quieter Paris to attend to the practical side of their existence. She did the grocery shopping, paid bills, kept up the checkbook.

She'd never minded that her mother and sister were beautiful and that she was simply passably pretty with a talent for steadiness and responsibility. It meant she took after her father, Jasper O'Hara, a kind and practical man who'd kept their lives together while Camille acted in New York or modeled in L.A. He'd been an accountant and he'd died of a coronary five years before.

Then that comforting sense of who she was exploded a year ago when she was taking an investigations class that involved blood testing and blood typing. She'd tested her own blood and discovered she was type A, scientifically impossible when both her parents were type O. Several years ago, her parents had given blood at a Red Cross blood drive and her father had come home joking that they were "Oh, oh,'' giving it the inflection that suggested trouble. He'd said that that exclamation usually applied to everything they did.

It certainly applied at that moment when she tested her blood a second and then a third time. She couldn't be Jasper O'Hara's daughter.

She'd rushed home that weekend to confront her mother about it and watched the color drain from her face. Her mother had sat her on the sofa and explained that she was the result of an affair she'd had with a bit actor just before she met Jasper O'Hara.

''Why didn't you tell me?'' she'd demanded.

''Because I married Jasper before you were born and he's truly been your father. There was no need. We were happy. You were happy. It was…irrelevant.''

Irrelevant? Paris had wanted to argue but had been too shocked to find the right words, the right questions.

''You are who you are,'' her mother had insisted, ''and it doesn't matter a damn who your father was. Besides,'' she'd added, almost as an afterthought, ''he's dead. He was killed in a car accident right after you were born.''

Paris had insisted on a name.

''Jeffrey St. John,'' her mother had finally revealed. ''He's dead, Paris. It doesn't matter. Jasper O'Hara was your father.''

Paris had gone back to school but found herself unable to focus on her studies. She felt as though the very foundation of her life was cracked and unable to support the future she'd planned.

She'd come home, needing a dose of the stability of her old life before she could decide what to do about her future. She knew that didn't make sense because her old life was based on her mother's fabrication. But even though Jasper O'Hara hadn't been her biological father, he'd been her biggest fan, and there was comfort in being where he'd been.

It saddened her to think that the steadiness that she'd always thought had come from him hadn't. So where had it come from? A bit actor? Somehow, that seemed unlikely.

She reached instinctively for the chocolate stash in her wallet, forgetting that it was at the fire station. Great. Broke and without chocolate. Life was a cruel master.

With no pickups pending, Paris pulled into a parking spot across from the Common to wait for Prue.

The sight of the Maple Hill Square, or Common, had a grounding effect on her. Life here went on very much as it had two hundred years ago, though the *Maple Hill Mirror* had up-to-the-minute equipment instead of the old labor-intensive printing method that required inking by hand and rolling one sheet at a time. The early residents of the town had never heard of the mochaccinos produced at the Perk Avenue Tea Room down the way, and would have been horrified by the lengths of the skirts in the dress shop window.

Otherwise, the restored colonial buildings that framed the square looked the same, a colonial flag flew, and Caleb and Elizabeth Drake, who'd once fought the redcoats, still stood on the green, their images bronzed to remind Maple Hill of its heritage.

This was part of what she'd come home for, Paris thought. The eternity of life here, roots in the deep past, finger on the pulse of the future. To someone who felt lost, it provided a handhold on permanence.

Prue probably never felt lost. She had the temperament of an artist, but seemed always so sure of herself.

Now she was part of a committee headed by Mariah Trent to raise funds for an addition to the library and more books.

Prue met Mariah while volunteering at the Maple Hill Manor School outside of town. Mariah had once been a dorm mother there, but now had a husband and two adopted children, and was the backbone of community fund-raising.

When Prue had been living in New York with her senator husband, she'd apprenticed with Shirza Bell, a famous couturier. Prue's life long dream had been to design clothes, and though she now helped to make a living for the three of them as Paris and their mother did, she still sketched at night and designed in her dreams.

Paris was jealous of her passion—and her face, and her body, and her wonderful ease with people.

She could see her coming from across the street. Late afternoon traffic was light, but Prue Hale stood out like a flame in the cool sunlight of late September. She was several inches shorter than Paris and attractively round without looking plump. Her hair was long and golden and always flying around her in appealing disarray. She had a penchant for long skirts and sweaters, and always looked like a social butterfly on her way home from afternoon tea.

Today, her skirt was a slim gray houndstooth, and she wore a dusty-rose sweater and a brightly colored shawl with a black-and-bright-pink pattern, which hung loosely on her shoulders. She had on black leather shoes with a small heel, a matching pouch purse, and a smile Paris could read from yards away. Paris wondered if Randy Sanford would change his mind about wanting to date her if he could see Prue.

Something good had happened to her sister. Paris would have to listen to every detail as she drove her home. God, she wished she had her chocolate.

Prue pulled the front passenger door open and fell into the cab, filling the small space with the fragrance of White Diamonds.

"Hi!" Her breathy voice burst into Paris's silence. "You'll never guess what happened!"

Paris pushed away every other thought to talk to her sister. A conversation with Prue always took up all the space in her head. Randy Sanford resisted being pushed, but she pushed harder.

"What?" she asked.

"Mariah wants to have a fashion show for the fund-raiser, and guess what else?"

"What else?"

"Featuring *my* designs!"

"That's wonderful, Prue!" Paris was sincere.

Prue's face was glowing, and Paris could only imagine how much it meant to her to finally have a place to show off her clothing line. Granted, it was just a small community function, but word had a way of getting around. And after finding her husband in flagrante delicto with an intern in his office, Prue's ego needed the boost. Then Paris began to worry about the practical aspects of the opportunity. "But won't it be hard to transfer the designs to the real thing? How much time do you have?"

"A little over four weeks," Prue replied, her excitement dimming just slightly. "I thought about that. But I think I can do it. If you help me."

Pulling away from the curb, Paris was filled with trepidation. "Prue, I can't sew a stitch."

"I know, I know. I can handle that part. But I need you to model." She said those last words quickly, probably anticipating Paris's reaction.

"What?" Paris demanded, stopping right in the middle of the narrow, tree-lined road. Someone behind her honked. She drove on to the red light at the corner. "Are you crazy? I don't know a thing—"

"You don't have to know anything," Prue argued eagerly, "you just have to have the body, and you do. You're perfect. Tall, slender, long legs, great hair. You'll be perfect."

Paris stared at the passing traffic and determined that God had to be paying her back for all the tricks she'd played on Prue in their youth. Her little sister had been trusting and gullible, and it had been easy to convince her that candy was poisonous and should always be tested by a big sister, that curly hair reflected dishonesty that could only be overcome if the curls were cut off, that she'd been left as a baby at the secondhand store where their mother and father had bought her for a bargain.

Curious, Paris thought now, that *she* might have been the one abandoned to someone else's mercy, considering her doubtful beginning.

"Prue, I'll only embarrass you," she pleaded.

"You will not," Prue insisted. "And I've been thinking about it. I knew you'd need incentive, so I thought we'd make a deal."

A deal? Oh, this couldn't be good.

"I'll design and sew during the day," she bargained, "then drive for you from four to midnight, if you'll do this for me. You can make more money if Berkshire Cab is available from nine to twelve. There are all those people going home from late meetings who hate to drive after dark, or in the wind and rain."

"But *you'll* be driving after dark. And the wind and rain will be here before you know it. I don't like it." It would be nice to be able to expand her hours, but 6:00 a.m. to 6:00 p.m. was the best she could do alone. "And what about your job at the dress shop?"

Prue sighed. "Patsy's closing up. I've got my walking papers. Will's been transferred to New Jersey and they'll be gone in a couple of weeks. I need employment, anyway." She hesitated a moment, then added, "And you wouldn't deprive me of this chance, would you?" Prue's tone contained just the right element of little-sister pleading.

Paris groaned. "Prue, I'll model for you, but you don't have to drive for me."

"Yes, I do," Prue insisted. "Nobody's complained that I took a simple minimum-wage job so I could continue to play with my designs. Well, this is my chance to make something of them and make a bigger contribution to the household. Please don't argue with me. I'm starting tonight, anyway, right? You have calls to make, or something?"

"Prudie..."

"You'll have to cut back on the chocolates until after the show," Prue said.

Paris groaned. "You could have told me that before I agreed."

"Not if I wanted you to help me."

"One thing."

"Yeah?"

"I think I dropped my cab wallet at the fire station. Would you mind picking it up tonight?"

Determined to look casual, Paris stared at the road as she felt Prue turn to look at her. "What were you doing there?"

"I...had a fare."

"A fireman called a cab when they have those great trucks to ride in?"

Paris ignored her, concentrating on the turn that would take her to Lake Road.

"Did you go to see that EMT Addy Whitcomb's trying so hard to fix you up with?" Prue said it teasingly, but when Paris didn't reply and her color rose instead, Prue shifted in her seat and asked excitedly, "You did?"

"Just to tell him that I wasn't interested in dating him," she corrected quickly, "and to assure him that I knew he didn't want to date me, either. I've... I'm just clearing the decks. I'm tired of my life being this mass of confusion."

Prue was silent for a moment. "Is this the thing about your father again?"

"I've just got to get some answers," Paris said with a shrug of her shoulder, "and it'll be easier while Mom's gone because I know how she hates my interest in it. I know you don't understand." She forestalled her sister's protest with a raised hand. "I don't expect you to. Just let me do what I have to do without criticism, okay?"

"I wasn't going to criticize," Prue assured her. "I was going to tell you that I understand what motivates you. If the man I'd thought was my father my whole life turned out not to be, I'd want some answers, too. I just don't understand why you think it'll change anything. He's dead."

Paris blinked, a little surprised by Prue's empathy. "I know. I just want to know more than Mom's willing to tell me."

"Okay. But a search for details about your father doesn't mean you have to dismiss the possibility of having an interesting man in your life, does it?"

"He doesn't want me, either. He apparently has his own reasons for avoiding Addy's romantic maneuvers."

Prue nodded knowingly. "His fiancée died."

Paris glanced at her sister. "How do you know that?"

"Mariah knows him. He works for Whitcomb's Wonders, you know. He's on a janitorial crew that services her husband's building. Randy and his fiancée had been through medical school together and were interning in the same hospital when she got cancer."

"Jeez."

"Yeah. What did you think of him?"

That was hard to simplify into words. He was handsome, annoying but oddly appealing, a little bossy, yet seemingly concerned for her welfare. She didn't know how she felt about him—just that an image of him lingered in her mind.

"Um..." She shrugged again, trying to minimize his impact on her. "Nice-looking, thinks he knows everything, tries to be charming. You know, typical guy."

"I don't think he's very typical. Mariah says she saw him save a man's life at the gym. The man collapsed on a treadmill, wasn't breathing, and he brought him back. The ER doctor said he wouldn't have made it if Randy hadn't been there. I know it's what he's trained to do, but Mariah thought it was pretty amazing close-up."

Paris could imagine that that was where his confidence came from. Saving a life was pretty big stuff.

"About the wallet..." She tried to divert the conversation.

"I'll get it. But you can search for information about your father," Prue insisted, "and still get to know Randy."

Paris pulled into the driveway of their home and left the motor running, turning to her sister with a firm expression. "If you pressure me and cause me stress," she warned, "I'm liable to turn to chocolate. And if you expect me to wear that red wool thing you showed me the sketch of the other day…"

"All right, all right," Prue said defeatedly. "I just think if you're presented with the gift of a nice guy with romance on his mind, you should take it. But what do I know? Thanks for the lift. I'll take over for you at four."

"Six," Paris corrected. "Have a good dinner, be sure to fix yourself a thermos of coffee, and I'll turn the cab over to you. If you promise you'll keep in touch throughout the night."

"I promise."

"All right. See you at six."

"Do I get to say ten-four?"

"No."

CHILLY HAD ALREADY GONE home to his wife, and Randy had finished restocking their vehicle and was in the office, checking out, when he noticed the leather wallet with the broken chain still sitting on Kitty's desk. There was no note on it to indicate that Kitty had spoken to its owner, a procedure she usually followed when something was left in an ambulance.

Randy opened it, consulted the business card inside

the flap and dialed the number. He would show Paris O'Hara that he could be businesslike even if she couldn't.

A familiar voice answered. "Miss O'Hara?" he asked.

"Ah...used to be," the voice replied. "Now I'm Mrs. Hale. Actually, that's not quite right because I *used* to be that, too. But I'm not anymore."

Good grief. Her sister? Did everyone in her family think everything to death?

"Berkshire Cab?" He tried another tack.

"Yes," the voice replied. "Always Safe, Always Friendly." She recited the slogan on the business card. "Can I pick you up?"

Now, there was a line a man liked to hear. Well, most men did. With his determination to have relationships on his terms, he had to be selective.

God, he was sounding just like the O'Hara sisters.

"I'm calling from the Maple Hill Fire Station," he said. "We have your wallet."

"Aah." There was something speculative in the quiet way she drew out the word. "Randy Sanford?"

"Yes," he replied.

"My sister asked me to pick it up, but I've been busy since I came on. I'll be there in about ten minutes."

He met her in the driveway so that she wouldn't have to get out of the cab. But she seemed to want to. She leaped out from behind the wheel and offered her hand with a warm smile.

"Prudence O'Hara Hale," she said as he shook her

hand. "I guess if I just use both names, I don't have to explain as much." She laughed over her earlier dithering.

"You don't have to explain at all," he said, handing her the wallet. "I'm just a stranger, trying to return something your sister dropped."

"Ah, but you're not a stranger at all," she corrected him, accepting the wallet. "Thank you. Addy makes you sound like a cross between George Clooney and the surgeon general."

He had to laugh at that. Addy was enthusiastic about her matchmaking avocation.

"I suppose my sister came on all cool and distant," Prudence guessed, opening the wallet and peering inside.

"She did," he agreed.

She glanced up at him. "She's really not like that at all. She's usually very warm and open, but she's got a crisis going at the moment."

He nodded. "Don't we all."

"I'm sorry about your fiancée," she said without warning. It always unsettled him when someone brought it up when he wasn't expecting it. Often conversations led that way and he was prepared. But sometimes he wasn't.

"Thank you," he replied, wondering where she'd learned that information. Addy?

"Mariah Trent is a friend of mine, too," she explained. "She's also hoping you and Paris give each other a chance."

"Your sister was pretty adamant that she wasn't interested."

"She lied," Prue said as though completely convinced that was true. "She was a little flustered after she left here. Paris is never flustered."

"Really."

"Yes. She thought you were handsome and charming. She tried not to make it sound as though those were good things, but I think they made an impact on her. And she's trying to ignore it because she's struggling right now."

He wasn't sure if it was okay to ask what she was struggling with. Then deciding honesty had always served him better than calculation, he asked, "A man?"

She smiled, but there was curiously little humor in it. "Yes, but not in the way you'd think. She could use a friend. Sometimes a man understands what a devoted mother and sister just don't get."

That was cryptic. He wasn't really into mysterious women. He liked them openhearted and easy to understand. Still, this woman was warm yet distant—a contradiction in terms. There was that scientific element that fascinated him despite his usual preferences to the contrary.

"You didn't eat the chocolate," Prue noted, closing the wallet.

"I thought it was probably as important to her as the money."

Prue grinned. "Even more so at the moment. I'm a dress designer on the side, and she's going to model for me at a library benefit. I made her promise to cut way back on chocolate.''

He raised an eyebrow. ''I thought she looked pretty great.''

''I'll tell her you said that.'' She offered her hand again. ''I have to tell you I'm now officially on Addy's side. Nice to meet you, Randy Sanford.''

''Nice to meet you,'' he replied. Though the experience was a little like being mowed down by a runaway train.

He waved her off as she drove away, then went to his car, smiling at the thought that Paris O'Hara had been flustered.

By him.

CHAPTER THREE

"THE MIRANDA POOLE AGENCY." A slightly bored voice with a pseudo British accent answered the telephone. Paris felt her courage wane. Her mother had often talked about her very first agent, and Paris had looked her up on the Internet, somewhat surprised to see that she was still in business. But would her mother's agent know about Paris's father?

She might very well know *something,* Paris answered herself with a fortifying toss of her hair. One of the few bits of information her mother had given her was that they'd been represented by the same agent. That was how they'd met.

Paris assumed a tone of voice a shade deeper and more authoritative than her usual courteous manner. "May I speak to Ms. Poole, please? This is Paris O'Hara calling."

There was a momentary pause. "Does Miss Poole represent you?"

"No, but she represented my mother some time ago."

That was almost a non sequitur, but not quite. The voice didn't seem to know what to make of it.

"Who was your mother?"

"Camille Malone."

"Hold on a moment," she advised.

A cheerful New York voice came on the line almost immediately. "Miranda Poole," she said. "Camille, is that you?"

"No," Paris replied, sitting up straight at the kitchen table to sustain her woman-in-charge attitude. It was threatening to bail on her. "This is Camille's daughter, Paris. I was wondering if you could answer a few questions for me."

"About Camille?"

"About…another actor you represented at the same time. Jeffrey St. John."

"Ah, yes," Miranda replied. "He and Camille were in the chorus of *Damn Yankees* together as I recall."

"That's him." Paris's heart thudded against her ribs. Now came the tricky part. She had to make her willing to share information without revealing that he'd gotten her mother pregnant, something her mother claimed no one had known. If she could at least confirm where he'd come from, she'd have somewhere to start in an effort to find out what kind of man he'd been. "I understand he was from Florida."

"That's right," Miranda replied. "Still is, last I heard. Got one of those photo cards from him at Christmas. He and his sons have formed a band and they're working clubs from Daytona to Miami Beach."

Still is. The words rang over and over in Paris's ears. For a moment she couldn't speak.

"Paris?" Miranda asked.

"He's..." Paris had to clear her throat and try again. "He's alive?"

"Of course he's alive. You kids, honestly. A person turns sixty and you think the warranty automatically runs out. I'm eighty-three and still placing the best talent in New York." Paris heard the sound of paper being shuffled on the other end of the line. "I don't seem to have kept his number," Miranda said, "but he shouldn't be hard to find if he's working clubs. Performers like privacy off duty, but they can't make themselves too hard to find or they won't get work. I think it was a Fort Lauderdale address."

Paris was still speechless.

"How is your mother?" Miranda asked. "She was such a game girl. Once played a pickle in one of the first commercials for Burger Bungalow. A lot of actors won't take those roles, but your mother paid her rent with whatever came her way. Not too many actors like that today."

"She's fine," Paris replied, finally regaining a fraction of her composure. "She's in Africa on a fashion shoot right now."

"She was a beautiful girl. I suppose she's matured into a handsome matron."

"She has," Paris confirmed, then thanked Miranda for her cooperation. She hung up the phone, thinking that it was a good thing her mother had experience playing a pickle, because she was going to find herself in one the moment Paris got a hold of her.

Paris paced the living room with its unobstructed view of the lake, but failed to notice the setting sun, the ducks sheltering in the reeds, the lone sailboat dawdling across the middle of the lake, its running lights streaking a pattern across the water as it moved. She usually took such pleasure in the beautiful, quiet moments when she was alone in the house without her charming but chattering mother and sister.

Tonight, all she could think about was that her mother had lied to her. Twice! First, she hadn't bothered to tell her that Jasper O'Hara was not her biological father, then, when confronted with Paris's evidence to that effect, she'd lied again, and told her her father was dead.

To think Paris had waited a year, trying to respect her mother's sensitive feelings on the subject. Only the need to pull her life together after a year of floundering had made her desperate for more information.

She couldn't believe it. What had motivated her mother to do such a thing? It wasn't as though Jeffrey St. John had been some demented villain. Certainly, the plain-spoken Miranda Poole would have said something about that.

Paris guessed that her mother decided life would be simpler without an ex-lover's involvement in it, so she'd lied.

Then she paced a little more and realized that probably wasn't true. While her mother often had the quality of a diva about her, she wasn't prone to selfish decisions.

Camille Malone O'Hara had been a beauty queen, then a model, then an actress, and a beautiful face and body were still very much a priority with her. She ate only healthy foods, worked out every day at the gym and chose her wardrobe with skill and care. And she was always after Paris and Prue to do the same.

Prue had a natural inclination to fall into step, but for Paris, all her mother's encouragement had done was remind her that she took after her father and would never be gorgeous.

So, her mother could be…superficial. But, usually, when it came to her daughters, she did everything in her power to be supportive.

Still—she'd lied twice, so maybe in regard to this particular issue, her maternal instincts could not be relied upon.

Angry and exasperated after hours of thinking about her situation and her mother, Paris tried to call her. She stopped first to try to figure out what time it was in Morocco. Five hours ahead of Boston. She glanced at her watch. It was 11:00 p.m. It would be 4:00 a.m. She didn't care and called anyway.

She sympathized for just a moment with the sleepy sound of the voice that answered the phone. Camille, she was told, had taken off with a photographer and two other models. They would be back in several days. Until then, there was no way to reach them.

"You're telling me," she asked, "that in an age of cell phones, e-mail, faxes and global positioning, they're out of touch?"

The foggy voice sighed. "Is it an emergency?"

Yes, it's an emergency! she wanted to shout. Who the hell am I? I need to know. But she understood that while it was important to her, it didn't warrant sending out a search party or otherwise alarming everyone on the shoot.

"No," she replied finally. "I'm sorry I bothered you."

"Shall I have her call you when she comes in?"

"No," she replied. "Never mind. Thank you." She could pursue this herself without her mother's help.

Prue came home an hour later and sympathized while she made tea.

"Why would Mom have lied to me again?" Paris demanded.

Prue took the boiling kettle off the stove and poured water into a fat brown teapot she'd already warmed with hot water and fitted with a loose tea infuser. Had Paris been doing it, she'd have simply poured hot water into two mugs and dunked a tea bag, but Prue was into ritual. She carried the pot to the table, put a calico cozy on it, then went back to the cupboard for china cups and saucers.

"It's pretty obvious she doesn't want you to meet him, whoever he is," Prue said frankly.

"I have a right to know who he is."

"Not if he's going to hurt you."

Paris gasped impatiently. "Prue, life isn't all about hair and makeup and cups that match the teapot! Sometimes it's messy, and if that's my life, I have a right to know."

Prue frowned at her testy remark. "Yes. I'm not telling you you don't have a right to know, I'm just speculating on why Mom won't tell you."

"Well, I'm going to call him." Paris whipped the cozy off the pot and poured the weak but steaming tea into Prue's cup, feeling guilty for snapping at her. Then she poured her own. "First thing in the morning."

"What if you get his wife, who doesn't know he fathered a child that isn't hers? Or one of his boys?"

"I'll be careful. I won't talk to anyone but him."

"Okay." Prue dipped her spoon into the sugar bowl. "Want me to drive for you in the morning so you can make the call? I'm not sure it's a good idea, but I know you'll do what you want to do, anyway."

"The truth," Paris said loftily, "is always the right thing."

"Noble," Prue acknowledged, "but probably not always right."

"You can't pick and choose with it," Paris countered.

Prue stirred the sugar into her tea. "You should go back to law school. You certainly sound like a lawyer. All black and white, right and wrong."

"Before I can do anything relating to my future,"

Paris insisted, "I have to settle this. Good or bad, I have to know. And then I can go on."

"What if it's harder than you think?"

"I can handle it." At least, that was her plan.

Prue sighed. "Well, you're a better woman than I am. I'd be happy knowing Jasper loved me like his own."

"I do love knowing that," Paris said defensively. "I just also need to know who my biological father is. Then I can reorganize my life and get somewhere with it."

"I thought you were doing pretty well. You provide a much-needed service in this town."

Paris sipped at her tea. "I like the work, but anybody could do it."

"I don't think so," Prue argued. "Not everyone would let the old folks run a tab, or keep an eye out for runaways, or take the homeless to the clinic as a service to the community."

"It's a custodial world. We're supposed to take care of one another."

Prue shook her head at her. "That's radical thinking in today's world. Well, maybe not in Maple Hill, but almost anywhere else. You certainly don't hear that kind of talk in political circles, I assure you. Except for Gideon, and that apparently was just a front."

Paris decided they'd talked enough about her problems. Prue was doing her best to be supportive, and the least she could do was return the favor. "Do you miss that life?'' she asked. ''The politics and the power parties?''

''Sometimes.'' Prue pushed away from the table and went to the cupboard for a box of thin ginger cookies she claimed were a safe indulgence. Paris thought it a crime to waste valuable calories on something that wasn't chocolate or cream-filled, but she was determined to be cooperative. She took a cookie when Prue offered her the box.

Prue fell back into her chair. ''Then I remember all the nights Gideon came home after midnight, all the plans we had to cancel at the last minute, all the things we planned to do but never got to because something more important had to be taken care of. I accepted it at the time, but now that I don't have to, I'm happy to live for me.''

''It's hard to believe,'' Paris said quietly, ''that Gideon would have done that to you. The intern, I mean.''

Prue grew defensive. She always did when Paris suggested that fooling around with an intern in their summer home in Maine was unlike her brother-in-law's straight-arrow approach to life and politics. ''You always take his side, but I saw it with my own eyes. They were on the sofa, and she was in her underwear. How else would you explain that?''

''I don't know,'' Paris replied, ''but I think I'd have asked that he try.''

''He's a politician.'' Prue's eyes filled with turbulence, and her cheeks with color—other effects Gideon's name always had on her. "He can explain away anything. I know what I saw, and no one's going to make me believe that it wasn't what it looked like." She leaned back in her chair and sighed. "Washington does that to you. The success of your cause is worth whatever it takes to accomplish it. Men wheel and deal, gain power, make life-and-death decisions for millions of people and finally come to believe that they deserve whatever they want in recompense."

Again, that didn't sound like Gideon. Paris remembered him when he was an alderman in Finchbury, a town on the other side of Springfield, and fought big money and the almost rabid historic conservationists who wanted to oust every resident and retailer in a block of old buildings downtown and turn the area into an interpretive center. He'd slaved for a year to get the funding to restore the buildings, maintain the businesses and the residences, and turn a large upstairs room into a sort of miniconvention center. Everyone praised his efforts as the perfect combination of conservation and commerce.

But Paris kept that to herself. Prue's ignition switch was always hot where her soon-to-be ex-husband was concerned.

"Well, the best revenge is living well, they say." She reached across the table to pat Prue's hand. "And you're about to become a brilliant designer." She gave her sister a small grin. "And if I'm going to have to eat these ginger things until the fashion show, you'd better move up the date."

"SAINTS AND SINNERS!" A smooth voice answered the phone just after nine the following morning. Paris had stared at the phone for a full hour before mustering the courage to dial. She'd told Prue she'd make her call at 8:00 a.m.

At eight-fifteen, Prue had anxiously checked with her. "What did he say?"

"I haven't called yet," Paris had admitted.

"I'm sorry. I'm not rushing you."

"It's all right. I'm calling now."

Prue checked again at eight-thirty.

"I still haven't done it. But I'm going to. Now."

"You're sure you want to know?"

"I'm sure."

The voice was younger than Jeffrey St. John would be, Paris felt sure. She tried to sound like a prospective client.

"I'd like to speak to Jeffrey St. John, please," she said.

"This is Jeffrey St. John," the voice replied. "Did you want to make a booking?"

"Jeffrey St. John," she asked carefully, "who was in the chorus of *Damn Yankees?*"

The voice laughed. "That was my father. But I'm in charge of our scheduling."

"I need to speak with him please," she said pleasantly, but as though she would brook no argument.

He hesitated an instant. "Well...he's on the golf course. But I can page him and have him call you."

"That would be nice, thank you," she said, and

passed on the pertinent information. Then she paced and trembled for ten minutes while waiting for the return call.

Jeffrey St. John Sr.'s voice was a little gravelly and reminded her of Tony Bennett. She imagined him in her mind's eye when she introduced herself. "I'm Paris O'Hara," she said, sounding far more confident than she felt. "I'm Camille Malone's daughter."

"Camille Malone…" St. John repeated, as though having to think about it. Paris was immediately alarmed. Would a man have to think twice about the name of a woman he'd impregnated? Of course, her mother had said she hadn't told anyone. It had never occurred to her that she might not have told *him*.

"You were in the chorus of *Damn Yankees* together," Paris reminded him. "Miranda Poole represented both of you."

"I remember her," he said finally. "She was small and blond with a voice like Ethel Merman's! How is she?"

"Oh, fine," Paris replied, whipping up her courage. "She's modeling in Morocco at the moment and I'm…I'm sort of…on a search for my father."

"Ah," he said, as though he understood and was waiting for more.

She wanted him to volunteer it without her having to ask. But that didn't seem to be happening.

"Are you…?" she began, and stopped short when she heard his intake of breath.

"Now, wait a minute," he said, his voice a gasp. "You aren't thinking that's me?"

"I was, yes," she admitted. Then she asked candidly, "Are you?"

"No!" he insisted, his voice rising a decibel. Then he lowered it and repeated, "No. Your mother and I were friends, we hung out together in a group and enjoyed each other's company, but we were never intimate. I was married."

"Mr. St. John, I don't want anything from you," she said, certain he had to be lying to protect his family. "And I promise I won't tell a soul. Your family doesn't have to know. It's just that I need to know. Please. Tell me the truth."

"Miss O'Hara." A strain of sympathy mingled with the denial in his voice. "I'm telling you the truth. I understand your need to find your father, but...I promise you it isn't me. Wouldn't you do a better job of this if you asked Camille? What made you believe it's me?"

She didn't want to tell him that her mother had given her his name. It seemed like a betrayal, though this apparent third lie was seriously battering Paris's loyalty.

"I've been doing some investigating on my own while my mother's out of the country," she replied. "I...may have taken a wrong turn."

"What's your birthdate?" he asked.

"March 20," she answered, "1977."

"Okay, so..." He was apparently calculating. "I

did *HMS Pinafore* in London from April through November 1976. Miranda Poole can verify that. I wasn't even around. If memory serves, your mother was playing Martha Jefferson in *1776* on Broadway.''

If that was all true, it was convincing proof of her misdirected data.

''You are mistaken,'' he said gently. ''I'm sorry. Your mother was a wonderful friend and had I met her when I was still single…'' His voice trailed off, silenced by the possibilities. Then he went on. ''Dora is the mother of my sons. I wouldn't have done that to her, rest her soul.''

Paris heaved an accepting sigh. ''All right. I'm so sorry I bothered you.'' She talked over him as he apologized again. ''No, no, it's not your fault. I just got my clues a little twisted.''

''You should ask your mother.''

He was absolutely right. ''I should. Thank you for calling me back. Good luck with your career and your family.''

''Good luck to you, young lady. And…if you can't find him, I wouldn't mind standing in for him if you need your car tinkered with, rude clerks leaned on or sage romantic advice.''

She had to smile at that. And feel a little regret that he wasn't her father.

''Thank you,'' she said sincerely. ''I'll remember that.''

Paris hung up the phone and called Miranda immediately. She was clearly mystified by Paris's questions, but looked through her files and corroborated everything Jeffrey St. John had told Paris.

She felt as though she was going to explode. She reached for a cup of coffee, then changed her mind. She was so enervated, coffee would only make matters worse. And she couldn't reach for wine because she had to relieve Prue.

Chocolate! she thought. That contained caffeine, too, but it was charged also with serotonin, a mood booster. And her frame of mind was now somewhere below sea level. As she dialed Prue, she praised the scientists who'd made that discovery. Slender hips for Prue's fashion show would have to take a back seat— no pun intended—to her sanity.

"What do you mean, it's not him?" Prue asked as they stood in the driveway, the driver's side door of the cab open, the motor idling.

"I mean Mom lied to me again," Paris said calmly, doing her best to prevent her anger and disappointment from boiling over. "I mean Jeffrey St. John is not my father."

Prue studied her worriedly. "Maybe he lied, Paris. Certainly someone presented with that question and unprepared for—"

"He was in London when Mom got pregnant with me. Their agent confirmed that."

Prue wrapped her arms around Paris. "I'm sorry."

Paris held on for a moment, then pushed her gently away. "It's all right. I'll be fine. You get to work on your designs." She jingled the car keys. "I'm off."

"I could work until four. Give you time to…adjust."

Paris shook her head and slipped behind the wheel. "I'm okay. I'll probably work late, but if I get tired, I'll call you."

"Paris…"

"Thanks for this morning. You get to work. I'm going to drive and think about things."

"You should drive and think about driving!" Prue shouted over the sound of the motor.

"I will!" Paris promised as she drove away. "But, first," she said to herself. "I'm buying chocolate."

RANDY AND CHILLY WERE helping shred lettuce for Paul Balducci's famous taco salad when Kitty came into the firehouse kitchen with the call.

"Berkshire Cab was T-boned at the northwest intersection of the Common," she said urgently. "Single occupant, female. Caller says she's conscious but a little incoherent."

Randy and Chilly were already running toward the rig.

She drove for a living, Randy thought, edgy and anxious as he raced the rig to the scene. You'd think she'd be careful at intersections. And why was his heart thumping? He was always steady as a rock.

Because he was a compassionate human being, that's why, and he knew this woman. That was all it was.

But he felt a great jolt in his chest when they arrived on the scene and found the Berkshire Cab crunched. Fortunately, it was on the passenger side. But he couldn't see Paris for the people crowded around her. Chilly ran interference for him while Randy got their gear.

"How you doing, Miss O'Hara?" Chilly asked as he opened the door. Randy knelt on one knee and took her pulse. She was pale and her voice was strained when she tried to grin and said, "I'll bet the car that hit me was Addy's. She'll do…anything to get us together."

She sounded as though she was gasping for air, but her vitals were good. Her pulse was a little fast, but her heartbeat was steady and she was awake and responsive.

"Did you hit your chest against the steering wheel?" he asked as he worked over her arms, feeling for breaks.

"No," she replied. "The collision just…jarred me."

"Legs hurt?"

"No."

"Can you move them?"

"Yes."

"Do you know your name?"

The look she gave him was enough to tell him she hadn't sustained a blow to the head. "I'm the woman who refuses to date you, remember?"

"Is she okay?" A worried older woman clutching a quilted handbag stood on the other side of the open door. "I thought she saw me. She looked at me, but she kept on going. I couldn't stop in time."

"I think it was my fault," Paris said to Randy, that tight sound in her whisper. "The stop was on my side. I stopped, but…I didn't see her."

"That's right," a young man standing behind the older woman confirmed. "I saw it all. She stopped, but she mustn't have seen the car coming 'cause she took off again."

A police officer had arrived on the scene and was making notes.

"I'm fine. Really." Paris used the side of the door to pull herself to her feet.

Randy reached out to steady her, suddenly understanding the pained voice with no corroborating physical evidence of injury. It didn't reflect pain, but a strong effort to hold back tears.

"Chilly's gone for the gurney," he said, still holding on to her. "You seem fine, but we're going to take you to the ER and let them look you over to make sure."

"No, I'm…"

"Rules, Paris," he said, ignoring her protests. "Just relax. Here's the gurney. Just sit down and I'll swing your legs up. Tell me if anything hurts."

"Just my insurance premium," she joked thinly.

"Well, that's lucky," he said as Chilly drew the light blanket over her. "Because we can fix that without surgery."

He sat in the back with her while Chilly drove.

MAYBE IT WASN'T THE WORST day of her life, Paris thought, her head throbbing and her ears ringing as she held her breath, but it was running a close second.

Randy, leaning over her, frowned worriedly. "Relax, Paris," he advised, watching monitors. "Breathe. You're okay. Just breathe."

She expelled a breath because she just couldn't hold it anymore, and as she suspected, a loud sob erupted from her. She burst into tears.

She'd always scorned weakness in people. She'd loved her mother and her sister, but considered them a little frivolous according to the standards she'd set for herself. She was going to do big things. Go to law school. Defend the friendless.

Then one piece of bad news had thrown her for a loop. She'd been unable to go back to school, unable to pursue her dream. She'd started Berkshire Cab in an attempt to keep going, to help support the household. But now she'd run a stop sign, hit the car of a poor little old lady and probably damaged her driving record. Not to mention the cab.

She felt a gentle hand on her cheek.

"Hey," Randy said quietly. "It's going to be all right. I don't think you're hurt, and the woman you hit isn't hurt. That's about the best outcome you can hope for. There's no reason to cry."

For reasons she couldn't explain, she began to cry harder.

"My car!" she wailed.

"You had a good dent in the passenger side," he

said, that gentle hand stroking her hair. "But it looked like just body work to me. It's expensive, but I presume you're insured."

"I am." She sniffled and coughed. "But they'll probably drop me now. And I'll have to find something to drive until my car's fixed."

"Doesn't your sister have a car?"

She shook her head. "She had a Porsche she sold when she came back home. Mom's car is at the airport."

"Well, I'm sure there's a solution. You have to look at the bright side. None of the terrible things that could have happened did. You got off easy. And a couple of days' rest will do you good, I'm sure. When you're overworked, it's easy to be distracted."

She wanted to take offense, but her attention was diverted by the soothing hand in her hair, the thumb sweeping tears from her cheek.

"I wasn't distracted, I was…upset." She sounded petulant. She hated that. She drew a deep breath and tried to pull herself together.

"Is it something you need to talk about?"

She looked into his concerned eyes and considered sharing the strange stuff about her mother and how she kept lying about Paris's father. But he had his own problems. Also, she'd been trying to get rid of the distracting annoyances in her life. And he was one of them.

Though it didn't seem like that at the moment.

She closed her eyes. "No, thank you," she said.

"It was all my fault because I was going for chocolate and I'm supposed to have sworn off it."

She opened her eyes again to see that he was smiling.

"Right," he said. "The fashion show."

She looked surprised. She tried to sit up but he pushed her gently back. "Stay quiet," he urged. "Prue told me when she picked up your wallet."

Of course. Trust Prue to tell a handsome man her whole life's story—and Paris's as well.

"Chocolate's better when you're upset than a cigarette," he said, putting a hand on her waist to steady her as the ambulance made a turn. "Here we are. The nurse can call your sister for you."

"No," she said as he tightened the belt that held her to the gurney. "I don't want to bother her."

He grinned. "You can't take a cab home when you're released now, can you? You're the only service in town."

That was a problem she hadn't considered. "I'll get home," she said. Then the ambulance doors opened, and in a sudden hubbub of activity, she was hauled out of the ambulance and into the emergency room.

It took several hours to determine that she was fine. No bones broken, no muscles pulled, no impact injury to her head or stomach.

The only other good thing to come out of that morning was that the officer told her she wouldn't be charged with reckless driving. Her insurance agent had appeared, assessed the damage to the cab and the other woman's car, and assured her that she was covered. She thanked heaven for life in a small town.

She was released shortly after two in the afternoon. She was trying to decide who she could call to take her home when she noticed Randy walking into the ER in civilian clothes—a pair of snug jeans and a Maple Hill Marathon T-shirt stretched over muscular shoulders and tucked in at the flat waist of his jeans.

She felt a powerful jolt of physical awareness.

He strode toward her, intercepting her as she headed for the public telephone.

"You're looking good," he said with a smile and a somewhat clinical scan of her body from head to toe. "How do you feel?"

She nodded, embarrassed at the memory that she'd cried all over him. "Fine. I'm fine. I'm…going home. Are you still working?"

"No. I asked Julie to let me know when you were released."

"Julie?" she asked.

He pointed to the nurse who'd assisted the doctor.

Julie looked up from a computer screen as he said her name and winked at him.

He took Paris's arm and led her toward the door. "I'll take you home."

"I thought your shift didn't end until four."

"That's right. But I got somebody to cover my last two hours so I could take you home and show you what you're missing by not going out with me."

She rolled her eyes at him, knowing she should refuse but feeling very halfhearted about it.

He put an arm around her shoulders and continued toward the door. "I know what you're thinking," he said in a cavalier voice. "You're vulnerable, I'm charming, and I'm going to choose this moment to demonstrate my sexual prowess and make you incapable of resisting me. Am I right?"

She had to smile. "Not even close. I would never be incapable of resisting you."

He pushed the doors open and they stepped out into the warm and breezy mid-September afternoon. He challenged her with a look. "Well, that sounded pretty confident. Is that why you're afraid to date me? You don't want to be wrong about that?"

"I'm not *afraid* to date you," she corrected him, following as he pointed to a dark green LeBaron and led the way. She stopped in her tracks when she saw the Berkshire Cab sign on the driver's door. "What...?" she gasped.

He caught her arm and drew her toward the car.

"I had your car towed to the body shop but salvaged the magnetic sign. You said you needed something else to drive while yours was laid up."

"But whose...?"

"It's mine." He opened the passenger-side door and urged her inside. It had beige leather upholstery and had apparently just been vacuumed out. She could smell carpet freshener. "I have an old pickup I can use until you get the cab back."

He walked around the car, slid behind the wheel, then grinned at her as he started the motor. It purred with a strong, healthy sound. While she continued to stare at him, openmouthed, he reached a long arm into the back seat and handed her a white oblong box tied with a gold ribbon. Gold lettering on the lid of the box said it was a pound of Fanny Farmer chocolates.

She didn't even have a gasp left.

"Come on, now," he said with a smile into her eyes. "Tell me you're not just a little bit in love with me."

She knew the admission would upset everything, particularly her determination to keep her distance. But there were too many lies in her life to add another one.

"Maybe just a little," she conceded, returning the smile.

CHAPTER FOUR

"BUT IT MAY BE ONLY temporary," Paris qualified quickly, slipping the ribbon off, then removing the lid. "Chocolate's only a temporary gratification, you know." Then she sighed and he felt her turn to look at him as he left the hospital parking lot and headed for the road that would take them to the lake. A sudden quiet filled the car.

"Although, the thoughtfulness of lending me your car," she said in a slightly husky voice, "inspires a very permanent gratitude. I can't believe you'd do that for me."

He glanced at her, discovered that she looked worried about it, and didn't want that. "It's not a hardship," he said. "I assure you."

"But it's very sweet, all the same."

That wasn't entirely true, but he wasn't about to admit to that. He'd keep his ulterior motives to himself.

"Thank you," he accepted modestly. "So, you aren't as immune to my charms as you thought you were."

"Apparently not," she whispered.

"What was that?" he teased, holding a hand to his ear.

"Apparently not!" she repeated in a louder tone. "Do you want a piece of chocolate?"

"Please."

"Nut or soft center?"

"Surprise me."

He held his right hand out and she placed a peanut cluster in it.

"Enjoy that," she said, "because I'm not sharing any more." She selected a chocolate, bit it in half and made a soft sound of pleasure. "Oohh." There was a moment's silence while she finished the morsel, then she seemed to suffer eater's remorse.

She hit his arm with the box lid, then covered the chocolates. "This is going to set me back five or six pounds, at least!" she complained. "I'll never fit into the red dress, and Prue's going to be filled with re-criminations! I mean, we're just starting to get along, and this is one thing I can do for her, though I'd rather be shaved bald than walk down a runway in front of hundreds of people! And she's going to be furious with me because I'm going to look lumpy in her clothes! It's going to be like high school all over again!"

"What about high school?"

"We hated each other," she said, reaching over the seat to put the chocolates in the back. The action brought them into fairly close contact as she braced her hand on his shoulder to reach the back seat. He felt the softness of her breast against his arm and caught a whiff of jasmine.

Her eyes met his, just inches away, and he forgot completely about the road ahead.

She sat back quickly.

He was grateful that the road was straight, and that there was nothing in front of him.

"She was beautiful and I was…more cerebral. I hated her because every boy who came to our home noticed her and not me, and she hated me because I got the grades and she was always having to explain to our parents why hers were so low."

"That's just the usual kid stuff, isn't it?"

"It would be," she said, sounding distracted, "if the father we both adored growing up hadn't turned out to be her father, but not mine."

"That's what you were thinking about this morning," he guessed, "when you didn't see the oncoming car."

She nodded regretfully, then folded her arms, clearly upset with herself that she'd shared that. "I can't believe I didn't see that car. Well, I must have seen it, but somehow it just didn't register."

"I'm sure discovering that your parent isn't really your parent is pretty heavy stuff. You just found out?"

She told him how she accidentally learned in a college class that her father could not be hers biologically. About coming back to Maple Hill to confront her mother, who seemed to have explained away the situation with a series of lies.

"My mother left for a photo shoot in Africa a few days ago," Paris said. "And I determined that while she was gone, I was going to find out for myself who my father was.''

''But…you said she told you he was dead.''

''Yes, but she lied. Well, at least the man whose name she gave me is very much alive. And he denies being my father.''

''He could be lying, too.''

''I don't think so.''

''Then…I guess you have to somehow convince your mother that you can take the truth.''

''Take the truth.'' She leaned back against the headrest. ''Why would she think I can't take it? Certainly she wouldn't be the first unwed mother, if that's the case. Anyway, I'd just talked to Jeffrey St. John this morning—that's the man she told me was my father—and I was a little upset and on my way to the market to buy a giant candy bar.''

''There was half of one in your wallet,'' he said, turning onto Lake Road.

She made a face at him. ''Prue ate it when she drove last night.''

He laughed. ''You mean, she denies you but eats it herself?''

''She can,'' she said. ''She's very petite. It's that yellow house.''

She pointed to a big bungalow with a private dock and a considerable amount of lakefront. He pulled into a short driveway with yellow chrysanthemums on both sides.

Prue, wearing overalls and a broad-brimmed sun

hat, was weeding the beds. She looked up in surprise, then stood as he pulled up to the rear steps.

"Isn't she like a cover of *Better Homes and Gardens* magazine?" Paris asked. "Dressed in grubbies and somehow still a picture."

He had to agree. "She's a very attractive woman. But so are you. And while confidence is sexy, there's something about vulnerability that's very appealing."

She looked at him in surprise.

"What happened?" Prue asked, putting the basket and scissors down at the sight of Paris's pale face. Then she noticed the Berkshire Cab sign on the strange car. "Where's the wagon?"

Paris explained briefly about the accident. "The wagon's going to be in the shop for a couple of days, so Randy's lending us his car."

"That's very kind of you." She gave Randy a knowing look, as though suspecting his interest in her sister motivated his kindness. Then she returned her attention to Paris. "But are you okay? Have you seen a doctor?"

Paris started for the house, telling her sister about the trip to the emergency room. Then she seemed to remember him.

He was wondering if he was going to have to walk home when she studied him consideringly, then drew a deep breath. "I'm going to make him a sandwich, then you can take him home when you start your shift."

She glanced at her watch. "I'd better start early.

We have a Wednesday afternoon regular, don't we? Two-thirty?''

Paris put a hand to her forehead and groaned. "I forgot! The Lightfoot sisters and their weekly tea party with Mariah at Perk Avenue." The Lightfoot sisters ran the Maple Hill Manor School where Mariah once worked. "And I was congratulating myself on having picked a slow afternoon to have an accident. No calls backed up on the cell phone."

"Not a problem." Prue snatched the phone and whipped the sun hat off her head. "I'll take over now, then you can call me when Randy's ready to go home. I like it when you owe me." Then she used her hat to point at the box in Paris's hands. "Is that chocolate?"

Paris clutched it to her and her expression grew firm. "They were a gift from Randy when he picked me up at the hospital. You can trust me with them. We made a deal."

Prue nodded, looking unconvinced. "All I ask is that you remember the red dress."

"I will, I will," Paris promised.

With a doubtful look back at her sister, and a scolding look for Randy, Prue hurried off to the house.

Paris beckoned him to follow her.

The house looked like a place occupied by three women, though it had none of the colonial or sometimes Victorian air with which many of the locals decorated their homes. It was all bright colors and floral patterns in the upholstery and the curtains, lending it a sort of patio flavor. He wondered if the women's mother had tried to bring Southern California with her when she followed her husband here.

They walked into a living room that was painted bright red with white farm-style furniture upholstered in a slate-blue fabric covered with red-and-cream flowers. A coordinating plaid covered a fainting couch and another chair.

He heard Prue run up the stairs while Paris led the way into a huge cream-colored kitchen that looked very up-to-date. The cupboards had wire-mesh fronts, and several bottom ones were fitted with basket bins for produce. An old-fashioned iron stove attracted his attention, but upon closer inspection, he noticed that what appeared to be a wood box was really just an extension of a very large oven, and it wasn't iron at all, just designed to appear to be. The refrigerator and the dishwasher matched with the same convex black panels and gold filigree trim.

A long work island in the middle of the room boasted a small sink on one end and stools on the far side.

This made his Spartan apartment look even more basic, and muddled his impression of Paris and her mother and sister as three women struggling to get by.

"Wow," he said simply.

She had opened the refrigerator door and turned to peer at him in question.

He spread his arms to indicate the room. "I have a corridor kitchen that's about eight feet long with barely room to turn around. This is very elegant."

She nodded. "My dad was very handy," she said, then with a quick frown, corrected herself. "You know. Jasper. Prue's dad. My...stepdad, I guess." Then she seemed to tire of deciding what to call him and just went on. "He loved to putter in his spare time and Mom always had an idea of how to make things more useful and more beautiful. She has a real gift for decorating."

"I'll say."

"Turkey and Swiss, or ham and cheddar?" She held up deli packs of lunch meat.

He went toward her. "Is ham and Swiss out of the question?"

"Unorthodox," she replied, selecting those from her collection, "but not out of the question. Whole wheat or sourdough?"

"Whole wheat."

"Grilled or cold?"

"Cold. Can I do anything to help?"

She pointed to the work island. "Just pull up a stool and relax. We can eat out on the deck. It's my favorite place."

He obeyed. She seemed to be relaxing and he didn't want to do anything to interrupt the process.

She made the sandwiches quickly and efficiently while standing opposite him at the work island. She added a bread-and-butter pickle to each plate, then pulled a face at him. "Ordinarily, I'd add potato chips to this, but in view of the red dress, we'd better make it carrot sticks."

"*I'm* not wearing the red dress," he teased.

She raised an eyebrow at him. "You mean, you'd make me watch you eat chips while I have to eat carrot sticks?"

"Depends." He was suddenly aware of an angle he could work. "Do I have some sort of stake in this dress?"

She looked confused. "I don't understand."

"Well, it occurs to me that I could support your effort to get in shape for this notorious red dress," he bargained, "if you'll go somewhere with me while you're wearing it. Bearing in mind that I don't think training's really necessary. I think you look pretty terrific already."

She tried to withhold a smile at the compliment but didn't quite succeed. She pretended to concentrate on cutting the sandwiches at an angle. "It's for the fashion show," she said.

He nodded. "I understand that. But we could go somewhere after the show."

She put the knife down and frowned at him. "Why are you doing this," she asked, "when you were so determined to avoid me while Addy was trying to get us together?"

"Simple," he answered. "I hadn't met you then."

She handed him two cans of diet soda, then, carrying the plate, led the way onto the deck.

It had a magnificent view of Maple Hill Lake. It was absolutely quiet at the moment, nothing moving on it but a family of mallards several yards away. The afternoon sun shone brightly on it, bees hummed, and water lapped against the dock with a sound he'd always found quieting. The breeze was a little cool as fall took hold.

They settled onto a canopied glider fitted with cup holders. He put a soda can in each hole, and she placed the plate between them on the blue-and-yellow upholstered seat.

"But everyone who knows you," she went on, continuing their conversation from the kitchen, "says you're not interested in a relationship."

She took half a sandwich and gestured him to do the same. He did. "People always think they know what other people are thinking."

She leaned into a corner of the glider and met his gaze. He could tell she was going to ask him something difficult.

"Why did you quit medical school?" she asked.

He waited for the tightening in his gut that always accompanied questions about Jenny or anything that related to her, but the sun and the lapping water must be sedating him. He felt just a twinge.

"If my friends have been talking about me," he said, "then you probably know that my fiancée died while we were both interning at a hospital."

"Yes." Paris regretted asking the question when she saw a glimmer of pain in his eyes. But it disappeared as quickly as it came and he seemed to relax with an indrawn breath.

"I was so excited by what I'd learned, what modern medicine could do, that when Jenny was diagnosed, I was certain there had to be something that could be done for her." He drew another breath, this one a little ragged. "But there wasn't. The cancer was virulent and advanced. She lived only a few months." He put his sandwich down, popped the top of his soda can and took a drink.

"I went into medicine," he said after a moment, "determined, as every new doctor is, to save lives. But nothing could be done for Jenny, and then the fact that I was a doctor—or almost one—became a curse. I understood every subtle change in her appearance, the grim result of every test, the futility of every effort we made to try to save her. She was dying by inches and I knew everything that was happening to her."

She reached a hand along the back of the glider to touch his shoulder. He didn't seem to notice.

"Those four months were as deadly to my emotions," he said, "as they were to her body. It wasn't just that losing her was so awful. It was, but everyone loses someone at one time or another. You can't escape it."

"Then, what was it?" she asked gently.

He took another sip of soda. "It was knowing what was going on inside her that tripled the pain. I won't have a wife and give her children, when I know I can't support them through illness and pain. I stayed with Jenny until her last breath, but it killed the part of me that's willing to share that way."

She could almost understand that, though the life he'd chosen instead didn't seem to make sense.

"But you're still in medicine," she pointed out to him.

"I'm an EMT," he argued. "That's a different animal altogether. I stabilize victims and transport them to the hospital where saving their lives is someone else's responsibility."

That didn't seem to compute entirely, but she kept that to herself. And it became imperative to pull him back from the apparent agony of his memories.

"Then why are you looking for a relationship with me?" she asked lightly, biting the end off her pickle. "Do I look particularly hearty with a lengthy lifeline, or something?"

He smiled. Curiously, it relieved her.

"Well, you do." He grinned. "But we seem to be made for each other. You're on this quest thing for your identity and you don't want to get entangled with anyone until you find yourself. My parents were great, but they're gone. I have no siblings, so my life's my own. I don't want to get entangled with anyone at all."

She looked into his eyes, wondering if he was suggesting what she thought he was suggesting.

"Yes," he said, apparently reading the question in her eyes. "That's exactly what I mean."

Her heart thumped.

"But..." she said, her pulse accelerating, "even uncommitted relationships can get complicated."

He tipped his head to indicate it didn't matter. "I don't care if it gets complicated," he said, "as long as it doesn't involve promises. I had a sort of... physical friendship in mind."

The notion was both delicious and terrifying. She

was captivated by him, but it was one thing to let a relationship become physical while waiting to see how it unfolded, and another to set out on it deliberately, knowing it would never be anything else.

"Friendships often last forever," she said. She barely had a voice.

He nodded. "But there's no vow, no contract involved."

"Is it any less binding if it isn't written down and signed?"

He nodded again. "If you know you can't do the 'in sickness and in health, till death do us part,' it is."

"You've known me all of two days."

"Doesn't seem to matter, does it? I'll bet we'd have a great time."

It seemed to her that their efforts *not* to have a relationship had already complicated the last few days. She couldn't imagine that what he suggested could work for her.

But she hated the thought of never seeing him again.

"Could we get back," she asked, "to the red-dress alliance? You said you could support my efforts to look good in it. How?"

So CLOSE, HE THOUGHT GRIMLY, and yet so far. It had looked for a moment there as though she was on his side.

Well. He could afford to bide his time. He wasn't going anywhere and neither was she. He'd start by being a friend, and eventually, when she needed something more, he'd be there.

He suspected they could be good for each other.

"For a start," he said, switching mental gears, "I could take the chocolate back."

She smiled sweetly. "They'd never find your body. Any other ideas?"

"Ooh," he said. "A woman of action. I like that. Actually, I meant that I could keep them for you. When you're tempted, you'd have to come to my place and try to convince me to let you have one. Certainly that'd give you time to think twice about it."

She considered that a moment, then nodded reluctantly. "I guess that would work."

"And we both need more exercise. I used to run with the Wonders, but they run mornings and I don't have time anymore. Occasionally, I run in the afternoon or evening, but not as regularly as I should. We could help each other stick to a plan. Your sister takes over driving in the afternoon, right?"

"Right. Usually at four."

"Okay. I'm off tomorrow. I'll be by just after four and we'll get moving before we have a chance to sit down. The road around the lake is the best natural track there is."

She knew it was ridiculous to be excited about the establishment of a running regimen, but she was, anyway. Still, she tried to appear nonchalant.

A cool breeze swept across the lake in a sudden flurry of red and yellow leaves. A whiff of wood smoke came from somewhere in the distance, and the family of ducks flew off, protesting the disturbance.

Randy looked up at the sky, the mellow gold of the afternoon waning with the breeze. ''Things are changing,'' he said.

He meant the weather, but she took that pronouncement in a more personal way. Her whole life had been turned upside down and now that she was determined to right it again, she couldn't tell if this thing between her and Randy was going to help or hinder the process.

Then he turned to her with a warm smile and that appreciative look in his eyes that made her feel pretty and she decided not to worry about it. There were bonuses in it for her, anyway, whatever happened in the end.

CHAPTER FIVE

"To the cemetery, please." Ashley and Michael Morrison climbed into Paris's cab in front of the grade school. Ten-year-old Ashley had a cell phone, and this was the second time she'd called Berkshire Cab to take her and Michael, eight, to the cemetery.

Everyone in town knew the story. Melinda Morrison, their mother, had died during the Christmas holidays in a wreck on the Interstate. She'd been toy shopping in Springfield.

Clete Morrison, their father, operated a towing service and had been called to the wreck by a state trooper who hadn't known his connection to the victim. The man was understandably traumatized, and though, according to Addy, he was a loving father, he couldn't talk about that day to anyone, even his children.

Paris guessed that Ashley and Michael, needing to talk about their mother, settled for talking *to* her at her gravesite instead.

Both children were bright and precocious, though Ashley definitely was the power in charge.

"What happened to your station wagon?" Michael asked Paris.

"It's in the shop," Paris replied, surprised that he remembered that she'd picked them up last week in a different vehicle. Of course, cars were his father's business. "My friend lent me his car until mine is fixed."

Michael rubbed a hand over the leather seats. "This is cool."

"Don't forget to tell Mom about forgetting your words to the Thanksgiving play," Ashley told Michael. "She can help you remember." To Paris she added, "Michael's going to be a Pilgrim in the play at school."

"Are you sure?" Michael asked. "I mean, I know Grandma said Mom still loves us even though she's in heaven, but that's probably a thousand miles from here. I don't think she can reach us."

"Yes, she can," Ashley insisted. "Her spirit can help us."

"You mean, like her ghost?"

"No, I mean her...her..." Ashley floundered.

"She means that part of her that was your mother," Paris explained for her, finding their faces in her rearview mirror. Michael clutched a fistful of dandelions. "That's still very much alive, like her love for you. If you tell her what you need, I'm sure she'll try to help you like moms always do."

Except for mine, she thought wryly, who keeps lying to me.

"But how can she help me remember stuff?" Michael asked.

"If you write down the lines you can't remember,"

Paris suggested, "and read them over and over, she'll help you remember. I'm sure of it."

Proud of that piece of practical advice that would help Michael help himself, she pulled into the cemetery and drove to the top of the hill where she'd brought the children the last time.

"Will you wait, please?" Ashley asked in a formally adult tone.

"Of course," Paris replied with the same formality.

She watched the children find the grave under a wizened oak and sink to their knees. Ashley scraped debris off the flat stone that marked it, while Michael took the small flower receptacle to the faucet several yards over and filled it with water. He put the dandelions in it and carried it back to its little niche near the stone.

They lingered for several moments, talking to each other, probably talking to their mother, then Ashley consulted the colorful watch on her wrist and they stood to leave.

Paris drove them back to the day care where they stayed until their father picked them up after work.

"If Mrs. Ames asks why we're late," Ashley coached her brother, "just tell her we stopped to buy candy."

"Whoa!" Paris turned to Ashley. "You mean your dad doesn't know you're going to the cemetery?"

Ashley looked grim. "He doesn't want us to. He thinks it's bad for us. But don't worry. When we call you to pick us up, we get to the day care faster than if we walked from school, even when we stop to see

Mom. Except for today. We had more to talk about with Mom.''

Michael dug through his backpack and produced a Spider-Man wallet. He took out two singles and a fistful of change, which he handed to Ashley, who put it with a five dollar bill and handed it over the seat to Paris.

Paris, feeling guilty about colluding with children to deceive adults, took one of the singles and pushed the rest back. ''Thursday is bargain day,'' she said. ''All rides are a dollar.''

Ashley blinked in pleased surprise. ''Really?''

''Yes. But next time, you have to have your dad's permission to go. Okay?''

Ashley nodded dutifully, but Paris got the impression she intended to ignore that advice.

''I'll bet your dad won't mind your going to the cemetery if you explain why you want to.'' Paris offered that parting thought as the children climbed out of the cab.

Michael shook his head. ''He won't go, and he doesn't want us to go there, either.''

''Okay.'' Paris smiled at the children and waved them off. ''Have a good afternoon! And don't forget to do your homework.''

Ashley made a face at her. ''I never forget. Bye.''

The children, desperate to talk to their mother, reminded her of how desperate she was to talk to hers. But it did soften her attitude a little to remember that when she was Ashley's age, she'd had a loving mother to come home to after school. And when her mother was on a job, Jasper had been there.

For the first time since she'd discovered that not only was Jeffrey St. John still alive, but he wasn't her father, she began to wonder in a more sympathetic way why her mother had lied. Was she really trying to hide the fact that she'd had a youthful affair? A one-night stand? Maybe an indiscretion with a married man?

Then that concern was swept aside as a glance at the dash clock reminded her that she had to hurry if she wanted to be changed into sweats and running shoes by the time Randy arrived.

That excitement filled her being and pushed aside her problems—an unusual occurrence for her. She usually dealt with difficulties until she solved them.

She sighed as she drove home, wondering if she was losing ground in her efforts to clear the decks of her life.

Prue seemed preoccupied as she took the car keys, cell phone and clipboard, which were a sort of transfer of the badge of office of cab driver.

"Everything okay?" Paris asked, looking into her sister's unfocused eyes.

Prue seemed to call herself back. "Yeah. Sure. There's a cloak in your room I'd like you to try on when you get a chance. And look at the trim I've set out on your dresser. I'm having trouble deciding which to use. Tell me what you think."

"Did you have something to eat?" Paris asked, still concerned about her usually lively sister.

"I'll pick up something at the Barn." Prue smiled thinly. "See you tonight." The Breakfast Barn was the place to go in Maple Hill for an early breakfast or a late-night snack. It was more cozy than elegant and good home cooking made up for whatever it lacked in ambience.

Prue used to scorn its appeal when they were teenagers because it was a converted barn and the inside walls were painted red, but she'd come to appreciate it since she'd returned to Maple Hill.

"There's a chocolate bar in the toolbox in the trunk," Paris confessed. "If you need it."

Prue cocked an eyebrow, meeting Paris's eyes with real awareness for the first time since Paris had come home.

Without explanation Prue smiled and hugged her. "Thanks. I was really feeling unloved there." Then she ran out to Randy's LeBaron. She stopped at the driver's side door. "Would you turn off my CD player?" she asked, opening the door. "I forgot it."

"Sure." Paris nodded, then shouted after her as she climbed in the car, "You might need gas!"

"Okay!" Prue yelled back, then closed the door.

Paris forgot everything when she spotted the cloak. She'd intended to try it on when she returned from her run with Randy, but it was laid out on her bed, and the sparkle running through the dark blue wool caught her fancy. It would be like wearing the night sky, she thought, pulling off her jeans and sweatshirt. Music thrummed from the next room—the Three

Tenors at full volume. The drama their voices lent seemed appropriate as she slipped into the cloak.

The lining was silky and cool against her skin. She turned to the full-length mirror on her closet door.

The cloak was full cut, the sleeves wide, the hood deep, though it could be pulled closed with a cord. She giggled, thinking she looked as though she should be on a white stallion, riding through the English countryside in the moonlight, running from smugglers. Or maybe she was a smuggler, and she was running from the law.

Yes. That was a more appealing idea. Unsavory with an element of romance. It would be nice if the truth about her real life was that generous.

''PARIS?''

Randy had passed Prue on her way to the road as he drove toward the lake. She'd tapped her horn and waved at him, though she didn't seem her usual ebullient self. So Paris had to be home.

She didn't respond to his knock, however, so he pushed at the half-open door and called her name again. Still no response. The loud strains of something operatic came from somewhere in the house. He followed it cautiously, afraid of frightening her.

He went down a long, wide hallway and peered into the room where the music originated, but it was empty, except for a wide bed with a yellow-flowered coverlet with matching draperies. Fabrics and trims were spread all over it.

He started toward the next room and was startled

when something hooded in flowing blue flew out at him in a spin like some wild ninja. Self-defense training and simple instinct made him grab for a handhold and ready a punch.

Then he noticed that his attacker was considerably smaller than he was, that the scream emitted was high and distinctly feminine, and that under the flowing cloak—one side of it captured in his hand when he'd grabbed at the figure—was a slender and curvaceous body covered only by a lavender bra and panties.

He was momentarily paralyzed by the beautiful sight and couldn't help the instinctively male reaction to enjoy it an extra heartbeat.

"Randy!" Paris gasped.

He saw the color flood her cheeks and still didn't seem able to move.

Then she put her free hand to her eyes and groaned.

"I'm sorry." He finally freed her, unwilling to be the cause of her distress. "I called, but you mustn't have heard me. Did you think I was an intruder?" he asked.

Her color deepened and she wrapped the cloak around her. He was surprised when she giggled.

"I wasn't attacking you," she said, giggling again. "I was escaping."

"Escaping?"

She nodded. The hood had fallen off her head when he grabbed her and the disheveled blond mass of her hair shone in the dim hallway. She ran into the other room and turned off the music.

"Escaping," she confirmed, leaning one shoulder

against the wall. She pinched the fabric of one sleeve. "Prue asked me to try this on, and I got a sort of wild fantasy image of myself running from the law."

He folded his arms, thinking this woman was even more complex than he'd originally thought. "That's a wild leap of imagination."

She nodded, a dreamy quality lingering in her eyes. "I'm a smuggler."

He smiled, completely charmed by this side of her. "Of what?"

She thought, then frowned. "I don't know. What did people smuggle in the old days?"

"Oh…" He reached out to the hood and pulled it back onto her head, trying to capture the dream as she saw it. "Where are you? England? Early part of the nineteenth century?"

She nodded.

"Whiskey, I think," he replied. "Fine textiles, pearls."

She seemed to like that and nodded, her expression pensive. "Wouldn't it be fun if that was who I turned out to be?"

He had to agree with her. "It would. Not likely in this day and age, but it would."

The moment seemed to be stretching dangerously for him. The hallway was shadowy and his brain was still filled with that glimpse of her lavender-covered charms.

As though she'd read his mind, the fantasy in her eyes seemed to leave her and she tensed a little. She didn't draw away, but simply looked into his eyes, reading the emotions he made no effort to hide.

For just an instant, she looked as though she wanted to respond. As though if he moved toward her, she would open her arms and let him in.

Then she slapped the hood off her hair and smiled at him. This one was forced.

"Well, I guess if I'm going to be running from the law," she teased, "I should get my shoes on and practice."

Disappointed, he gestured in the direction of the living room. "I'll be on the sofa."

"Good. I won't be five minutes."

True to her word, she was in sweat bottoms, a T-shirt and running shoes before he could quiet his racing pulse. He wasn't quite sure what was happening to him. He hadn't reacted to a woman like this since Jenny. He'd pretended interest in them because he'd thought he had to for appearances' sake, but he'd been fairly sure serious attraction was a thing of the past.

Yet here he was, running beside her on the Lake Road, shortening his stride so that she could stay abreast of him, and feeling as if he'd like to get a good lead on her and just keep running.

But at the same time, he wanted to stop and take her in his arms.

He hated that. He was never ambivalent about what he wanted. It was obvious that he was attracted to her, but it was entirely possible he was giving the whole thing an emotional element that really wasn't there because he liked Paris, and he didn't want her to feel used.

Not that he'd done anything, but it was certainly on his mind.

Other joggers using the road rounded the bend half a football field away, and Paris sprinted ahead of him to make room for them to pass. Randy groaned when he saw the baby stroller and recognized the man pushing it as he ran and the woman jogging beside him. Another couple followed behind them.

"Oh, no," he said.

Paris stopped in front of him and he collided with her, taking hold of her shoulders to steady her.

"What?" she asked. "Pull a muscle?"

"No," he said, indicating the group coming toward them. "Nothing that simple."

She frowned in the direction of the runners closing in on them. "That's…well, I recognize Mariah Trent. But the others, I'm not…"

Before she could finish the thought, the lively group was upon them, his nosy, buttinsky friends smiling widely and taking special note of Paris.

Mariah hugged Paris. Only women, Randy thought, would hug each other after jogging for an hour.

Mariah introduced Paris to her husband, Cameron, and their friends, Evan and Beazie Braga, mercifully relieving Randy of the responsibility. That allowed him to squat down near the baby and be treated to a gummy smile brightened by the presence of two little teeth while avoiding his friends' interested looks.

Evan Braga, part of the Whitcomb's Wonders team

and Randy's friend—or so he'd thought—shook his head at Paris. "I have to question your choice of jogging partners," he said with a doubtful look at Randy. "He may look all right, but he cheats at poker."

"I didn't cheat," Randy corrected him, his index finger caught in the baby's fist. "You just lost. And how did an ugly guy like you produce this beautiful baby? All the credit must go to Beazie."

Beazie, a pretty redhead, her short hair caught back in an infinitesimal ponytail, nodded modestly. "Thank you. The baby's up all night and carries on a lot—I think he got that from Evan. Otherwise…"

Evan caught her neck in the crook of his arm and kissed her into silence.

"You're Prue's sister, aren't you?" Beazie asked. "I'm sure I've seen you with her."

Paris nodded. "I'm the one without design talent. You'll love what she's doing for the fashion show."

"I can't wait to see her designs," Mariah said excitedly. "I understand you've agreed to model."

Paris laughed. "Hence the jogging. Randy's helping me get in shape."

"I'm glad he's well employed," Evan said, both arms wrapped around his wife's waist. "He tends to get in trouble if we don't have activities lined up for him. You coming with him to the picnic a week from Sunday?"

Paris opened her mouth to make a quick excuse when Randy replied for her. "She is."

She would have given him a dirty look, but his friends looked so pleased, she hated to contradict him.

"Can you bring a salad or dessert?" Mariah asked. "We're barbecuing steaks the company bought, and we're keeping it simple."

"Sure," Paris replied. She was a good baker. "Chocolate cake?"

To her surprise, Mariah asked gently, "Wouldn't salad be safer considering your chocolate weakness?"

When Paris's mouth fell open, Mariah said with playful seriousness, "Prue told me all about it. We don't want you to fall back on your promise. I understand Randy's even holding your supply of chocolate."

Paris gasped. "Is nothing sacred?" she asked half playfully, half seriously.

"No!" the group replied en masse.

"Okay, then," she replied, shrinking closer to Randy and pretending fear. "I'll bring a salad."

"Good." There was laughter, handshakes, calls of goodbye, shouts to remember to bring utensils. Then the group jogged away.

"Just a minute," Paris said, holding back as Randy would have run on.

He stopped, jogging in place, an eyebrow raised in question.

"You know, you've completely lost your cardio momentum."

"And you've lost your mind," she countered. "Why did you tell them I was coming to the picnic when you haven't even mentioned it?"

"Because if I go with a woman, they won't spend all afternoon trying to fix me up with one. Addy will be there, you know, because she runs Hank's office, and she'll probably bring a small army of single women to fix up with all the Wonders who are single. Please, Paris. Help me out here.''

''You might have asked me.''

''You said you didn't want to go out with me. You're only here with me now for the exercise.''

She gave him that dirty look again and jogged off. He caught up with her and kept pace beside her.

She hated to admit that there was something delicious about the ground flying under her feet, the sweet air filling her lungs and a strong man beside her, looking wonderful in his T-shirt and shorts. And going to a picnic with him and his friends sounded more appealing than it should.

''I'll get you for this,'' she threatened so that he wouldn't see her pleasure in the moment.

He cast her a glance, his expression curiously reluctant yet accepting. ''I think you've already got me,'' he said.

CHAPTER SIX

PRUE CAME HOME JUST BEFORE midnight, the distracted expression she'd worn that afternoon had developed into a serious depression.

Paris pulled out a stool for her at the work island and put on the kettle. "You'll be happy to know," she said lightly, hoping to cheer her sister, "that I jogged for over an hour, and that Randy's picking me up tomorrow at the same time, and every evening after that. I'm even bringing salad to a picnic his friends are having. I volunteered chocolate cake, but it seems *someone's* been talking about my problems with chocolate to Mariah Trent."

Prue, her head leaning on her hand, roused herself to smile. "I wonder who that could be?" Then, without warning, her face crumpled and she hid it in her hands, trying to suppress tears.

Paris went to the stool beside her and put an arm around her shoulders. "What is it?" she asked. "And don't tell me it's nothing because I knew something was wrong this afternoon."

Prue lowered both hands to reveal tears streaming down a pale and distorted face. She reached into the pocket of her shirt and handed Paris a piece of paper that had been folded to two inches square.

Paris unfolded it to find that it was a check. "One hundred thousand dollars?" she gasped.

She couldn't imagine where that windfall had come from until she noticed that the check was written on Gideon Hale's account.

"He sold the condo," Paris guessed.

Prue nodded stoically. "He wasn't reelected, you know. Probably because of the scandal. So he's free to do whatever he wants." She began to sob. "It's really...over."

Paris couldn't quite believe it, either. Except for a certain volatility in their relationship that made them disagree and argue at high volume, Prue and Gideon had seemed perfect for each other. He was a hard-fighting politician, and she was the supportive wife, highly visible in the press for her work for literacy and against domestic violence.

Paris had been jealous of their open affection for each other and the excitement of their lives.

Then it had all fallen apart with the intern.

"But you said he cheated on you, Prue," Paris reminded her gently.

"I know!" Prue said between sobs. "I don't regret leaving him, I just miss...having him."

That probably made sense on some level, but Paris was too busy trying to cheer her sister to think that through. "This check allows you to move ahead. You can take a trip, put a down payment on a house, buy a car—maybe even all those things if you're careful."

The kettle whistled and Paris went to the counter to make their tea.

"Is it hard for you that I'm here?" Prue asked as Paris returned with their cups.

Paris didn't understand the question. "What do you mean?"

Prue bobbed her head from side to side. She'd tied her hair up in a loose knot for driving and even now, with her face blotchy and her eyes red, she looked angelic.

"I mean, considering what you've learned about Dad. Is it hard for you that I'm his daughter and you aren't? Do you hate having that in your face every day?"

Paris felt guilty that she had to ask. "Of course not. I hate that Jasper wasn't my father, and that I don't know who was. But I don't resent you because you are his daughter." Paris sighed and said what had been on her mind most of her life but withheld because she hated to admit it. "What I do resent is that you're small and beautiful like Mom. That you have all her style and ease with people while I'm this sort of awkward Amazon. But that's my problem, not yours. And now that we're spending time together, I'm learning that I like you anyway. I'm even learning to deal with your enthusiasm—" she grinned "—which used to drive me crazy and made me tired, but now that I sometimes get low worrying about my own past, it perks me up."

Prue studied her, as though assessing the honesty of her denial, then apparently deciding she could believe it, smiled thinly. "I just wondered because you suggested buying a house."

Paris shrugged. "I just meant it'd probably be nice for you to have more personal space to work on your designs."

Prue sipped at her tea, wincing when it was still too hot to drink. She put it aside and nodded. "Actually, I was thinking that, too. And I remember Mariah telling me that there's an empty room upstairs in the old Chandler Mill that Cam and Evan refurbished on the river. I think I'll go look at it tomorrow. Maybe I'll use this check to open a design studio."

Prue's eyes lightened at the prospect, and Paris felt great relief that her sister was smiling again.

"That's a wonderful idea!" Paris hugged her. "I'm sure there's going to be great demand for your stuff after this fashion show. The cloak is absolutely gorgeous."

Prue held on to her an extra moment. When she drew away, her eyes were clear and her smile wider. "I'm going to look at sewing machines, go to Springfield to look at more fabric, and maybe a used car. I wish you could come with me, but I guess somebody's got to drive the cab."

Paris nodded regretfully. "Someday, when we can serve a wider area, we can hire help." Then she realized what she was saying. "Why am I saying 'we'? In order to put that money to work, you have to stop driving and pay attention to your designs."

"No." Prue took another sip of her tea and, finding it drinkable, took a deeper sip. "We made a deal. I can do both. And I'll pay for having the cab fixed."

"No…"

"Yes, I will. You've been taking up the slack for a long time, and now that I can contribute my share, I insist." She slid off her stool and went toward the cupboards. "Do we have anything we can put in this tea so we can toast my new venture?"

Paris pointed to a lower shelf. "There's apricot brandy in with Mom's chardonnay. That should go with peach tea."

Prue retrieved the chunky dark bottle and brought it to the bar to pour a small amount into each cup. Then, giddy with new relief, poured a little more. She put the bottle down and lifted her cup.

Paris clinked hers to it. "What are you calling your studio?"

"What about, Prudent Designs?"

Paris laughed. "I like it! To Prudent Designs!"

"And fame and fortune for the O'Hara sisters!" Prue added.

They drank, then Prue insisted Paris try on the cloak for her.

Paris went to get it, remembering with a sudden flush of color to her face the expression on Randy's when he grabbed her and the cloak opened. It had been flatteringly appreciative, even lustful. A little thrill rippled along her spine as she remembered that.

"And bring the trims!" Prue shouted from the kitchen.

Paris snatched up three trims Prue had left on the dresser and hurried back toward the kitchen. Life, she thought, was taking an upward turn.

Now. If she could just figure out who her father was, she could really enjoy it.

THE WONDERS PLAYED football as though it was Armageddon and it had been decreed that only those who played for blood survived. Randy had noticed that they had the same attitude about baseball and basketball.

For a group of family men who adored their wives and children and would die for one another, they had a curiously lethal approach to competitive sports. It gave them an edge their family lives had blunted, Randy guessed. When they got together in the spirit of play, they remembered who they were before this unusual Maple Hill fellowship had turned them into friends and pacifists.

So, he concluded, as the Wonders' Old Guard squared off against the Upstarts, those hired within the last year and a half, it was not a good time to be holding the ball. Hank, Cam, Evan and Gary Warren were coming at him with blood in their eyes.

But he had a killer instinct of his own that had developed to help him survive Jenny's death, and Chilly, who ran bravely ahead to block for him, had put himself through med school by teaching martial arts. That was a skill not entirely compatible with football, but no one seemed to care.

Cole Clements and Paul Foster, both relatively new hires, flanked him and followed him toward the line. He didn't know their stories yet, but they were screaming threats as they ran and he guessed they hadn't been preachers before joining the Wonders.

He remembered a bone-jarring collision, flying through the air with stars flashing around him, and an awareness that he still had the ball tucked under his arm. "Good," he thought as he felt consciousness recede. He might die here, but he was taking the ball with him. The Upstarts were going to score.

He struck the ground and thought he'd died.

But when he realized he hurt too much to be dead, he opened his eyes and focused fuzzily on Paris leaning over him.

"Good Lord!" she was shouting at him. "Have you never heard of the pass? Gary was clear!"

"Ah...Paris..." someone was saying.

But she was apparently upset and not listening. "It's just a game! I don't see why you all have to put your lives on the line! I mean, it's not like you had money on it or anything. Why didn't you just pass to Gary?"

"Paris..." Someone else tried to stop her.

"He was hanging right out there. Why would you burst bodily through four men who were obviously out to kill you?"

He dragged in oxygen and decided he was going to live.

"Because," he told her, catching her arm to stop her, "Gary was playing for their side."

"Paris, he's okay," Hank's voice said from somewhere behind him. "And carrying the ball through is his style. He likes the abuse."

Hank and Cam pushed and pulled him to his feet, and Jackie, Hank's wife and the mayor of Maple Hill, offered him a paper cup of water. "Paris is right," she said, passing a reproachful glare among all the men. "There's no need to take a life-and-death approach to a picnic football game. This isn't Omaha Beach, you know. It's just a friendly get-together."

"And, anyway," Beazie declared, wielding a spatula, "the steaks are ready."

There was a unanimous roar of approval and the group broke up to retrieve utensils and form a line around the gas grill Cam and Mariah had brought to the park. Glory, who was married to Jimmy Elliott and was nanny to Hank and Jackie's brood while studying accounting, had been supervising the children on the playground. She now herded them all toward their parents.

Paris went to the dark blue chenille throw she'd brought to sit on and delved into the cooler. She straightened with a glass bowl containing some kind of layered salad and a fistful of utensils. She looked delicious in jeans and a simple yellow camp shirt.

Randy remembered her look of concern when the guys flattened him in the tackle, and used an interest in the salad to get closer.

"Do we really have to share that?" he asked, trying to take it from her.

"I'm afraid so." She held it away from him.

He reached around her for it and they were suddenly nose to nose, their lips mere inches apart. "I have a chocolate bar in the glove compartment of the truck,'' he taunted.

She fought a smile while her eyes explored his face. ''You're supposed to be helping me resist temptation.''

She was in his arms now, the salad bowl held away from her.

Mariah came and snatched it from her. ''I'd better rescue this before it ends up in the grass,'' she said with a grin as she carried it away.

Randy noticed that Paris's eyes never left his.

''I know you're thinking about kissing me,'' he whispered. Her concentration on him made him lose track of everything else. ''And you can't fight temptation on too many fronts. So I thought I'd help you out with the chocolate.''

Her eyes were now focused on his mouth. ''Because…you don't think I could resist you?''

''Because I know,'' he whispered, lowering his mouth to hers, ''that I'm not going to help you try.''

The instant they connected was electric. Every effort he'd made over the past week to soft-pedal his desire for her abandoned him when her fingers wandered into his hair. Gooseflesh rose along his scalp, then drifted to his shoulders, where her other hand rested—apparently for steadiness, because her grip on him was a little desperate.

Her lips were soft and warm, and clung to his with the same determination and purpose he felt. Sensation rioted through him with the old pre-Jenny vitality and fervor he never expected to feel again. He was aware for just one instant how miraculous that was, then she nipped at his lip and he forgot everything else.

PARIS HAD TO ADMIT that she liked Randy's approach to a kiss. Or had it been her approach? No, she'd been captivated by the notion, but the move had definitely been his.

She'd always thought kissing was awkward. Men were often clumsy or indecisive, making her feel as though the whole thing was a mistake. She'd been either crushed, or held so loosely, she began to wonder if the man was having second thoughts. Then, if she escaped the old where-do-the-noses-go? problem, there was still the actual meeting of the lips, which could be just okay or not at all appealing, but never the wondrous experience Prue had once claimed kissing Gideon was. Never the stuff of novels and movies.

But it was here. Randy had a firm grip on her waist that allowed her to breathe while making it clear she was precisely where he wanted her to be. He dipped his head and tilted it so that their noses never even bumped, and his lips were warm and dry and completely certain of their mission.

Wrapped in his embrace, responding to his flatteringly ardent kisses, she felt the flinging open of a door inside her that had been closed for as long as she could remember.

Paris O'Hara was somebody, the news seemed to reach her from beyond the door. And not just because she had a man's undivided attention. It was in the way that he held her, and not just in the fact that he did. It was in his confident yet reverent touch, the passionate yet tender way he kissed her.

She was not a shadow of her mother, or a pale image of her sister, but *somebody*.

It occurred to her that she still had no idea who, but it didn't seem to matter for the moment. She basked in her own womanliness when Randy finally raised his head and looked into her eyes with desire in his.

Then she was forced back to the picnic and the out-of-sync normalcy of steaks and salad.

"Well," he said, having to clear his throat. "What do you have to say for yourself?"

She blinked at him, staggering from the experience. Fortunately, his arm, which was still around her, prevented her from stumbling. "Me?" she demanded.

"Yes," he said, catching her hand in his and drawing her toward the end of the line formed near the grill. "You've completely seduced me."

She looked into his innocent expression and made a face. "Right. And you're blameless?"

"Blameless?" He frowned, taking issue with the word. "It's not something we have to assign blame to. I think it's something that deserves credit, applause, cheers."

"But seduction," she pointed out, "implies a subjugation of oneself to the other person. If you don't want a committed relationship, I don't think you want to be seduced."

He frowned over that and placed her ahead of him

in line, his hands on her shoulders. "Are you claiming to be unaffected?"

Considering she was still trembling and he could probably feel it, it would be silly to say that she was. "No," she admitted after a moment, keeping her head turned away, though the tone of her voice suggested it hadn't been as momentous as he seemed to think.

The front of the line was getting raucous, Cam trying to push ahead of Evan. She pretended interest in the fracas so she wouldn't have to look at Randy, but he turned her to him and tipped her face up. He looked into her eyes and finally smiled with satisfaction.

"You can lie all you want," he said, tugging at her ponytail. "I can see the truth in your face."

"Then, I'd think that would upset you rather than make you look smug." She spoke quietly because Addy Whitcomb, several people ahead of her, was looking back at them with interest. Of course, Randy's plan in inviting Paris had been to make his friends think they were seeing each other so they'd leave him alone.

He leaned closer to ask quietly, "And why is that?"

"Because you made it clear that all you're interested in is an affair," she replied in the same tone.

He raised an eyebrow. "I believe I called it a physical friendship."

"Well, call it want you want," she replied. "Semantics aren't the issue. Permanence is. And if someone is completely seduced, I think permanence becomes part of their plan.''

''I thought it wasn't part of yours.''

''It isn't, but then I didn't claim to be seduced. Is it part of yours?''

''No. And you can claim or not claim whatever you want, but it's right there in your eyes.''

Paris was becoming increasingly annoyed with the fact that she was attracted to him in a big way. She'd thought it would be simple enough to admit just so much, to let it all go just so far, but it was clear that was never going to work. She'd always been an all-or-nothing kind of woman. And if they were going to have to argue about everything every step of the way, she didn't think she'd be able to stand it.

''Then,'' she said as the line moved ahead, ''it's a very good argument for why we shouldn't see each other anymore.''

''Yeah, well that's not going to work, is it?'' he asked mildly. ''You've got my car, and I've got your chocolate.''

Paris gasped at the truth of that when she found herself face-to-face with an enormous steak. She stared at it in amazement. She also remembered the red dress. ''I couldn't possibly eat all that,'' she said.

''We'll share it,'' Randy said from behind her.

''It's medium-well,'' Hank cautioned. ''I seem to remember you like yours medium-rare.'' Then he grinned. ''Or is this a case of self-sacrifice for the little woman?''

''Something like that.''

Hank cut the steak in half on the griddle, then put half on Paris's plate and half on Randy's. "Sharing a steak is pretty serious stuff," he teased. "Next thing you know, it'll be a house, a checking account, a child."

"Thank you, Dr. Phil." Randy pushed Paris gently toward the salad table. "We'll save children for tomorrow."

Paris smiled at the teasing but noted as they made their way back to the blanket, their plates heaped with salads, that Randy's friends were watching them with interest. And as the day wore on, their attitude toward her took on a subtle change.

She'd been welcomed from the moment they'd arrived late that morning, but she'd been treated like a guest. Now that the group had probably witnessed their kiss and heard them argue, she was accepted as one of them. She was invited to help serve ice cream to the children, volunteered for cleanup, and held Evan and Beazie's baby while they packed the folding table into their van.

Gary brought out a guitar, and the party Paris thought was winding down took on a different, more intimate atmosphere. With children snuggled in their parents' arms, or bundled up and asleep on the blankets, couples leaned into each other and listened to the light and moody songs Gary played.

He had an interesting repertoire of current Country Western music, old ballads and a few timeless tunes of life and love. As dusk enveloped them, the air grew cool and breezy, and everyone shrugged into jackets or wrapped their blankets around them.

Paris, who'd been a little flustered about spending the afternoon with Randy, had forgotten a jacket. She was chiding herself for behaving like a foolish adolescent when she felt a silky fabric being wrapped around her and realized Randy had put his dark-blue-and-white baseball jacket on her shoulders.

He sat behind her, a knee propped up for her to lean on, and drew her backward into his arms. She went without struggle, the scented breeze, the music and the delicious ambience of a few dozen people all happy in one another's company eliminating the concerns she might otherwise have felt in the situation. He wrapped the sides of the jacket around her and held them in place with his arms. She could have died of contentment.

As everyone grew more relaxed, and the songs more familiar, the crowd joined in to sing a few university fight songs, "Amazing Grace" at Addy's suggestion, and a few Frank Sinatra favorites everyone seemed to know.

It was after ten when couples with sleeping children reluctantly began to pack their things, and those who had to be up early for work the following day folded blankets and carried things to their cars.

There were hugs goodbye and promises to meet for various upcoming events. Most of the men would probably see one another at the Wonders' office within the next few days, and the women were often crossing one another's paths at community events, but it had been a special day that somehow underlined their special connection. It seemed to Paris a miraculous thing to gather twenty-some people together and make each and every one of them glad they'd come.

"Now, remember," Mariah teased Paris as she handed her her empty salad bowl. "The library will be able to build a children's wing if you look sensational in Prue's clothes. Not to mention what it can do for her."

Paris rolled her eyes, pretending impatience. "I know, I know. Watch my diet, keep exercising, remember the red dress."

Mariah hugged her. "You read my mind. Are you coming with Prue to check out the space in the Mill?"

Paris shook her head. "I'll be driving cab. But she's very excited about it."

"It's a big open space," Mariah said. "She'll love it. Thanks for coming, and thanks for bringing that wonderful salad. After the library event, you can treat us all to your chocolate cake. Deal?"

"Deal. Thanks for inviting me."

Mariah hugged Randy, then he followed the exodus of vehicles, all honking their goodbyes.

He was uncharacteristically silent most of the way to Lake Road.

"What are you thinking?" she asked as they approached the turn to her mother's home.

He sighed as he guided the car in the turn. "I'm wishing I didn't have to take you home," he said. "I'm wishing we could figure out what we want from each other.'' Then he cast her a wry smile visible as his headlights reflected back on them from the Lake Road sign. ''I mean, I know what I want. But I want you to get something out of it, too, and I'm not sure what you want.''

''Neither am I,'' she admitted. ''I thought I knew, but things have changed on me.''

''Maybe you've changed.''

''I don't know how that can be,'' she said, ''when I'm not sure who I was in the first place.''

He stopped the truck abruptly and let the motor idle.

''Don't you think you're putting too much emphasis on biology,'' he asked gently, ''and not enough on the simple fact that you're you, whoever you came from?''

''Maybe.'' She'd long ago accepted that that could be true. She just didn't seem to be able to feel differently. ''The fact remains that I have to know, whether I am or not.''

He frowned for a moment, then finally nodded, as though he, too, accepted it. ''Okay. I just hate the thought of you hurting yourself over this.''

''The truth is the truth,'' she said, ''however it affects me. I have to know it.''

''Okay.'' He put the truck in gear and drove on. ''Remember that I'll help you if I can.''

She put a hand to his arm, that affectionate gesture a suddenly easy thing. ''Thank you,'' she said. ''I appreciate that. And thanks for the loan of the jacket.''

She leaned forward to pull it off, but he stopped her. "You can give it back to me tomorrow afternoon. For now, just stay warm."

Just stay warm. Those simple words played in her brain as he turned into her driveway and his headlights swept over the back of a small silver import.

"Company?" he asked.

"No." She swallowed, a pall falling over her wonderful day. "My mother's home."

CHAPTER SEVEN

RANDY CAUGHT PARIS'S wrist as she would have opened the door. "Hold on," he said. "I'll get the door."

"But, I…"

"Give yourself a minute to think." He walked around the hood of the truck and offered her a hand down.

She was distracted, anxious, all the emotional highs of the day swamped by a dark eagerness to confront her mother. She forced herself to remember her manners.

"Thank you, Randy," she said. "I had a nice time."

It was dark, except for the meager light from the back of the house. She caught a whiff of wood smoke and damp grass.

He took her face in his hands. She was momentarily annoyed by the stillness it imposed on her when she was anxious to get inside. Then the soft strength of his touch quieted her nerves and reminded her of how she'd felt that afternoon when he'd kissed her.

Paris O'Hara was somebody.

"Remember to go easy," he cautioned gently.

"Okay? I don't know your mom, but if you're half her, then she has to be something special. So she must have had a reason for keeping the truth from you."

She didn't want to argue that right now. She just wanted to know what it was.

He nodded, apparently reading that in her eyes. "Okay. If you need…anything, I've got your chocolate."

Then he gave her a quick hug that was more about comfort and support than anything sexual. "I'll see you tomorrow afternoon," he said, and waited by the front of the truck until she got into the house.

Prue was apparently not home yet, but show tunes were turned up at high volume in the living room and her mother's exotic, musky scent filled the kitchen. The coffeepot was on, Paris noted, and the toaster was on the counter. Her mother's favorite quick snack was a whole-wheat English muffin and a slice of cheese.

Paris wondered absently if even overseas flights weren't serving food anymore.

She squared her shoulders, tried to rid her mind of all thoughts of Randy, though his words and his touch persisted, and tried to remember that she wanted to discuss what had happened with her mother, not attack her.

She found her in Prue's bedroom, placing a bolt of fabric and a silver bracelet on her bed. The fabric was beautifully patterned in a stylized leaf or heart shape in shades of beige and terra-cotta. Prue would love it.

Camille O'Hara straightened and turned away from

the bed, then spotted Paris and gasped with a hand to her heart.

"I didn't know you were home," she said, coming to wrap her arms around Paris. She had the same gift Prue had for looking wonderful whatever time of day, whatever she'd been through.

She wore simple cotton slacks and a big shirt in a flattering shade of blue. She'd gone gray at forty, but colored her hair a pale blond and wore it in a very trendy spiked style. Her fragrance wrapped Paris as tightly as her arms.

A million questions sprang to Paris's lips, but the inane question she asked was "Did you have a good flight?"

Her mother rolled her eyes and caught Paris's hand, leading her across the hall to her bedroom, where her bags still lay all over, several open and spilling their contents.

"Between having to get to the airport so early, the security and the lack of food, I don't think there are any good flights anymore. Oh, I understand it has to be that way, I just wish I had a yacht or something."

"That's a goal to shoot for," Paris said, watching her mother delve through a wheeled carry-on. "Can we just sit for a few—"

A fairly large item wrapped in brown paper was thrust at her before she could finish. Then a bracelet just like the one she'd left Prue was added to it. Up close, Paris saw it was set with an amethyst stone.

Camille took the brown-wrapped package from her and unwrapped it herself. It was a tribal mask.

"I bought this in a souk in Marrakech," she said, holding it up for Paris to study. It looked friendly, if a little wild-eyed. "It's from Central Africa and it's worn during a mating dance while men and women present themselves to each other in disguise to lend an air of mystery to the pairing up."

Curiously sensitive to masks and mating dances tonight, Paris thought that sounded like trickery, but kept the thought to herself. It would have appeared ungrateful, and she knew she was in a fragile state at the moment and should probably keep most of what she was thinking to herself.

"It's wonderful," she said, reclaiming it. "Thanks, Mom. And I love the bracelet."

"Amethyst is supposed to be good luck."

That wouldn't hurt.

"Where's Prue tonight?" Camille asked, pulling a makeup bag, a pair of slippers and a *Vogue* magazine out of the carry-on and tossing them to the middle of her cluttered bed.

"She drove today," Paris explained, both eager and reluctant to get to the point with her mother. "I went on a picnic."

Camille kicked her shoes off and put on the slippers. "She drove? When did that start again?"

"Well, I should let her tell you all the details, but the dress shop is closing. The owner's husband is being transferred. So Prue's designing a line of clothes for a library benefit, and she coerced me into modeling them by promising to drive from four to ten for me."

Camille grinned broadly. "She must be thrilled to get to show her designs." Then her eyes went over Paris's form in her jeans and T-shirt. Paris didn't remember until that moment that she was still wearing Randy's baseball jacket. "And...I'm sure modeling will be good for you."

You won't be good for it, Paris heard, but it'll be good for you.

Her mother pointed to the jacket. "That something new?"

"A friend lent it to me," she said, fiddling with the zipper pull. "It got cold at the park when the sun went down."

Her mother's eyes went from the jacket to Paris's face. "Judging by the size of it, your friend is male?"

Paris waved both hands as though to erase the subject. "Yes, but I'll tell you about that later. Can we just sit for a few minutes?"

"Sure. Want a cup of coffee?" Camille dragged bags aside to clear a path to the door. "I can't bore you with photos yet, but I have some funny stories for you if you're not too tired."

Paris nodded. "Good. I want to talk." She followed Camille to the kitchen.

She had tried to put that casually, but her mother paused while opening a cupboard to look at her. "Something wrong?" she asked, a worry line appearing between her eyes. "Did Prue's divorce come through?"

"I don't think so." Paris went to refrigerator for milk, irritated that her mother presumed the problem was Prue's. It was silly, she realized, but like many sibling differences, it just was. "Though Gideon did sell the house. She just got a check for her half."

Camille pulled down hand-painted china cups and saucers. "I'm glad he's being fair." She poured coffee into the cups and carried them to the work island.

Paris picked them up again. She didn't want to discuss her father while her legs dangled on a stool. "Let's sit in the living room where it's more comfortable," she suggested. At her mother's look of surprise, she added, "I've been running for exercise and my legs are a little creaky."

"Sure." Camille reached for an elegant round tin on the counter. "Want a rice cake?"

Paris declined politely. Her mother and sister often curbed their hunger with the popped-rice things. To Paris, they always tasted like what she imagined those round rubber feet one put under furniture to protect hardwood floors would taste like.

Paris placed their cups on the glass-topped coffee table and they settled on the sofa, her mother leaning against the pillows at one end, she facing her a little stiffly at the other.

While her mother added cream to her coffee, Paris wondered where to start so that her mother wouldn't feel as though she'd launched this search and learned these discrepancies in her mother's story out of mistrust or selfishness.

Unable to find a starting place, she said simply, "What's funny story number one?"

Camille sat back, cup and saucer in hand, and

crossed her legs gracefully as though cameras were rolling. Paris knew she couldn't help it; her grace was an instinctive thing, and her long history with modeling and movies made her every move a little piece of art.

But Camille shook her head. "No, I want to hear what's bothering you. There's lots of time for my stories."

"Mom…"

"Tell me." It was softly spoken, but it was an order.

Paris didn't allow herself time to think. She simply sat up and blurted, "I've been trying to find out about my father."

Camille's graceful movements turned suddenly awkward and mechanical as she uncrossed her legs, sloshed her coffee into the saucer, then bent toward the coffee table to put down the cup.

Her expression hardened and her eyes flashed anger. "Paris, I told you—"

"You told me he was dead," Paris interrupted, facing down her mother's displeasure, "And you told me his name is Jeffrey St. John, which isn't true."

Camille was silent for a moment, but Paris knew she had her. Her mother's face was pale and tight. "And how did you come to these conclusions?" Camille asked. "Knowing you, there's data to back it up."

Unable to decide if that was a criticism or a compliment, Paris explained about her telephone calls. "When Jeffrey St. John denied that he could be my father, I called your old agent back, thinking it was possible he just didn't want to admit the truth. But she confirmed that he was in London at the time you got pregnant.''

Camille had closed her eyes and curled both hands into fists in her lap. ''I don't suppose you'll believe me,'' she asked in a dead voice, ''if I tell you it's better just left alone?''

Paris didn't even have to think about it. ''No, Mom. I have to know.'' Then, feeling guilty because it was so obvious her father had hurt her mother, she made an effort to try to smooth the way for the truth.

''Mom,'' she said, moving a little closer, ''you don't think I'm going to hold it against you if you had an affair with a married man, or...or...''

Her mother looked up at her with a look of such pity that for the first time since Paris determined to find the truth, she was almost afraid of it. Then she reminded herself that the truth existed as it was, whether or not she knew it, and nothing could change that.

She swallowed and reached for her mother's hand. ''Is he in jail?'' she asked.

''No,'' Camille replied, tightening her grip on her hand.

''Was he running from the law?''

''No.''

Paris was now wound so tightly, she wasn't sure she could stand it if her mother didn't stop saying no.

''Well, was he a spy? A terrorist? A...a rapist? What?''

She watched her mother's expression change at that last suggestion and felt as though she'd run headlong into a brick wall. It hurt. It broke something inside her. It left her with air trapped in her lungs, moving neither in nor out, just stuck there.

Her mother emitted a painful-sounding sob, then began to cry.

Paris tightened her grip on her hand and tried to concentrate on breathing. She gasped her own little sob, which expelled the air and finally allowed her to speak. The words were like sharp-cornered bricks in her brain, painful to think about, agony to say aloud.

"My father was a rapist?" she whispered. "Mom, please. You have to tell me."

Camille swiped at her eyes, then met Paris's gaze with real heartbreak in hers. Paris realized that she was asking her mother to relive what had to have been a shattering, horrifying experience, and now she hated herself for it. But there was no going back.

"He was a producer," Camille finally said, her voice broken up with sobs she couldn't hold back, "On…on the *Forsythe Family Show*. It was…a really big deal at the time and everyone wanted to get on it. Big cast. Drama, laughs. I…I was only eighteen."

Mesmerized in a kind of horror, Paris nodded, encouraging her to go on.

"When he invited me to his office, to…to congratulate me on getting the job, I thought…I thought that's all it was." Her face contorted and she looked her age suddenly for the first time in Paris's memory. "But he locked the door and explained to me that I had to be grateful to him because he'd put in a good word for me. Another pretty little brunette with better legs almost got it, he said, but he'd told the backers he…wanted me.''

She shrugged, tears streaming down her cheeks. ''I was so innocent. I thanked him, told him I so appreciated all he'd done. Then he closed the blinds.'' She began to sob again. ''You hear stories like that and think to yourself, she could have fought him off. She could have gotten away. Why didn't she fight? Why didn't she scream?''

Paris went to the desk for a box of tissues and put one in her mother's hand. She felt as though she was being tortured, but knew by the grief in her mother's eyes that she was the one who'd been through hell that night.

''I'm not thinking that,'' Paris said.

''He was big,'' Camille said, regaining her composure for a moment, dabbing at her nose. ''I was terrified. I remember that I couldn't get air to breathe, much less scream. He said I'd lose the job if I ever told anyone, and he'd see that I never worked again.'' She looked down at her hands. ''I needed the job. Grandpa drank everything he made, and I was the only one keeping Grandma and me and Aunt Rosie alive.''

For one moment of blinding truth, Paris was able to put her own shock and horror aside and see her mother as if for the first time. She'd always loved her—it was impossible not to. But everyone else's mother looked like a mother and did the things mothers do. Shopped for groceries, did laundry, picked you up at school.

But not Camille. She modeled clothes, went to lavish openings, and even now that her career had quieted down, she was still somewhat of a celebrity. And she'd been raped at eighteen.

Paris got a rolling pain in her stomach, trying to remember what she'd been like at eighteen. She'd thought herself sharp and clever and destined to stand before a judge and plead for the poor and disenfranchised. She'd been idealistic and clueless. She couldn't imagine she'd have been able to survive a rape and go on to be successful.

She'd been stopped in her tracks by learning that Jasper O'Hara wasn't her biological father.

She took her mother's cup from the table, wiped off its wet underside with a tissue and handed it to her. "Drink," she said. "I'll get you some brandy."

Hands shaking, she went to the cabinet where the brandy was kept and pulled it down, remembering that just last week she and Prue had toasted Prue's soon-to-be design studio. It felt like years ago.

She hurried back to the living room and poured a small amount into her mother's coffee.

"I wanted you to trust that I knew what was best for you," Camille said, staring into the cup. "But, no. You always have to get to the bottom of everything. Just like a lawyer. Can't take anybody's word for anything."

Paris pushed the cup gently toward her mother's mouth and made her drink.

Camille lowered the cup to her left hand. "Now you'll never be able to forget it," she said mournfully. "And you'll hold it against me."

Rage was all entangled inside Paris with sympathy for her mother, and she was having trouble deciding what to react to. Then she remembered what her mother had been through, and added another slosh of brandy to what was left in her cup.

"No, I won't. I'll hold it against him. Is he alive?"

Camille shook her head. "No, he's dead. I swear he is. I read the notice about ten years ago in *Variety*. Light-plane crash on a skiing trip."

Paris didn't know whether to be angry or grateful. God, she wished Randy was here.

The thought came as a surprise, then seemed to fill her brain, to be the light at the end of her black tunnel. She wanted to be with Randy.

"I was horrified," her mother said with a frail, apologetic smile in her direction, "when I learned I was pregnant, but I decided to keep you because I knew it was the right thing to do." She squeezed the hand she held. "Then I felt you move for the first time, and it became the *only* thing to do. You were real and alive, and you were part of me."

Camille drew a ragged breath and looked Paris in the eye. "And that was the only thing I ever thought was important. I understand your need to know who your father was, but in my heart, I didn't think you needed to know how you happened to be because you'd make so much more of it than it is. You're *you,* and that should be enough for you and whoever you invite into your life.''

More of it than it is. Paris turned those words over in her mind and wondered how knowing who'd composed half of her being could ever be considered too much knowledge. But she made herself focus on her mother. There'd be enough time to think this all through later.

''Your father…'' Camille went on, then stopped to clarify. ''From this moment on, when I say 'your father,' I'm talking about Jasper. He was there the last three months I carried you, he was there when you were born, and he considered himself your father. Whatever personal journey you have to embark upon to put your life in order, that will always be the truth for me. And I was there for both men's contributions.''

Those words firmly spoken, she tossed her head as though to clear her mind, dabbed at her eyes and smiled. ''You know we met in a taxi when I was in a hurry to get to the studio, and he wanted to go to the airport.''

Paris nodded. Her mother had often told her daughters the story. ''He rode with you to the studio, tried to get your phone number, and when you tried to put him off, fibbing that you were seeing someone, he insisted you were fair game, since you weren't married. Then he missed his plane, was a day late for his meeting with his fiancée's parents, which was for the best since he broke up with her, anyway, then he came home, took you to dinner and asked you to marry him on the second date." She'd just never mentioned that she'd been pregnant at the time.

Camille's smile widened. "It's gratifying to know that you sometimes do listen to me." Sadness tugged at her smile, but she held it in place. "God, I wish he was here now. He always understood you better than I did. And that's a curious thing when you consider the circumstances." She took the last sip of her coffee. "I always thought it significant that when you learned he wasn't your biological father and you came home to...to organize your life, you started a taxi service."

Paris was a little surprised to realize she'd never made that connection. Her mother was probably giving it more significance than it deserved, but it was interesting all the same.

"And you know that we named you Paris," her mother said, putting her cup down, "because we honeymooned there and discovered how truly in love we were."

Paris had always thought her name was odd, but liked the notion that it reminded her parents every day of being in love.

"Yes," she said dryly. "And I was always grateful you hadn't honeymooned in Budapest."

Camille freed Paris's hand as though realizing that though the truth had brought them together, Paris had to deal with it on her own.

"Is there anything else you need to know? Do you want his name, so you can verify that I'm not lying about his death?"

After her determination to know the truth, Paris was surprised to experience a real aversion to hearing his name. Then she remembered her bold declaration to Randy that the truth remained the truth, whether or not she knew it, and that nothing would change it. She realized grimly that she'd been right.

"Yes," she said. "Please."

"His name was Glen Griffin," Camille said, knotting her fingers in her lap. "He was tall and dark, and though you might get your height from him, I don't see him in your features. You look like my mother." She smiled thinly. "A prim, proud lady with a heart of gold and a spine of steel."

Paris wasn't sure why she wanted to cry. Relief that she didn't look like him, perhaps?

Camille reached for her hand again and angled her chin, as if she was having difficulty with what she was about to say. "What I want you to remember is that while it was an ugly experience for me, your father helped me get around it. And though you and I often have difficulty understanding each other, you're a piece of my heart, Paris Elizabeth, and I've been grateful for you every moment of your life."

Paris wrapped her arms around her mother and held on for a moment. "Thanks, Mom," she said. "I'm not sure I'd have been as strong. Or as loving, under the circumstances."

"You were as welcome as any other baby born to two people in love."

Paris finally drew away. "Thanks for telling me the truth. I'm sorry you had to feel the pain all over again, but I had to know.'' She gathered up their cups and saucers, needing to put the discussion behind them. ''Now, can I help you put your stuff away so that there's actually room for you on the bed?''

Camille studied her analytically. It was a mother's look, filled with the suspicion that trouble continued to brew.

''What are you going to do?'' her mother asked.

''I'm not sure at the moment,'' Paris replied honestly. ''I have to let it all sink in, then decide where to go from here.''

''Back to school?''

''Maybe.''

The front door opened and Prue walked in, looking completely cute in a big taupe sweater and pencil-slim slacks. Her hair was caught atop her head and wrapped in a brightly colored scarf tied in a bow over her left temple.

While understanding that it was totally unfair to her sister, Paris felt Prue's sparkling, feminine appearance destroy the delicate wall Paris had maintained between herself and the truth she'd just learned. Prue was charming and beautiful. Paris was half...wrong. Half bad.

''Hi, Mom!'' Prue got halfway into the room, clearly excited about their mother's return, when she seemed to sense the vague tension that filled the room.

Paris knew she had to get herself out of it.

''What?'' Prue asked, stopping still near the coffee

table. Then her expression tightened. "Did something happen to Gideon?"

Paris handed her the cups and saucers. "Gideon's fine, I'm sure. Mom and I have been talking. She'll tell you all about it." She took the keys still dangling from Prue's fingers.

She turned back to give her mother another hug. "I love you, Mom. I've just got to go out for a little while."

"Okay, but…be careful. It's late."

"What happened?" Prue asked worriedly.

Paris hugged her, too. "Mom'll tell you. I'll see you later."

She hurried out to Randy's LeBaron that now served as Berkshire Cab and hoped that it knew the way to his apartment.

CHAPTER EIGHT

THE COFFEEMAKER WAS DEAD. Randy stared morosely at the empty carafe, a funeral dirge running through his head. He had the same addiction to coffee that Paris had to chocolate. He didn't care that it was nearing 11:00 p.m., he needed a cup. A day spent in Paris's company, while delicious on one level, made him edgy and confused on another.

He'd thought he was so clever when he'd gotten her to agree to jogging with him every afternoon. He'd been sure the forced proximity would make her want him as much as he wanted her.

It was working—a little. Only trouble was, he was no longer sure what he was after. Oh, he wanted her body, all right, but when she looked into his eyes now, it was as though they gripped at something inside him, held on, refused to let go. Thoughts of her lingered long after they'd parted company.

He didn't want that. He didn't. He'd had that with Jenny, given it everything he had, then something inside him died right along with her.

He needed coffee!

He glanced at the clock, saw that the market was closed, and he seriously considered trying to get to the Breakfast Barn when he heard a knock on his apartment door.

After eleven?

He went through the dark living room to the front door in his sport socks, still wearing his jeans and T-shirt. Paris stood there, drowning in his baseball jacket, her eyes welled with misery.

He could only imagine the discussion with her mother hadn't gone well. His heart bled for her.

He opened his arms and she flew into them. He held her tightly and kicked the door closed. "Easy," he said quietly. "It's okay. Just relax."

She clung to him, her anguish apparently too deep for tears as she gulped deep dry sobs.

He rubbed up and down her back and felt her trembling. He drew her to the sofa and pushed her onto it. "I'm going to get you a brandy. I'll be right back."

He poured it quickly and handed it to her. "It'll help more than chocolate right now."

Whatever had happened with her mother had left her with a grief that looked big and pointed. He waited patiently, his hand rubbing her while she took several wincing sips of the brandy.

Then without preamble, she said, her eyes dark with distress, "My father raped my mother, Randy." Then tears burst out of her like a break in a hurricane wall.

"What?" He asked the question on a note of instinctive disbelief. Of course, she wouldn't be joking about something like that.

"Most people are born because of an act of love,"

she wept, as he took her cup from her and put it on the coffee table, "but I'm the result of an act of violence!"

He took her in his arms again and just held on.

"I was so...so cocky about having to know the truth," she sobbed against him, "about being able to take it, whatever it was. Now..."

"You were probably right about it," he said, holding her tightly, stroking her shoulder and her back. "It's an ugly truth, but it doesn't change you."

He felt her shrink a little closer. "Half of me is made up of someone bad enough to hurt an eighteen-year-old girl that way!"

"No, you're not," he insisted. "You're all you, a woman you made yourself from components given to you by your genes. Nothing about you suggests anybody who could hurt another human being."

"But it's in there. Science says so."

"I don't think so," he disputed. "But if it was true, we're all capable of being bad or cruel. Whether or not we respond to those inclinations is our choice."

"The truth is," she admitted on a squeak of self-deprecation, "I wanted him to be a war hero, or an astronaut, or a judge."

"I know," he sympathized.

"Instead..."

"Stop it," he ordered quietly. "He was nothing more than a sperm donor. From what you've told me, your father was Jasper O'Hara, and you were very lucky to have him. He'd probably be turning over in his grave if he knew you were discounting his influence on you just because it wasn't biological.''

Paris pushed against him to sit up, her face contorted, her eyes still spilling tears. ''I know all that, and I adored him and I miss him every day. But…it doesn't change Glen Griffin's contribution to me.''

''Have you ever been aware,'' he asked practically, ''of any urge within yourself to hurt someone else? To demand what you want without considering the cost to whomever else was affected?''

She thought a moment, then sighed, her shoulders sagging. ''I've had it in for Prue, sometimes.''

He struggled to maintain patience. She was too upset to see how absurd that was. ''Paris, that's just sibling stuff. She's crazy about you. That's not what I'm talking about, and you know it isn't.''

She nodded agreement, then her eyes seemed to lose focus and he knew she was elsewhere, though she continued to speak to him. ''There was a time when I…loved my mother, but didn't really like the idea that I was half her. I thought she was all beauty and clothes and the ability to say the right thing. I wanted to be brainy and make more important contributions than fashion magazine covers and silly movies.'' She hesitated, her eyes still unfocused, but sharpening on some misery he couldn't see. ''But when I think of what she must have gone through. And that she kept me…''

He had to bring her back to him. He put a hand over her mouth to stop her and drew her back into his arms. She came without protest, starting to cry all over again. "I hurt her."

"Because you didn't understand."

"Because I wouldn't listen."

"Because you had to know. Now you just have to get your mind right about it and use the knowledge in a positive way. Don't focus on the fact that a sleaze contributed sperm to your being, but that a brave woman really gave you life."

"I know." She quieted, leaning heavily against him. "I don't care about him, I appreciate all my mother did and I'm no longer angry that she kept it from me now that I understand why, but...I just hate the thought that he's part of me."

"He's not. He contributed biology, that's all."

A moment passed in silence, then she pushed away from him to look into his eyes. The room was dark, but he could see the gleam of tears in hers.

"Do you still feel the same?"

He wasn't quite sure he understood the question. "You mean, if this had happened to me?"

"No, I mean do you still feel the same about *me?* I mean, knowing how I came to be?"

The question seemed to have an importance to her beyond the need to feel secure despite her parentage.

"Of course I do."

"You wouldn't be afraid that I'd do something cruel and hurtful to you?"

He shook his head. "That isn't you. You have to get that straight in your mind, Paris. You're not him."

She looped her arms around his neck, a hint of

sexual longing now mixed with the sadness in her eyes. Excitement and trepidation flamed in him at the same instant. She wanted him! But why now, after all her firm denials? She was hurt, vulnerable. He had to move carefully.

"Do you still want that physical friendship?" she whispered, then she leaned closer to plant a light kiss on his lips. It was gentle, seeking, not at all seductive.

He returned it in kind. "I do, but do you?"

She leaned into him, her cheek against his, her breath in his ear. "I do," she said softly. "I feel as though I need to generate good energy, good thoughts, good emotion." Then she leaned back to look at him again. "I need to find the good woman in me, and…we do so well together in other ways." Now she looked worried. "Would that make you feel used?"

Under other circumstances, that would have been a laugh-out-loud question. As it was, he couldn't prevent a small smile. "I think I could deal with that," he said, pushing her hair back with his hands so that he could look into her eyes, "as long as you're absolutely sure of what you're doing. You've had a major blow to your equilibrium here. Maybe you should…"

All attempts to suggest she think twice and go slowly were swamped when she leaned closer to kiss him again. There was no artifice in the gesture, just a desperate need for him in her hands and her lips that made mush of his resolve.

PARIS HAD NEVER FELT this way before. Well, of course not, she thought with her last vestige of sanity as Randy's hand reached under her sweatshirt and rested like warm suede on the jut of her ribs. She'd never known about her dark beginnings before.

But this need for Randy seemed to exist in and of itself, without connection to the past or the future. It was born of the moment, of his kindness and compassion, of the quiet, shadowy room and the feelings for him she'd suppressed since she'd met him, because she didn't think she could commit to anyone without knowing who she was.

Now that she knew, it was as if the floodgates had opened and everything she'd denied herself in the interest of self-knowledge could now be hers. She knew who she was. She didn't like it, but she knew.

And if she'd had any concerns that Randy would think any less of her, those were laid to rest when he lifted her into his arms and kissed her with a reckless abandon that meshed perfectly with her need to get lost in him. Then he carried her to a dark bedroom. It was as cold as outdoors in it, and smelled of wood smoke and fall. She shuddered against him.

He deposited her in the middle of a casually made bed, then went to the open window and closed it.

"Sorry," he said, coming back to sit on the edge of the bed. "I always sleep with it open. Fresh-air-loving outdoorsmen in my background." He grinned, rubbing her arms gently. "Want to go back to the sofa?"

"No." She bounced once on the soft mattress.

"This is comfortable. And I'm sure we can raise the temperature in here." And just to prove it, she pulled off her sweatshirt, then ran her hands up under his T-shirt. He took the hem from her fingers and pulled it over his head.

"Are you protected?" he asked, suddenly serious.

She grinned. "It isn't cost effective. I haven't had a date in months. Can you take care of that?"

"Happy to."

She flattened her hands against his pectoral muscles, needing to feel the warm strength of him, to know that this was really happening. She almost forgot what had brought her here, just knew that they were here together and that she'd wanted this for some time now.

He wrapped his arms around her, unfastened her bra, then closed his hands over the small globes of her breasts. She felt their tips bead in his palm and the sensation sink quickly and deeply right into the heart of her womanhood.

Then he was on his knees and pushing her back to the pillows, untying and unzipping her snug jeans and pulling them down her legs. Her panties went with them and both were tossed aside. He added his own jeans and briefs to the pile.

His hands explored her with what appeared to be sincere fascination. This adoration of her body was so new, so gratifying in its flattery, that she felt like someone else, pulled out of the vague memories of her mother's revelation and placed in some cosseted, well-born woman's life.

His hands were everywhere, causing her nerve endings to first tingle with awareness, then riot and ignite as his fingertips stroked and strummed. She began to lose her ability to think, her grasp on the tenuous thread that connected her to reality.

A little afraid of the encroaching mindlessness, she tried to take control, grasping his shoulders and attempting to push him to the pillows. He resisted, caught her hands and put them at her sides.

"Don't move those," he said, a small smile on his lips. His eyes flashed and his white teeth shone in the darkness. "It's all right. You don't have to be in charge tonight."

"I have to…think," she heard herself say in some distress.

"No." His fingertips stroked the line of her collarbone, then created their own line down the middle of her body. "You have to feel. Just let it be, Paris."

"I don't think I…" she began to protest, certain she couldn't simply abandon herself to the experience. That wasn't her way. Then his finger traced that line over her belly, then right into her womanhood.

She gasped, already on the brink of that torturous advance and retreat that promised fulfillment. She forgot his directive and wrapped both arms around his neck.

"You weren't supposed to move," he said, amusement in his voice.

"I want you…" she began, unable to form the complete thought before his artful fingers brought fulfillment crashing in on her like the broad side of a storm. It beat her back to the pillows, though she still held on to him, rolled over her on its way in, pummeled her with its tender ferocity, then rolled over her on its way out. She trembled with its impact.

"Randy!" she whispered.

"Right here," he assured her.

She wasn't sure what she wanted to tell him, just that she was overflowing with sensation and the desperate need to know that again, to share it with him.

RANDY COULDN'T DENY a certain pride in knowing that he'd brought the heretofore organized and clear-minded Paris O'Hara to speechlessness. He didn't know what she wanted to say, but he could guess. Even in the dark, he could see that her eyes were filled with wonder. He reached into the bedside table drawer for their protection.

Apparently accepting that she couldn't put whatever it was into words, she simply framed his face in her hands and kissed him with unutterable tenderness. In a moment that tenderness changed to determination and she pushed on him until he was lying on his back.

"Now you're going to use me, aren't you?" he teased. "You did warn me earlier—"

She kissed him into silence. "No talking," she said, "or I might lose my train of thought."

He pretended disappointment. "You're going to use thought?"

"Only to remember," she whispered, nuzzling him as she climbed astride him, "all the lovely things you did to me. Now, shh."

He wasn't sure he could speak, anyway, with her silken thighs draped over his hips and her warm lips dropping kisses over his rib cage, across his stomach, down even farther.

He'd been needing her touch since she fell apart in his arms a few minutes ago, a quivering, silken bundle of little cries. But the instant her lips touched him, he had to recapture control or embarrass both of them.

She was smiling when he caught a fistful of her hair and said urgently, "Paris!"

She caught his hands for balance as he entered her, then settled onto him with a little groan of contentment that sent him right over the edge. He was aware of climbing, climbing, flying as her body closed tightly around his and shuddered as his did in a lengthy climax.

They drifted down, fingers entwined, then Paris fell onto his chest, wrapping her arms around him as though he were the parachute bringing her to earth.

"Randy!" she said again with that same urgent sound in her voice.

"Right here," he told her again.

"I know," she said against his throat as he settled her into his shoulder. "I know. It's a miracle, isn't it?"

A miracle. Yes, quite possibly. He was different. He probably looked the same, but he could feel changes. Jenny had been moved from the forefront of his brain and tucked away in his memory. Grief had been erased and replaced with the buoyancy of spirit he used to have in the old days. That might just be the residual effects of good lovemaking and possibly not permanent, but he felt it all the same.

And he no longer owned his heart. It belonged to Paris.

"I'm...sleepy," she said with a long sigh.

He kissed her bare shoulder, then stroked her hair. "Then go to sleep."

She kissed his throat. "What if I hog the covers?"

He laughed lightly. "Won't matter. With the grip you have on me, if you're covered, I'm covered."

"Who'd have ever thought," she asked on a yawn, "that I'd turn out to be clingy?"

"Cuddly is different from clingy."

"Thank you."

"Go to sleep."

Randy felt her awake with a start in the middle of the night and sit bolt upright. He feared this was the moment of wakefulness when a woman often regretted the night before.

He put a hand to her bare back. "Need something?" he asked.

"Bathroom," she replied.

"Across the hall a few feet to your left," he said.

"Okay. Be right back."

Be right back. That was good. No regret in her voice, no excuse to leave.

She ran back in a moment later, her ivory form a ghostly image racing through the shadows and into bed. She snuggled into him, shivering. He wrapped the blankets around her and held them tightly to her.

"You sleep in flannel when you're alone?" he teased.

"My mother's always cold and my sister's a bit of a hothouse flower, so our house is probably ten degrees warmer than you keep your apartment."

"I can turn up the heat."

"No." She snuggled closer. "This is nice. Did I snore?"

"Not that I noticed. You do kick a lot, though."

"Sorry."

"I'll get some shin guards."

"Does that mean you're inviting me back?"

"No." He felt her little start of surprise and kissed her temple. "It means I'm not letting you leave."

She pinched his shoulder punitively. "I have to be up to drive cab at six."

"If you can get up at five," he said, "I'll take you to the Barn for breakfast."

"To plan strategy?" she asked.

Oh-oh. "Do we need strategy?"

"Well...I think maybe. Now that we're physical friends, we're probably going to need some rules. I mean, it'd be easy to cross the line."

"What line?"

"Between lovers and friends."

"Ah. Well, I don't think I can make that distinction until I've had bacon and eggs."

"Okay. Five o'clock."

Holding her to him with one hand, he reached to the bedside table with the other for the simple old alarm clock with the analogue face that had awakened him every morning since medical school. It was 3:37 a.m. He set the alarm for five, hating the thought that he had only another hour and twenty-three minutes to hold Paris like this.

She'd had such a shock about her natural father yesterday, and they'd had such a mind-bending night together. He had an uneasy feeling she'd regret everything in the light of day.

But maybe not. There was a new positive-thinking element to his nature since making love to her. He decided to indulge it.

PARIS AWOKE TO THE SENSATION of being carried. She couldn't ever remember feeling so tired. She knew the shoulders she clung to belonged to Randy because he seemed to have somehow become incorporated into her being.

"Tell me we're not in the restaurant," she said groggily, her eyes still closed.

"We're getting into the shower," he said. "It'll save time if we shower together."

"Can't get my hair wet. Takes too long to dry."

"I don't have a shower cap."

"Towel."

He put her on her feet on a bath mat, then handed her a dark green towel. "That do it?"

"Mmm," she said, wrapping it around her hair. Then she leaned into him again and closed her eyes. "We could skip breakfast."

"Food will wake you up." She felt him lift her into the shower. The mat was cool under her feet.

"I don't want to wake up," she said testily as he climbed in with her, then quickly changed her mind when he directed the spray on her and began to wash her back. She groaned at the perfect temperature of the spray, and the rigorous scrubbing with the loofah between her shoulder blades. He swiped it over her bottom, down her legs, then moved her bodily to put himself under the spray.

She took the loofah and worked over his broad shoulders, down the artful curve of his back, over his neat buttocks, then down his strong legs.

She was congratulating herself on their clinical adherence to the plan when she was overcome by the need to plant her lips on the curve of the shoulder she'd slept on all night long.

"Paris..." he warned a little hoarsely.

"Right." She dropped the loofah and pushed the shower curtain open, prepared to step out of the tub and reach for a towel.

But he caught her by an arm and pointed to the medicine cabinet. "You give up awfully easily," he complained. "Condoms in there."

She felt him react to her, felt the molten little puddle already forming inside her. She retrieved a condom and returned to the shower.

"I thought you were serious. Here, I'll do it."

"Only about you," he said. "We can get breakfast to go."

He lifted her into his arms and stepped back under the flowing water. "Okay," she said. "But...we're not really going to make love in here, are we? Standing up?"

He rolled his eyes at her, bracing a foot on the side of the tub. "Yes, we are. We're invincible."

"If you slip and I get my hair wet..." she began to threaten, giggling.

With both arms wrapped around her bottom, he swatted her hip. "Pay attention. I'm defying physics for you and all you can think about is your hair?"

Then he entered her and the giggle died on her lips. It was last night all over again, the warmth, the strength, the passion, the delicious sense of security she felt in his arms.

She ripped the towel off her hair and tossed it through the curtain and onto the floor.

CHAPTER NINE

PARIS'S PURSE RANG at ten minutes to six. She and Randy were still wrapped in each other's arms, loathe to abandon the night. With a groan, he reached over her to retrieve her purse from the floor and hand it to her.

She reached into the front pocket for her cell phone. "Hello?" she asked, her voice heavy with sleep and lovemaking.

"Hello," a female voice said uncertainly. "Is…this Berkshire Cab?"

"Yes." Paris cleared her throat. "Berkshire Cab."

Randy rolled off her and grabbed for his clothes at the foot of the bed.

"Paris?" the voice asked.

"Yes."

"It doesn't sound like you. It's Starla."

Paris combed her hair into order with her fingers, as though that would somehow give her voice a more professional sound. "It's me, Starla."

"Rita Robidoux's called in sick at the Barn," Starla said, "and I promised to cover for her. Are you driving this early?"

"Yes." Paris swung her legs over the side of the bed. "I can be there in five minutes."

"Thanks. Did I…wake you?"

"Ah…no. I was just a little slow starting this morning. And I was on my way to the Barn, anyway. Be right there."

Paris pulled her clothes on on the run and collided with Randy, coming out of the bathroom. He was barefoot and bare-chested in jeans, one arm slipped into the sleeve of a dark blue shirt.

"Did I hear you say you've got a fare to the Barn?" he asked as he kissed her cheek.

"Yeah. You know Starla McAffrey?"

"Yeah. But I thought she usually worked dinner and evenings."

"She's covering for Rita, who called in sick."

"So we can still have breakfast if you don't have another call after you deliver Starla?"

"Yes. I don't see why not."

"Good. I'll follow you in the truck."

Starla McAffrey was tall and slender and in her middle thirties. She'd spent the past seven years caring for sick parents. Her mother had been an invalid since Starla was a teenager, and her father, her last remaining family member, had died six months earlier.

Everyone in town had speculated about what Starla would do with her new freedom. They'd expected her to move to the big city, or at least take a vacation. Instead, she'd worked longer hours at the Barn and joined Addy Whitcomb's quilting group.

Prue had been surprised. "I can't believe she didn't take off for somewhere different. I mean, for most of her life as a young woman all she's seen is the restaurant and that house on Adams Street that's had a hospital bed in the living room for as long as I can remember.''

That was true. Paris could remember selling Girl Scout cookies there in fifth grade, and Starla's mother had been in a hospital bed in the front window with a big orange cat in her lap.

But Starla always looked serene. Paris watched her run out of her house in her uniform, pristine apron and serious athletic shoes. She wore her hair in a straight bob that just skimmed her shoulders, bangs adding softness to an angular face. Paris wondered if her life of service had pushed all personal expectations out of her reach, or if she was happy to finally have no one dependent upon her but herself.

She climbed into the back of the cab, bringing with her the spicy scent of carnations.

''I have got to get a car,'' Starla grumbled good-naturedly. ''Then I wouldn't have to get you up at the crack of dawn.''

''It's my job.'' Paris smiled at her in the rearview mirror. ''And I start at six every morning. Sometimes I don't have a fare that early, but I'm ready to go. What's the matter with Rita?''

Rita, in her late fifties, was an institution at the Barn. She'd been providing friendly harassment and personal counseling there longer than Paris had been alive.

''Just the flu, I think. I heard about your accident. Are you okay?''

"I'm fine, thank you. I guess with all the driving I do, the odds were bound to catch up with me." She didn't want to admit that she'd been distracted by personal problems. "But you're perfectly safe, Starla."

Starla laughed. "Oh, I know that. I've always admired your competence. I was proud of you when you came home from law school."

"Came home from law school?" Paris frowned at her in the mirror. "Don't you mean, when I went away to law school?"

"No. I mean when you came home. I know how difficult it is to grapple with a family problem when it'd be so much easier to just stay away and do what you want to do."

Paris stopped at a red light and continued to stare at her passenger in the mirror. She didn't think anyone knew why she'd come home.

"Oh, I don't know the details," Starla assured her. "But I always admired your style."

"You're sure you don't have me confused with my sister?"

"No. Prue's beautiful and remarkable in her own way. And we all know about your mom. But you seemed to maintain a charm and attitude all your own, as though you weren't at all intimidated by them. Being kind of a plain-Jane, I admired that." Then she seemed to regret the way that sounded. "Not that you're plain. You're very pretty in an…"

Paris stopped her, unwilling to allow her to risk personal salvation by lying.

"Please, Starla. I'm not pretty and we both know it. But I appreciate the point you're making. And I pretend to have style so no one will guess that I have no idea what I'm doing."

Starla laughed. "Well, don't tell anyone." Then she sighed and grew serious again. "And I understand your coming home. I went for half a year to Boston College, then had to come home when my father couldn't deal with my mother on his own. I imagine your mother had difficulty coping when your father died. He seemed so strong and steady."

"He was." Paris could agree with that. "But my mother was doing fine without all of us. She just copes. But I came home to…sort of…find myself, I guess. That sounds so trite, but I was confused and needed to come home."

"Yeah. It's perfect here, isn't it? Real life but right in the middle of the small-town, old-fashioned nostalgia for the past that brings all the tourists here in the summer. When things are scary, Maple Hill grounds you. It survived the British, the Civil War, and every other war we've sent men to. It's remained warm and charming in the face of condos and corporate high-rises. It makes you feel that you can survive, too."

"You don't miss Boston?" Paris asked as she pulled into the Barn's parking lot. "I mean, you could probably finish your education now, if you wanted to. I'll bet there's funding available for a single woman…."

"No." The word was polite but firm. "I've been

waiting so long for my life to start. I know school would give me certain advantages, but I'm thirty-six, for heaven's sake, and I've never had time for romance, for parties, for just hanging out. I loved my parents dearly, and don't regret a moment I gave them, but this time is finally for me and I'm going to take advantage of it.'' She rolled her eyes and sighed. ''But so far, I'm batting zero. It's hard to meet a really good man, you know? Many of my customers are married, or I see them cheating, or I know they drink too much. Still…'' Her voice took on a positive note. ''I'm determined there's someone out there for me.''

''Good for you!'' As Paris braked to a stop, she was ready to carry Starla's banner into battle. ''Do you have a particular man in mind?''

Starla made a face as she leaned over the front seat to hand Paris a bill. ''Actually, I have a date for Saturday night. We're going to a play in Springfield.''

''All right! Anyone I know?''

She shook her head. ''I don't think so. He's on a sales route between Springfield and Boston. He just passes through and has a meal. Rita's waited on him a lot, though. She doesn't know much about him, but says he's always very polite.''

That worried Paris a little, but she was sure Starla was old enough to know what she was doing.

''Be careful,'' Paris advised. Then she grinned. ''But have a nice time.''

''Okay. I'll report later.''

''I'll be waiting.''

Randy pulled open Paris's door as Starla disappeared inside the restaurant. "Any calls?" he asked.

"Not a one." She grabbed the cell phone off the console and it rang. She made a face at Randy as she pushed the On button.

"Berkshire Cab," she said.

"Hi, it's Prue," her sister's worried voice said. "Where are you? Where have you been?"

"With a friend," she replied. "I'm fine, and I'm on the job."

"Mom's worried." Prue hesitated a moment, then added on a grim note, "She told me everything. I'm sorry, Paris."

"I'm a big girl," Paris assured her. "There's nothing to worry about, or be sorry about, except that that happened to Mom. I'm just going to…I don't know…pretend it isn't there, or something."

"Paris…"

"Okay, that's probably not healthy. I'll just live around it. We all have issues we can't quite reconcile, so we just keep stepping around the hurdle. Like you and Gideon. You don't want to be with him, but you can't quite let him go."

Prue was silent another moment. Paris closed her eyes and sighed, wishing she hadn't brought up her brother-in-law.

"I've let him go," Prue said finally. "Mostly."

"Well, that's good. Now, if you'll let *me* go, I'm going to try to have breakfast at the Barn before I get a call. Okay?"

"Okay."

"Tell Mom I love her." Paris pushed the end button and dropped the phone in her purse, tucking the big fare wallet in beside it.

"That was close." Randy held the door open for her, then pushed it closed when she stepped out beside him. "I thought we missed our opportunity when the phone rang."

"Just my sister."

He put an arm around her shoulders as they walked to the door. She liked the easy gesture and leaned into him in response.

"She's probably worried about you."

"I'm fine."

"No." He squeezed her shoulders and laughed when she looked up at him in surprise. "Actually, you're magnificent."

"Please," she said with theatrical modesty, "you'll give me a swelled head."

"That's the only part of you we can allow to expand." He opened the door for her and pushed her gently through when she stopped to groan over that reminder. "At least, until after the fashion show."

PARIS LOOKED BEAUTIFUL. There was a small trace of sadness in her eyes that worried Randy, otherwise she appeared to thrive on their lovemaking. Her hair was piled atop her head in a casual knot that spilled silky strands down the back of her neck. Her skin glowed, though he hadn't seen her apply makeup, and he liked to think that the dark color of her lips was due to his kisses. She wore the same yellow shirt she'd worn last night, but she'd put his jacket back on over it, and he couldn't deny the possessive way it made him feel.

He was starting to worry about himself. He'd never expected to be affected this way. Oh, he cared for her and he'd known making love to her would deepen their relationship, but he'd expected the change to be primarily sexual.

He felt as though his entire being had opened and taken her inside him. He felt possessive and protective and fiercely tender where she was concerned. He suddenly hated the thought of her driving all over creation with strangers, but knew how she'd react if he told her that.

He hated that she had the burden of knowledge about her natural father and didn't know what to do about it except "live around it," as she'd told her sister she intended to do.

He hated that the circumstances of her conception made her feel that her value as a human being had been somehow compromised and that she couldn't trust herself to be who she knew herself to be.

He wanted to hold her close to him and fix it all for her.

He smiled to himself as he imagined her reaction to that suggestion.

"What?" she asked him, accepting a menu from Starla.

Starla smiled from one to the other. "So, you weren't kidding about being on your way here, Paris. I know you want coffee with cream," she said to her, but questioned Randy with a raised eyebrow. "Coffee for you?"

"Black, please," he replied.

She disappeared.

Paris looked at him over the top of her menu. "Why are you watching me?" she whispered, holding back a smile.

He folded his forearms on the table and leaned toward her. "Because I'm going to have to spend most of the day without you, so I'm committing you to memory."

She blushed. It melted something inside him.

"Everybody's going to know what we've done," she said, looking around to see if they were being watched, "if you keep looking at me that way!"

"I'm sure people are always speculating on who's doing what with whom. The Barn thrives on gossip—we're just doing our part for the emotional health of the community."

She rolled her eyes at him and looked back at her menu. "What are you having?"

"Sausage, eggs, potatoes, English muffin. You?"

She gasped. "What about the red dress?"

He laughed. "I'm not wearing it."

"But you promised to be my exercise mentor, my health guru. What if I'm so tempted by your choice of breakfast that I decide to have the same thing?"

His attention was caught by the opening door and the pretty young woman stepping inside, accompanied by an equally attractive older woman who looked a lot like her. Both women were scanning the room. He could guess who they were looking for.

"I'd say that probably won't happen," he said, moving his place mat and utensils to her side of the booth and stepping out to wave and call attention to the newcomers. "The serious food police have just arrived."

"What?" Paris peered around him to see what he was talking about and put a hand over her eyes when she spotted her mother and sister. "I don't believe it," she groaned.

"Hi, Randy!" Prue said cheerfully, giving him a quick hug. "I presume I can be this familiar if you're my sister's boyfriend? Mom, this is Randy Sanford. He's an EMT. Randy, my mother, Camille O'Hara."

Randy held out his hand, but the woman ignored it and wrapped her arms around his neck. He had to lean down to accommodate her. "I'm so happy to meet you," she said. "Addy can't say enough nice things about you. Jackie and Hank speak highly of you, too. As does the fire chief." To Paris she added, "And he's not just an EMT, he's a paramedic—an EMT of the highest rank. I've done my research."

"Thank you. But I think everyone speaks highly of someone who can start their heart beating again, or unclog their airway. You don't want to be on the wrong side of someone like that."

Camille grinned as though she appreciated his sense of humor. "Possibly. But I think they were talking personally rather than professionally. Beazie Braga, particularly, has a lot of praise for you. She says you helped her when she appeared on Evan's doorstep, practically unconscious. And you were even off duty at the time.''

"Evan's a good friend. Would you like to join us?"

"If you don't mind.'' Camille slipped right into the booth opposite Paris, and Prue followed her. They were a breathtakingly beautiful pair, he noted, sitting beside Paris. She had very similar features and coloring to her mother and sister, but her height and angularity made her more elegant than pretty, probably an inheritance from her father.

Paris looked from her mother to her sister. "What are you doing?'' she demanded. "Randy does not have to pass inspection from you to go out with me.''

Camille looked affronted. Randy could see that it was an act. Passing inspection was precisely what she was doing. "What a thing to say!'' She tsked and said apologetically to Randy, "Sometimes I don't know what to do about her manners. Frankness is one thing, but—''

"We just came to get acquainted,'' Prue interrupted. "And Mom was just a little…you know…worried.'' Then she added candidly, "I'm sure if Paris stayed the night with you, you know what went on at our house last night.''

Paris groaned again.

"Yes, I do,'' Randy admitted. "And I imagine you wanted to make sure she didn't come to me as a defiant step over the edge.''

Camille seemed surprised that he understood that.

"Yes, that's what I wanted to know. Your praises have been sung by absolutely everyone, but a mother wants to be sure. Paris is hurt and vulnerable right now, and a lot of that is my fault. So I wanted to know..."

What she wanted to know had to wait when Starla arrived with two more menus, two cups and the coffeepot. She poured, greeted Prue, who'd apparently driven her a few times, exchanged a few pleasantries with Camille, who knew other members of the quilting club, then put the pot down, tucked their menus under her arm and took their orders.

"I wanted to make sure," Camille continued the moment Starla was out of earshot, "that you were someone who'd understand her. I'm sure there are a lot of perfectly nice men who wouldn't. She thinks too much, analyzes everything, wants it all to work out. And life isn't like that."

"I'm well aware of that." Randy pushed the sugar toward Camille when she reached for it. "She's just trying to make order out of a difficult situation. I did the same thing when my fiancée died. I thought if I organized everything, put everything in place, her death would make sense."

Camille nodded sympathetically. "Addy told me about that. I'm sorry."

Paris put a hand on her mother's in an attempt to silence her. Then she turned to him with a shake of her head and apology in her eyes. "I'm the one who's sorry. These two think because they're cute and charming they can burst in anywhere—"

He stopped her with an arm around her shoulders. "It's okay," he said. "I don't mind answering questions."

"It's barbaric."

"It's a family's prerogative. And since I don't have any, I kind of like the way it feels to know there's one operating the way a family should."

Apparently resenting that he'd come out on her family's side, she gave him a warning look, though her voice remained mild. "I thought you didn't believe in permanence and commitment."

He wished her mother hadn't heard that, but he knew Paris's purpose had been just that—to put him in trouble with her mother. For some reason he didn't understand, she didn't care for their alliance.

"In man-woman relationships," he said honestly with a reluctant glance at her mother, "it doesn't work for me. But it's a good thing to see in families."

Camille watched him, probably altering her assessment of him. But she frowned as though not knowing what to think.

"You don't believe in commitment to a woman?" she asked.

He explained about watching Jenny die. "I know I could never do that again with a wife and children," he explained, "so it seems better to keep relationships…open."

"You mean…she can see other men?"

"No, Mother," Paris objected, clearly exasperated but trying to remain polite. "He means open. So that I can leave when I need to, and so can he."

Camille blinked at her. "Okay, but I don't see the advantage in beginning a relationship by planning to leave it."

Randy had to admit that she had a point. He waited with interest for Paris to counter it.

She opened and closed her mouth several times. "We're not *planning* to leave it," she said finally, her hands fluttering as she tried to explain, "we're just…just…leaving our options open."

Camille looked mystified. "And you're in agreement with that, Randy?"

Her maternal eyes looked deep into his soul and the casual answer he'd intended to prevent Paris from running away in terror simply refused to be spoken.

"I used to be," he said.

Three pairs of eyes turned to him, one pair filled with accusation. "It's comfortable for the moment," he amended, to placate Paris and ease her mother's fears. "But life changes us every day. Who knows what tomorrow will bring?"

Paris evaded his gaze, then everyone sat back as Starla brought their food. Sweet and spicy aromas mingled and Prue passed her mother the pepper, laughing lightly as she pointed to Paris's plate. "I wouldn't worry about Paris's plan for an open relationship," she said. "She hasn't managed to stick to her diet."

Everyone frowned over Paris's plate with its sausage, eggs, potatoes and English muffin.

Camille grinned with delight.

Randy raised an eyebrow at her grimly as Paris

took the bowl of oatmeal and fruit Starla had mistakenly placed in front of him and gave him his sausage and eggs.

"That was Starla's mistake," Paris said quietly, "not mine. Now, if everyone would mind their business and give me credit for knowing what to do with my own life, we'll get along just fine."

Paris was halfway through her oatmeal when her phone rang. "Berkshire Cab," she answered, looking at her watch. "Okay, Jackie, I'll be right there. Yeah, mine's in the shop." She listened a moment. "Randy Sanford lent me his LeBaron. No. Well, we're having breakfast together, but my mother and sister are here, so I don't think that qualifies as a hot romance. See you in five minutes."

Randy excused himself to Camille and Prue and followed Paris to the parking lot.

"You *used* to think an open-ended relationship was a good idea?" she asked grumpily the moment they were outside. The sun was higher, but clouds were moving in. She marched to the car and yanked open the door.

He caught her arm before she could slip inside. "I used to think it was a good idea," he said firmly. She had to know things were changing. "Are you telling me last night did nothing to shake your concept of how things should be between us?"

Something flickered in her eyes, but it came and went so quickly, he couldn't quite identify it. "No, it didn't." She stood toe-to-toe with him, as though she thought he had to know things were *not* changing. "It was wonderful, and it helped me realize that I have a lot of love and hope in me despite my natural father. But lately my life's been one shocking discovery after another. I'm not promising anything to anyone until I know the discoveries are over.''

He didn't get that. ''You know who your father is. There should be no more shocks.''

''Yeah, well I'm still not sure who *I* am.'' She yanked free of him and got in behind the wheel.

''Oh, hell.'' He was really getting tired of that excuse. ''I can tell you who you are,'' he said, holding the door open as she tried to close it. ''You're the woman who's just looking for an excuse not to have to perform. Big bad Paris with the dangerous genes. Give me a break. If you claim you're still on this personal Zen journey, then you don't have to go back to school, you don't have to fall in love, you don't have to get on with your life.''

She pulled on the door, and out of a fondness for his fingers, he let it go.

''Well, you can journey till you're old!'' he shouted at her through the window as she turned the key in the ignition. ''But the earth's round. It's going to lead you back to me!''

She drove off with a screech of tires and probably in the wrong gear. He guessed he was about to lose his car and his girl.

Randy turned with a disgusted growl to go back inside and found Evan Braga standing in his path, looking at him over the top of his sunglasses. ''That was a good line,'' he praised, offering a sympathetic smile as he fell into line beside him to walk toward the restaurant. "But you have to deal with women with a little less volume in your voice. Shouting turns them off, or makes them feel superior, which is even worse."

Randy glared at him as they kept walking. "Hey. I remember when you weren't doing too well with Beazie. Purple hair. Remember?"

He nodded good-naturedly. "Oh, yes. Loving a woman is a rare and humbling adventure. But that one's special. We want you to work it out."

"We?"

"The guys."

"The guys," Randy told him as he opened the restaurant door, "have nothing to say about it."

"We've already taken bets. I'm sorry, but my money says you're together by Halloween."

He couldn't help a scornful sound. "How appropriate. I'm sitting with her mother and sister. You want to join us?"

"Ooh. Good company, but no, thanks. I'm meeting a prospective client. You working on my building on the weekend?"

Randy nodded. "Yeah. Why?"

"Prudent Designs moved into that middle space upstairs and Prue doesn't want it cleaned until after the fashion show. Just wanted to warn you. Something about endangering the fabrics and all that."

"Okay. I'll leave it alone."

"Good. Cheer up. Your day's got to get better from here."

Camille and Prue were still in the booth, but his plate was gone.

Camille hailed Starla as he resumed his seat. "I had Starla keep your breakfast warm," Camille said, pointing to him so that Starla could see that he'd returned.

"Thank you." He heard an ungracious note in his voice, though he hadn't intended it.

Prue was sympathetic. "She makes us cranky, too. But it's okay. She just has these emotional crises, then she gets over them. You're still coming by to take her running this afternoon?"

He nodded as Starla placed his food in front of him. "Thank you, Starla," he said, then added to his companions, "but the way we parted, we may be running on opposite sides of the lake."

Camille surprised him by laughing. "She's trying to scare you away because she's scared. Don't let her do it. Promise?"

He was making a world of misery for himself, but he knew what he had to do. "I promise."

CHAPTER TEN

IT RAINED, MAKING IT a bad day for cab drivers. The day's take was good because everyone who usually walked small distances to the grocery store or the post office called a cab instead. But then no one on the road seemed to remember how to drive in the rain since they hadn't seen it since spring.

And Paris had the old station wagon back, the LeBaron safely parked at home until she could return it to Randy that evening. She was sure she'd put an end to their running "dates," so she'd have to drive it to his apartment.

She had no idea what was wrong with her. She'd loved everything about last night. She'd loved his touch, his kisses, the tender way his body invaded hers with the utmost tenderness and complete possession. And she'd loved waking up in his arms, turning over to find him smiling at her, bumping into him in the bedroom as they got dressed, planning to breakfast together.

It had something to do with her mother and sister showing up. Something to do with their easy acceptance of him and his camaraderie with them—his ability to be honest with her mother and still charm her.

How could he get along with them so easily when it was a constant tactical effort for her? And what did he mean by telling her mother he *used* to agree that a casual relationship was a good way to go?

How could he have changed his mind? Knowing she could leave Maple Hill whenever she chose to continue this journey of self-discovery, or to go to law school, or to simply just go, was the only reason she'd agreed to let him into her life. It was the only reason she'd gone to him last night.

Well, it wasn't fair. They couldn't embark on a relationship with one set of rules, then change everything midstream.

She was driving back from Springfield in the middle of the afternoon when traffic was stopped by a police officer and a lineup of flares. A Maple Hill police car, a state police vehicle, and an ambulance pulled up to a collision at a spot where a small country road intersected with the highway. Someone pulling out onto the highway had apparently been struck by the other car heading south.

She recognized Randy immediately. He was on his knees in the road, working over a figure too small to be an adult.

Chilly and another police officer had their hands full trying to keep a woman back while Randy worked. Her head was bleeding, and she was crying hysterically.

Traffic from the other direction stopped, and the policeman directing it waved her on. She proceeded with a sick feeling in the pit of her stomach and said a prayer for the child on the pavement and the bleeding woman.

She took Starla home, delivered Mr. Kubik to a doctor's appointment, then picked up the mayor to take her to the hospital on the edge of town. She looked grim.

"Everything okay, Your Honor?" Paris asked, wanting to think about something other than the image of the accident.

Jackie sat moodily in the middle of the back seat, looking out at the rain. "No, it's not. One of our staff went to pick up her son at home to take him to a Cub Scout meeting and they were hit by another car. The first rain of the season is always so treacherous."

Not the change of subject she'd hoped for, but Jackie looked so distressed and probably needed to talk about it. "I saw that accident," Paris said. "Randy was working on the boy when I drove past." She was almost afraid to ask. "Did the boy... survive?"

"He's hanging on, but he has two broken legs and a couple of broken ribs. One punctured his lung." Her voice cracked and she hesitated, then drew a steadying breath. "He wasn't breathing when the ambulance arrived, but the word is that Randy brought him back. Spencer was at our house for a birthday party just last week. Smart, special little boy. Right in the middle of my horror and sympathy for his mother is the gratitude that it wasn't one of mine. Isn't that selfish?"

"Of course not. I'm sure every mother would feel

the same way." Wanting to distract her, Paris asked, "Is she okay? I noticed her head was bleeding."

"Mild concussion, a few cuts on her forehead and a broken arm. Chilly said she tried to reach out and protect her son when she saw what was coming."

"Children are strong," Paris said. She wasn't sure that was true, but people always told each other that when they were in danger. "Let's believe he'll be just fine."

Jackie smiled at her in the mirror. "We'll do that. You're very positive. I'm glad your romance with Randy is going well and that he has someone to share the burden of his work. I know how much he hates accidents where children are involved."

So much for her plans to put Randy out of her life and wallow in self-pity tonight, she thought grimly as she picked up speed on the straightaway.

"RANDY, WHY DON'T YOU come and have dinner with us," Chilly asked as he went into the office to check them out for the day. It was almost six. Everyone had crowded into the office, still talking about the accident. Randy avoided them and kept walking, anxious for fresh air.

He hated kids.

No, he hated the vulnerability of kids, the ease with which they could be hurt, lost, kidnapped, broken. He hated working on an injured one while his mother wept with worry. He hated the thought of ever having his own.

Well, that would make Paris happy if she was here.

When he'd been drunk on their lovemaking and so cocky about their future only this morning, he'd managed to forget about how much he hated the thought of having his own children.

"Thanks, Chilly," he said as his friend caught up with him and they walked out the front door. "But I just want to sit in the dark with a beer and a ham sandwich and be grateful I'm single."

"You saved the kid," Chilly reminded him. "He's going to make it. Kids are tough. Hey! Look who's here!"

Randy looked up to see what accounted for the sudden cheer in Chilly's voice and saw his LeBaron parked next to his truck. Paris stood beside it in a yellow sou'wester, the front of the hat tipped up. Rain fell in sheets. Chilly shouted goodbye and ran to his little import.

Lust raged in Randy at the sight of Paris; a strange, life-affirming reflex, he guessed, considering the day he'd had. He pulled up his collar against the rain.

It was a good thing she'd left angry at him that morning. This wasn't going to work after all. He'd thought for a time that he could forget his resolution about a wife and family and find new courage. But he'd been proved wrong today.

"Hi," he said, going to her. "Got your cab back?"

"Yes." She looked him over as though checking for signs of something. Apology? he wondered. Capitulation? "I'll follow you home."

He shook his head. "Thanks, but just leave it. I'll leave the truck home tomorrow and walk to work."

"No," she insisted, straightening away from the hood. Rain fell in a little stream from the brim of her hat. "As a thank you for lending me the LeBaron, I thought I'd take you to dinner."

He was a little surprised by her amiability concerning their argument, but he was in no mood to sit across from her at a table and talk about nothing.

"Thanks, but I've had a tough day." He smiled flatly. "And you don't owe me anything. I was happy to lend it to you."

She stepped in his path when he would have gone to the truck. "What about our run?" she asked. "You aren't forgetting your promise to the red dress?"

He couldn't imagine what had gotten into her. Why was she suddenly insisting on his company when she couldn't get away from him fast enough this morning? He held a hand up to catch the rain. "We'll get drenched."

"The country club," she said a bit smugly, "has an indoor track."

"I don't belong to the country club."

"I do," she countered. "That is, my mother does."

Apparently subtleties weren't going to work. "Paris, I'm in no mood to—"

"I know." She cut him off and opened the passenger door of the LeBaron. "I know what happened today and you're not going to go home and brood about it. You saved the boy's life, he's hanging on, and it won't help to ponder life's fragility and the pain of loving and losing."

He hated having his mind read—even by her.

"Pretty pushy for a woman who wants an open-ended relationship."

"I'm just pushy in any situation. Get in the car."

He drew a breath. "I don't react well to being pushed."

"Do you react well to being chased around the track, fed Chinese take-out, then made love to?"

The breath left him as though he were a balloon bumping against a lightbulb. He had to take a moment to steady himself. "In that order?" he asked.

"In whatever order floats your boat," she replied, then with a wry look at the torrential rain, she grinned. "Not a bad expression under the circumstances."

He got in the car.

When she followed him into his apartment so that he could change his clothes, she hurried into the kitchen to avoid puddling water on the carpet.

He looked at her glowing cheeks, saw the compassion and affection in her eyes that had firmly refused to let him spend the evening alone, and decided to scramble the sequence of the events she'd suggested.

He swept the dripping hat off her head and tossed it onto the counter, then pulled at the snaps on her coat. He was a little astonished to find her wearing a tank top and shorts—creamy skin visible at her collarbone and shoulders and along her long, smooth thighs. He had a vivid, debilitating memory of them clasped around him last night.

"I thought sweats would be too hot for running...in...doors," she explained distractedly.

He was kissing her before she could finish and carrying her into his room on the last word. Considering all they'd fought about, it occurred to him that this made absolutely no sense, but she was cooperating rather than fighting him, and he wanted her more than he ever had. He could worry about the irrational quality of their love for each other when he wasn't dying of desire.

They made love with heat, urgency and a desperation he was surprised to find he completely understood. They didn't want to love each other with this intensity, but they did. He validated her image of herself as a loving woman, and she made him forget that people got hurt or ill, sometimes lay broken in the road, and often died.

Lovemaking was all about identifying each other as soul mates—if only for the moment—and celebrating life and the gifts two people could offer each other.

Yes. There it was. That sensible argument he'd believed and held to until he'd grown temporarily irrational and thought he could put it aside. Yes. He was in his comfort zone once again. Whew.

AT THE COUNTRY CLUB, Paris was recognized and ushered through the elegant lobby to the dressing rooms below. She pointed him to the men's dressing room on the opposite side of a carpeted lounge. "There's a bank of lockers at the back of the room for visitors. Just put your stuff in there and meet me back here."

The track ran like a gallery on the second level around the basketball court visible below. The wall had been papered in travel posters, he noticed, as he followed Paris.

He caught up with her to ask, "Ever been to Paris?"

She shook her head. "Not yet. I'd like to. You?"

"Yes," he replied. "For two days on a see-the-European-capitals-in-two-weeks tour one summer when I was in college."

"Did you like it?"

He grinned. "I think a man should see Paris with a woman, not two other guys."

"Maybe I can accompany you back some day."

He nodded. That was a nice thought. A little casually spoken maybe—as though they might still be enjoying each other's company "some day." But that was the way he wanted it. The only way he could deal with caring about her this way. He wouldn't allow himself to be taken over to this degree if he wasn't sure he could escape.

Although at the moment, Paris was running so hard *she* seemed to be the one trying to do just that.

PARIS RAN AND RAN AND RAN, as though some giant hand pushed her and she had to keep moving her legs to keep up with the thrust.

It felt a little like she was trying to outrun something. Certainly not Randy. He'd just made love to her in a way that convinced her that all her arguments about open-ended relationships were absurd. This was too big to hold back, to contain, or to escape. Her feelings for him were woven inside her being and had taken root.

Then, what was she running from? The realization that despite all his claims this morning, the accident this afternoon had reminded him why he could never make promises.

She couldn't help but wonder if they'd ever be on the same page about anything.

They brought home two Golden Pagoda specials and sat in front of the television with a pot of tea, paper containers covering one side of the coffee table, and their ankles crossed side by side on the other as they ate.

Randy offered a carton to her. "Last few pieces of General Tzo's chicken?"

"I'd love it," she said, pushing the carton back toward him, "but I'm trying to remember the red dress."

"You ate mostly vegetabley stuff."

"I know. I can't wait until this show's over. Choc-olate-white-chocolate-macadamia-crunch ice cream would taste so good right now."

"Your chocolate stash lives here, remember?"

"I know. But I don't think I could stop at one bite tonight," she admitted.

"Problems?" He grinned. "I mean, besides your mother, your sister, your identity and your dangerous choice of lovers?"

She hooked her arm in his and leaned her head on his upper arm. "No. I've just tried so hard to organize everything, to find the answers to everything, thinking it would somehow clarify the present and help me decide what to do with my future. But the more I learn, the more I think I should just do what I want to do. I don't seem to be able to affect anything, so I may as well just be happy and worry later about how best to deal with whatever happens.''

She felt him kiss the top of her head. ''Can you stay tonight?''

More than anything, she wanted to climb into bed with him, make love again and sleep in his arms until morning. But she'd promised Prue.

''I promised my sister I'd be home to try on a pants outfit I'm supposed to model.'' She sighed. ''I don't feel like moving, but time's getting short and she's getting a little frantic. And her helping with the driving has made a big difference in our income this week. I owe her big time.''

''Isn't she driving tonight?''

''Yes, but she's going to pick up the outfit at her new studio and bring it home with her when she's finished.''

''Okay. I'll take you home when you're ready.''

She couldn't tell if he sounded disappointed or simply tired.

''If I stayed the night,'' she joked, ''my mother and sister would probably invite themselves over for breakfast, anyway. And you wouldn't want that.''

He laughed. ''I like them. I wouldn't mind if they showed up for breakfast.''

''I usually like them, too. It's just that sometimes,

they make me crazy. Like when they get involved in my life.''

"Isn't that what families are supposed to do?''

"No. They're supposed to just cheer you on, whatever you choose to do.''

"Not if they think what you choose to do is bad for you.'' He aimed the remote at the television and turned it off. "About that…''

She'd known this conversation was coming. For most of the evening she'd been waiting for it, wondering how to behave when it came. And she'd concluded that the best thing she could do for herself was agree with him, then put all her energy over the next few weeks into proving him wrong.

She kept her grip on him, but tipped her head back to lean it on the sofa so she could look into his face. He patted her hand on his arm and she thought she detected apology in the gesture.

"Yes?'' she asked.

"I feel differently about what I said this morning.''

"Ah. The earth's flattened out, huh?''

THERE WERE TIMES WHEN RANDY didn't know what to make of Paris. A lot of times. He braced a foot on the coffee table, took hold of her shoulders and turned her in his arms so that she could lean back against his knee, her legs stretched out. There was no evidence of sarcasm in her watchful expression.

"That accident today,'' he said, "reminded me why I have to stay…'' He hesitated.

"Single?'' she asked guilelessly.

"Not solitary," he replied. "Just not committed."

"Right." She smiled at him with no evidence of confusion or hurt feelings. He began to wonder if she'd even listened to him that morning. "Seems to me that's what I was arguing for this morning. You were the one who seemed to forget the plan."

He felt relief that she understood. Sort of.

"Last night was pretty powerful. It made me think that I could forget my promise to myself. But I can't."

"I understand."

He brought her up against his chest to kiss her gently.

"Then you're still in agreement?"

"Of course. It's the only way to play it safe."

Play it safe. Was that what he was after? Protection from his own life?

Yes. Probably.

"Good."

He put her back beside him, wrapped an arm around her and turned the television back on. They watched an old movie until just after ten, then he drove her to her mother's place, feeling vaguely edgy and annoyed. It was disappointment, he told himself, because she wasn't staying with him tonight.

He walked her to the door, and she turned before going in to kiss him with all the fervor he could have hoped for but would have preferred not to be reminded of as he drove home alone.

THE PANTS WERE DARK GREEN silk with pencil legs, and they highlighted every curve and line of Paris's hips and thighs. She looked at the back of her in the long mirror in Prue's room and raised an eyebrow in doubt. "You're sure about this?" she asked.

Prue nodded. "They're perfect. Put on the top." She handed Paris a cropped top that stopped at the midriff, beaded fringed silk falling to her waist.

"I have a Jennifer Lopez backside," Paris complained.

"It'd be nice if you could make us her money." Prue buttoned the top, then turned her to face the mirror. "What do you think?"

"It's beautiful." Paris was being completely honest. She just wasn't sure it was right for her. It was outrageous and sexy and moved tauntingly with her.

Prue caught the back of Paris's hair and held it atop her head. "You should wear it up for this outfit. It's beautiful when it's down, but also distracting. And we don't want anything to call attention away from the fringe and your hips."

Paris gave her sister a judicious look. "This show is for the library. I doubt there'll be loggers and sailors in the audience."

Prue grinned. "All the Wonders will be there and there are a lot of single ones. And I'm sure every married man in the place will be able to appreciate what you do for my clothes."

"As long as they place orders for the clothes. I'm counting on you to support me in my middle age so I can travel."

Prue helped her take off the top and put it on a

padded hanger. "You're not going back to law school?" She put the top in her closet and picked up the slacks as Paris stepped out of them. "You've got all your answers now, and you know they don't affect who you are one bit. So, what's to stop you?"

Paris was about to pull her flannel nightshirt over her head again when Prue stopped her with a raised hand. "One more thing. The little black dress. Every show has to have one."

Paris expelled a sigh. "As long as it's not the red dress. Randy and I had Chinese food tonight."

"Paris!"

"I had a spoon of pea pod chow yuk, one of vegetable chop suey and two small pieces of General Tzo's Chicken. That's it. I thought I exhibited great control."

Prue shook her head at her. "Yes, you did, but if you were going down a haute couture runway, the designer would be firing you right now. Fortunately, it's just mine." Prue delved into the closet and brought out a flirty little black dress with a sequined scooped neck, long sleeves and a short skirt of black tulle.

Prue held it over Paris's head while she reached her arms up and into it. Prue tugged it down, then stood behind Paris to zip it up. It was beautiful, and the cinched waist and flared skirt gave Paris a fragile look unlike her usually sturdy appearance.

Paris ran a hand worriedly along the neckline, which showed the swell of the top of her breasts. "Is this okay?" she asked.

Prue nodded over her shoulder. "Not only is it okay, but I think we'll get you a push-up bra."

"Prue!"

"Paris!" Prue laughed. "I swear to God, I don't know why you don't dress like this all the time. Look at what you do for clothes! Look at what they do for you!"

Paris had to stare at herself an extra moment. It was like looking at an alter ego she hadn't known existed. All the same features but with a glow and a curvaceous sensuality she'd never suspected she'd harbored inside the law student turned cab driver.

Had love done this to her? she wondered. She'd been so sure she'd inherited dark qualities from the man who'd raped her mother, only to find that when she was with Randy all she felt was love, generosity, hope, sunshine, flowers.

Then she remembered his honest admission that he wouldn't be able to love her after all, despite this morning's shouted declaration. He couldn't risk the pain.

"Paris O'Hara," Prue said, her voice quietly grave, "you're gorgeous."

She was, she let herself admit. Well, it was only for this moment, in this dress, with thoughts of love lending a glow to her cheeks, and the very real potential for loss lending drama to the depths of her eyes.

She realized for the first time how it would feel if Randy one day decided that they'd grown too close and he simply couldn't stay anymore. The woman who'd once thought knowing herself meant every-thing, now realized that knowing him did.

Pain ripped at her right where the dress clung tightest. She reached behind her to unzip it, knowing that when she pulled off the dress, she would no longer be beautiful. She would be the old Paris O'Hara who wore jeans and sweatshirts and drove a cab, who wasn't entirely thrilled with whom she'd turned out to be, but had found that loving someone else was more revealing than knowing yourself.

Prue picked the dress up off the floor and Paris turned toward the mirror to yank her nightshirt over her head and run Prue's brush quickly through her hair.

She was stopped cold by the fact that she still looked…pretty. The glamour the dress had given her was gone, but in her eyes was a sort of—and she had to look twice to believe this—a sort of confidence that had never been there before.

She stared at it, the brush clutched to her chest, and realized after a moment that it was the confidence of a woman who knew who she was. Paris O'Hara. Daughter of Camille O'Hara and the cruel and thoughtless gene-contributor,

Glen Griffin. Adopted daughter of Jasper O'Hara, sister of Prue Hale. And she was the woman who loved Randy Sanford.

The impact of self-discovery might have knocked her right over, but she was steadied by that confidence in her own reflection.

"You didn't answer me about law school," Prue reminded her, hanging up the dress.

"I don't think so," she replied. "I like driving the cab, and I love being here." Suddenly bathed in the light of self-knowledge, she gave Prue a hug. "And I love watching you become a designer. Maybe I'll become a transportation entrepreneur, or something. I don't know. The possibilities are out there."

Prue studied her in mild concern. "Because of Randy?"

"No," Paris replied. "Because of me."

"He's a darling," Prue said, "but that arrangement he claimed was working for both of you sounds like trouble. It's one of those relationships that needs an early-warning system, you know what I mean? It'll go along very well and you'll slip into happy complacency, then one day he'll decide he's hemmed in and he'll be gone and you'll be wondering what happened."

It took Paris a moment to realize that her sister had just described her own situation. At least, the way she saw it.

Paris put an arm around her shoulders. "I know. But I'm working on a plan to change his mind."

"You can't change men. Don't you read the books about relationships?"

"Not the man," Paris clarified, leading Prue out of the room. "Just his mind."

"A man believes and behaves the way his mind tells him to. You can't change a man's mind without changing the man."

Paris pinched Prue's shoulder. "Please don't confuse me with logic. I have a plan, and I think it can work. Want some tea?"

"Are you going to explain the plan to me?"

"Only if it works."

"If you wear that black dress when you explain it to him, maybe it will work."

Paris made a mental note to try that.

CHAPTER ELEVEN

RANDY VOLUNTEERED TO work Paul Balducci's days as well as his own the following week while Baldy went to Buffalo, where his mother was ill. He'd miss his days off, but emergencies were seldom that close together in Maple Hill that he wouldn't be able to find time to sleep. "You and Paris going to run mornings, then?" Chilly asked as they prepared their famous molten lava black bean chili and pork—otherwise known as Chilly's Chili.

"No, she starts driving at six," Randy replied, "and I'll be tied up here this week. We'll have to work something else out."

"She's sure looking good." Chilly drained water from the beans that had been soaking all night. "Not that she wasn't always gorgeous, but Beth and I ran into her the other day in the market and she was all smiles and good cheer. Loving you must agree with her."

Randy felt a pinch of guilt he didn't understand. He'd noticed himself how she'd suddenly seemed incandescent.

"I told you a little about her search for her natural father and what she'd discovered."

"Yeah."

"I think just finding out the truth has helped her get on with her life. And she and her sister are involved in that fund-raiser fashion show thing. What woman doesn't glow over clothes?"

Chilly added seasonings to the cubed round steak he was cooking in a big Dutch oven that had served the station for many years. Then he turned his attention to Randy.

"You're getting scared, aren't you?" he asked.

Randy, in the process of chopping onions and green pepper, turned the knife in his hand in a teasingly threatening gesture. "Of what? I probably outweigh her by sixty pounds."

"She's getting to you," Chilly guessed.

"Nothing gets to me," he denied.

"The kid about to breathe his last got to you."

Randy dropped the knife to the cutting board with a bang. "Chill," he said impatiently, "it got to you, too. Who wouldn't it get to? It has nothing to do with—"

"Yes, it does." Chilly took the cutting board from him and swept the onions and peppers into the pan. "You're not as insulated from what goes on around you as you thought you were. You're falling in love with Paris O'Hara, then you saw this poor injured kid, listened to his mother screaming, and thought you couldn't deal with death ever happening around you again. So you're going to back off before you're in too deep."

"You're wrong."

"How am I wrong?"

Randy glared at him. "Because I'm already in too deep."

WITH A WEEK OF SUNNY DAYS following the rain, the cab business slowed down a little and Paris took advantage of the quieter pace and Randy's busier schedule to drive full-time and let Prue have more time to work at her studio. The fashion show was just a week away, and her sister was obsessing over the red dress.

Randy had left Paris a message about taking on several back-to-back shifts, and she decided this was the perfect time to begin implementation of the plan. Though she hated the thought of not even seeing him for a week, she left him a cheerful message telling him she understood, that she'd be driving full-time, anyway, and, signed off with "I'll see you when I see you." It was carefully casual and sufficiently unconcerned to really annoy him if his feelings were more involved than he wanted her to believe.

Of course, there was the chance that they really weren't involved—in which case she was up a creek.

She was grateful for the call on the Friday of that week that took her to the airport. The deciduous trees were just brightening to red and gold among their evergreen counterparts on the hillside. They reminded Paris of the sun-and-shadow quilts Addy Whitcomb made with bright splashes of color amid more somber patterns.

She'd almost reached the airport when she sensed a subtle change in the sound of the cab's motor, a slight decrease of power. She was about to curse the garage that had fixed it when the sound and the power were suddenly back to normal and she began to wonder if she'd imagined the whole thing.

Her fare had said he'd be waiting on the only bench in front of the small airport's very small terminal.

Paris pulled into the spot reserved for taxis and spotted him immediately. He was very tall, probably six foot five or six, and handsome though completely bald. He wore dark slacks, and a gray-and-black houndstooth jacket over a red turtleneck. She took him for a big-city type. Which was all right, because she'd once been a big-city type herself and she knew how unfair it was to categorize people by where they lived.

He stood as she jumped out of the cab and walked around to help him stow his things in the trunk.

"You're very prompt," he said, waving her hand away from the heavy bag he'd placed on the ground while he stowed the smaller one. "Let me get that. You said twenty minutes, and here you are."

"Berkshire Cab does its best to be on time," she said, liking him instantly. She wondered if he was just visiting or intended to stay. "Where to?"

"Well, I'm not sure," he said, climbing into the back as she walked around to the driver's seat. "Is there a hotel in town?"

"There are a couple of inns." She started the cab, pulled away from the curb and turned on the meter as she headed out of the airport. "The Yankee Inn and the Old Post Road Inn. But they're both a little way out of town if you're not going to have transportation.''

''I'll rent a car when I get to town. All the airport rental had was a small car, and my legs are too long. There is a car rental in Maple Hill?''

''There is. It's connected to the garage. Do you want to go there first?''

''No. I'm here looking for someone. I really need to find a phone book first.''

As Paris pulled up at the stop sign at Airport Way's connection to the highway, she reached under her seat for the telephone book she always kept there. She handed it over the seat.

''Who is it?'' she asked. ''Maybe I can help.''

''Camille O'Hara,'' he said, his voice sounding vaguely distracted as he flipped pages of the phone book.

Paris couldn't help the gasp of surprise that escaped her. She turned to look at him in disbelief. ''Camille O'Hara is my mother.''

He blinked once, then smiled. ''You're Paris.''

''Yes.''

He laughed, stepped out of the cab, then opened the front door on the passenger side and climbed in. He offered his hand. ''I'm Jeff St. John.''

Paris was now confused as well as surprised. She shook his hand and opened her mouth to speak, but didn't know what to say.

He took care of that by smiling and looking her over feature by feature. ''I can see her in your hair and your eyes.'' The smile widened. ''But you look like you could change a tire if you had to, or fix the plumbing. Your mother would have to hire somebody.'' His expression gentled. ''How is she?''

She still couldn't imagine what he was doing here, but focused on answering the question. ''She's great. She just came back from a fashion shoot in Africa. She probably doesn't look too different from the young woman you remember.''

He ran a hand over his bald head. ''Well, the same can't be said of me. I used to have a full head of curly brown hair.''

She made the turn onto the highway and, with no one around at the moment, proceeded slowly toward Maple Hill. ''I hope my call didn't upset you so much that you…felt you had to come.'' That call seemed like an eternity ago. What she wouldn't give, she thought wistfully, if Jeffrey St. John were her biological father.

''Not at all,'' he replied, buckling his seat belt and settling back. ''But you sounded sincere and concerned and it made me remember Camille. I always thought that was her stock in trade as an actress. She meant everything from the heart and she worried about everyone. She could look right into a role and find that one thing that made an audience care.''

As she'd done often lately, Paris found herself wondering about her mother's life before her children had entered it—before Glen Griffin had hurt her and forced her to grow up, probably before she'd been ready.

''She still acts in our summer stock sometimes,''

Paris said. "But she likes modeling better these days. She says it's less grueling."

He nodded. "It was always so easy for her to sit there and look beautiful."

Paris glanced at him and caught the pensive look in his face as he looked at her. "Yes," he admitted. "I had a crush on her." He sighed and looked back at the road. "But I was married to a wonderful girl who gave me three very handsome sons. So Camille and I were just friends. I hear she married a banker, or something."

"An accountant," Paris corrected him. "He died five years ago."

"I'm sorry."

"Thank you."

"And I gather from your phone call, he wasn't your father?"

Paris shook her head. "He wasn't, at least not biologically. But he is my sister Prue's father. She's the one who looks just like Mom."

"Did you find your father?"

She'd known that question was coming. "I did," she replied with false good cheer. "So all's well. Shall I take you home?"

"Should I call first?"

"No, Mom loves surprises."

They found her in the kitchen, putting a bouquet of bronze-colored mums in a bright yellow vase. She wore jeans and a long pink sweatshirt and turned with a smile for Paris, then a questioning look for the man who accompanied her.

Paris waited for her mother to recognize him, but she didn't seem to. Camille turned away from the counter, her smile still welcoming but more reserved as she waited for Paris to explain.

Paris took Jeffrey's arm and drew him closer. "This is your life, Camille O'Hara," Paris teased, intoning the famous line from the old television show. "Don't you recognize this man from out of your past?"

Her mother's mouth opened in surprise, then a deep line formed between her eyebrows as she apparently tried to identify the stranger. She looked long and hard and was in the process of shaking her head, saying quietly, "I just don't..." when a sudden light went on in her eyes and a loud gasp of excitement and recognition turned into a scream of delight.

"Jeffrey!" Camille squealed. "Jeffrey St. John!"

"Camille." He caught her as she flung herself at him, closing his arms around her and grinning at Paris over her mother's shoulder.

They hugged and laughed, then Jeffrey set Camille on her feet and held her hands so that he could take a step back to look her over.

"What are you doing here?" Camille demanded. Then she apparently remembered Paris's phone call and frowned.

"Paris, you didn't..."

Paris raised both hands to stop her. "I didn't have anything to do with this. Did I, Jeffrey?"

"No, she didn't." He pulled Camille to him and hugged her again. "God, it's good to see you. After

I got Paris's call, I couldn't stop thinking about you. So I thought I'd stop by and see for myself how you are.''

"Where's Dora?" Camille asked.

"She died a couple of years ago. She'd had Alzheimer's for the past eight."

Tears rose to her mother's eyes. "Oh, Jeff. I'm sorry."

He nodded. "Thank you. She was ready to go, and I have my boys and my music, so life goes on. Never in quite the same old way, but I'm doing fine. Do I smell coffee?"

"Yes. Good heavens, where are my manners. Here, you sit at the work station, and I'll cut you a piece of Perk Avenue's chocolate-white-chocolate marble cheesecake."

Paris, headed for the door, turned to ask in distress, "You didn't buy one of those?"

Her mother winced guiltily. "Just two pieces. One for Prue and one for me because the food's been so austere around here since you…since we…since the red dress."

Paris swung a disgruntled glance toward Jeffrey. "My mother and sister put me on a diet because of an upcoming fashion show, but they eat behind my back."

He made a sympathetic sound. "I'm sorry, but since you aren't my daughter, don't expect me to share my piece."

"It's Prue's piece."

"Well, I don't know her yet, so I won't feel badly about eating it."

Well. He was okay. Paris blew him a kiss, waved at her mother and answered her ringing phone as she went back to the cab.

It was Prue.

"You'll never guess who showed up out of the blue!" Paris taunted.

When she heard Prue's intake of breath and the several seconds of heavy silence that followed her question, she wished she hadn't done it. Prue had obviously jumped to a faulty conclusion.

"Gideon!" she guessed on a whisper.

Hating that she was hurting her, Paris plunged on, pretending not to notice the plea in her sister's voice. "No. It's Jeffrey St. John." She told her about Jeffrey, remembering her mother's genuine delight at the sight of him, and her girlish rush of color. "He's eating your piece of chocolate-white-chocolate cheesecake as we speak."

Prue recovered quickly. "What does he want?" she asked.

"Mom, I think," Paris replied. "Did you need me to pick you up?"

"No. Actually, I was thinking I'd take you to Clea's for a makeover and to have your hair done this week to make sure we know what we're doing for the show. She says she'll open for us on Sunday so I can be with you. I wanted to make sure you and Randy weren't doing anything."

"No, we're not," she said lightly. She didn't feel

light; she felt troubled. And her plan had been in place only a couple of hours.

"How come?"

"He's practically living at the station this week."

"Oh."

"What time on Sunday?"

"One o'clock. I'll take you to lunch."

"So you can make sure I don't eat anything? Thanks a lot, sis."

"Darn right," Prue said. "When you're finished tonight, would you come to the studio so I can try the red dress on you?"

"Sure, but why don't you just bring it home?"

"Because, depending on how it fits, I'm going to do a little more work on it so I can dedicate the last few days before the show to the wedding dress."

"There's a wedding dress?"

"There was always a wedding dress at the end of a designer's show in the old days and I want to bring back the tradition."

Paris thought that was interesting, considering what had happened to Prue's marriage.

"I think that'll be nice."

"Maybe the dress will change your mind about a permanent relationship. Maybe it'll change Randy's, too."

"Maybe it'll make you want to get married again," Paris returned.

Prue sighed. "I'd have to be out of my mind."

"There, you see." Paris laughed. "First qualification covered."

"Very funny. You might remember I'm going to be pinning seams and hems on you tonight. You could be the first fashion-acupuncture experiment."

"Meanie."

"So, WE'RE GRACED WITH your presence today?" Evan Braga harassed Randy as they followed Hank, Bart and Cam as they jogged along the road that led around the lake. The fall morning was cold and their breath puffed out ahead of them. "We're good enough to run with when the lady's too busy to join you?"

"We're shorthanded," Randy replied, "and I'm covering somebody else's days so I've hardly seen her. Another guy covered for me so I could get a break and have the morning off.

"And you're never good enough to run with." Randy picked up the pace. "You run like the high school girls' track team. Can we get a little speed going here?"

"We're going for endurance," Evan yelled after him as he sprinted around his companions and set off at a dead run.

"That's as good an excuse as any," he shouted back.

Not a minute had passed before he heard his companions at his heels. He ran harder, a weird zest in him as he found yet more speed, more air.

He knew they thought he was insane. These runs around the lake *were* supposed to be about endurance, about building up the strength and stamina their often physical jobs required. But demons were driving him today. He'd tried several times to call Paris but the cab's line had been busy, and once there'd been no answer at all. He'd left a message that she'd returned—when he'd been out on a call.

He couldn't explain why it made him so edgy. Because it means she's not suffering as much as you are, obviously, he told himself. He hated to think he was that self-involved, that petty. But it was clear he was.

In a moment his companions had caught up and it was the picnic football game all over again. The morning's easy jog had changed to a high-stakes run and Hank took the lead. Somehow the competition redirected Randy's tension so that he was able to shoot out ahead of him and maintain the lead until they reached the midpoint on the lake where they always stopped to turn around. The other side of the lake was a little wilder, part of the road unpaved.

"Race you back," Randy challenged, running in place as everyone else caught up. "Last one back buys doughnuts."

"I can't eat doughnuts," Cam grumbled. "I'm playing groom to Paris's bride in the fashion show."

Randy bounced a light punch off his friend's flat stomach. "There's not an ounce of gut on you."

"I promised Mariah," he admitted grudgingly. "It's a European-cut tux."

Evan frowned. "What does that mean?"

"It'll be tight if he eats a doughnut," Bart interpreted. "So, even if you can't eat a doughnut, you can buy ours when you show up last." And he led the pack as they all took off, leaving Cam standing there.

It was a dead heat most of the way back until Evan tried to sprint ahead, managed to trip Hank, who reached instinctively for Bart as he went down. Randy, unable to evade the flailing arms and legs, involuntarily somersaulted over the lot of them.

As they all laughingly blamed one another, Cam jogged by. "I'll have an orange juice!" he shouted as he passed them, "a granola bar and a cup of yogurt!"

Hank reached out to snag his ankle and brought him down in the damp grass on the side of the road. Randy and his companions roared their approval.

"Poor losers," Cam said, sitting up and spitting out grass. He was trying hard not to laugh.

"I am not paying for health food," Hank said, getting to his feet and reaching down for Randy's hand. They helped the others up and stood in a still-laughing knot in the middle of the road. "Let's go to the Barn instead of the bakery and Cam can have an Egg Beaters omelette, or something."

"I'll buy," Randy volunteered. "I've been doing double shifts all week. I expect to need a tax break. I'll write it off as a gift to the developmentally disabled."

The guys cheered him, more interested in having breakfast paid for than in taking offense at his smart remark.

Rita Robidoux put two tables together for them

near the back and quickly set it up while they pulled off jackets and sat down, ruddy faced, eager for coffee and food.

"You guys been pillaging Springfield?" she asked, pushing Randy down into a chair. "You look loaded for bear."

"We've just had our morning jog," Hank explained, "and we're starved. What's the special?"

"Four-cheese omelette. Let me get the coffeepot while you're thinking."

Randy was debating the merits of the special over his usual favorite, sausage and eggs, when he looked up and spotted Paris, sitting alone in a booth near a window.

She was alone, and yet he felt a weird sort of jealousy. She was supposed to be driving now. Why hadn't she told him she was coming to the Barn for breakfast? Why hadn't she asked him to join her?

"Excuse me a minute," he said to his companions as he stood and crossed the room.

She saw him coming and smiled welcomingly as she dipped her spoon into a bowl of oatmeal.

He slipped into the booth opposite her, ignored her genial "Hi," and asked without preamble, "Why didn't you tell me you were coming for breakfast?"

She shrugged, looking a little surprised at the abrupt question. "I didn't know. I started at six as usual, but there was a brief lag a few minutes ago, so I thought I'd stop in and see if I could get a bowl of oatmeal eaten before the next call. What are you doing here?"

He pointed to the table where his friends were now engaged in earnest conversation and glancing their way. "Somebody's covering for me so I could get a break. I jogged with the guys this morning. We're having breakfast."

She nodded. "That's nice. They're such a good group. You didn't get suckered into buying everybody's breakfast, did you? According to Jackie, they're always racing or betting on something and the loser ends up with the tab."

"No, I volunteered. I've put in a lot of hours this week."

"Yeah, me too. But Prue's designs are coming along beautifully. You coming to the fashion show?"

It irritated him that she asked the question. "Of course, I'm coming. Why are things so casual between us?"

She blinked at him, confusion in her wide eyes. "Pardon me?"

He wondered precisely what he had meant by that. "Well...we're lovers. I'll be there."

"Okay." She studied him. "It was just a simple question. And we're not really lovers, we're just physical friends, remember? No strings on either side."

"Is that why you didn't return my call?"

She frowned as she apparently tried to remember what he was talking about. "I did. I left a message."

"But you didn't talk to me."

"You weren't there," she said emphatically, as though he were slow. "That's why I left a message."

"I haven't seen you all week."

"I know. You've been at the station all week. I don't see how that's my fault."

She had him there. That was true. What was wrong with him?

She seemed to be pondering the same question. "What's the matter with you? You tell me you can't commit but you want to continue our relationship, so I try to honor that by staying out of the way while you're working sixteen hours and you take offense because I left a message on your answering machine?"

"No." He heaved a sigh and tried to explain what he didn't understand himself. "I guess I'm just... missing you."

She smiled gently and patted his hand. "I miss you, too."

That small touch brought back wild memories. "What about this weekend?" he asked.

She spread both hands noncommittally. "Prue's working on the red dress this weekend and she wants me available for fittings. The show's Thursday night."

He couldn't decide if her excuse was valid or if she was putting him off. Love, he thought, was making him paranoid.

"I'm working with the janitorial crew tomorrow night in the Chandler Mill building. I might run into you."

"That'd be...good," she said, hesitating as her phone rang. She held a finger up in a "hold-on" gesture and answered it. "Berkshire Cab. Oh, hi, Parker."

Parker was a massage therapist and Mariah's sister. Also, the wife of Gary Warren, backbone of Whitcomb's Wonders' landscapers.

"Sure. Where we going?" Her eyes widened and she asked in whispered surprise, "You're kidding! *The* Bobby Rutland? Um…yes, I think your chair will fit in the cab. Yeah." Her eyes went to her watch. "Ten minutes? I'm finishing breakfast, and I don't think the Barn would like it if I ran off without paying. No, it's okay. It's just oatmeal. I'm happy to leave the last few bites to be able to see Bobby Rutland."

"Massage on the run?" Randy asked as Paris pocketed the phone and pulled out her wallet.

"Yes!" Paris slipped out of the booth, clearly excited. "Bobby Rutland's staying at the Yankee Inn learning a script and feeling tense. Jackie recommended Parker."

As well as being mayor, Jackie Whitcomb was proprietor of the Yankee Inn. It had been in her family since the early 1800s.

"Who's Bobby Rutland?" he asked, helping her on with his baseball jacket. He took the fact that she was still wearing it as a good sign. With all this fashion stuff going on, it might just be the cut she appreciated about it, not the fact that it belonged to him. God. Where the hell had this insecurity come from, anyway?

"He starred in that bank heist movie, remember? Ah…" She snapped her fingers, groping for the name. "*Also Known As...* That was it. He's supposed to be the new Brad Pitt. Really handsome and very intense. And I'm going to help Parker carry her chair up."

Then to his complete surprise, she put a hand on his shoulder, stood on tiptoe and gave him a kiss sharply at odds with the cavalier way she'd behaved since he'd come to her table. It went on and on, and he was happy to let it.

Then she drew away, kissed him quickly one more time, then excused herself to hurry to the cashier.

He snatched the bill from her and turned her in the direction of the door. "I'll get it. You can help carry the chair," he said, "but no contributions to the massage, okay?"

She laughed and hurried off.

Everyone in the restaurant was staring at him, and raucous cheers and applause were coming from his table.

Everyone should stare at him, he thought as he returned to his friends. He hadn't a clue what was going on. He felt completely out in the cold with Paris one minute, then as though she adored him the next. Was this his own insecurities at work, he wondered, or some cosmic plot to confuse and confound him?

He didn't know.

"Oh, you're not going to make it till Halloween," Hank said, pushing the cream pitcher toward him as he sat down. "You're going to be engaged by the fashion show."

"He doesn't believe in marriage," Bart said.

Evan snickered. "Yeah. Neither did I."

CHAPTER TWELVE

THE RED DRESS WAS absolutely scandalous.

Paris was usually not judgmental and figured that clothes were a telling expression of self, but the dress Prue held up on a hanger was about twelve inches long and not much wider than that.

"Is that…all…there is to it?" she asked in a horrified whisper.

"It's a cotton-Lycra blend," Prue said, whipping it off the hanger and handing it to Paris. "It'll cover more than you think it will."

Paris doubted it, considering she was at least three times longer than the dress in the torso alone, but one of the important lessons she'd learned on her quest of self-discovery was that her sister had a gift for design and it wasn't Paris's job to second-guess her.

She pulled on the dress and still couldn't help a gasp into the wall mirror Prue had had installed in her new studio.

The red was a rich, ripe apple color with a low-cut top, a back that dipped to the waist and a hem that was several inches above the knee on a very tight skirt. And it somehow looked…sensational. Scandalous, but sensational.

But there was no way she could appear in public in it.

"Prue, I can't..." she began to plead, but a look had come over her sister that Paris first thought was distress. Prue's eyes widened, she walked around Paris, then she began to cry.

"It's perfect," she whispered. "It's absolutely perfect. I designed the perfect dress." She wrapped her arms around Paris—or, really, the dress—and wept.

Paris tried to remember how she looked in it without her sister stuck to her. She was showing entirely too much bosom, too much back, too much leg, too much everything! And what wasn't bared, was clung to by the rich fabric that followed every movement, every breath.

While Prue enjoyed her emotional breakdown, Paris patted her shoulder and looked around the generous dimensions of the sparely furnished room. There was nothing in it but tables for working on, several sewing machines, a rolling rack of finished and half-finished projects, several overstuffed chairs she'd helped Prue haul from the secondhand store. There were shelves with bolts of fabric in them, drawers filled with trims, buttons, other sewing notions. Prue had the design studio she'd dreamed of at last.

But there was no way Paris was going out onto a runway in this dress.

"Prue, I cannot be seen in this dress," she finally said when it sounded as though her sister was pulling herself together.

Prue straightened and dabbed at her nose with a tissue. "What do you mean?"

"Well, look at it!" She held both arms out in the mirror, her eyes focused on what seemed like acres of bare flesh. "I guess it's beautiful, but it's....I mean...jeez, Prue!"

"Paris, you look gorgeous in it," her sister said, walking around her again. "Of course it's outrageous, but it's supposed to be. This isn't the little black dress, this is supposed to get you noticed, to tell the world you're a party girl in love with life, with your own womanly attributes, and with the man who'll appreciate you in it." She stood on a small stool as she spoke and wound Paris's hair into a loose knot. "I'm thinking we'll just do your hair up for that night."

There was a knock on the studio door. Prue pointed to Paris. "Don't move." She went to the door and opened it.

"Hi, Prue." Paris felt a frisson of embarrassment run down her spine when she heard Randy's voice. He couldn't see her in this dress! It revealed every...

She stopped her inner voice from arguing with her. He'd seen her naked; it didn't really matter what the dress revealed.

"Evan said I was supposed to ask you if you wanted anything done," Randy asked, still unaware that Paris was in the room. She looked around for somewhere to hide, and began to sidle toward the rolling rack of clothes. "I know you're working and probably don't want floors done or anything like that, but we can empty your trash cans, clean the bathroom, whatever else you'd like done. Then, when you're not busy, you can set a sched—"

He didn't as much stop talking as choke on the last word.

"Randy, I'm so glad to see you." Prue took his arm and pulled him inside the room. "Come and give us your opinion. I think my creation is brilliant, but Paris is afraid it'll horrify our audience. What do you say? Paris, stop hiding behind the rack and get out here."

Paris could feel the blush from her cheeks to her breasts as she walked to the middle of the room. But she angled her chin and threw back her shoulders, aware that though she did look scandalous, the dress was wonderful, and if he thought he really wanted to be uncommitted to all she had to offer him now that she had a stronger sense of self, he had another thought coming. And she had a plan to prove it. He was already not reacting well to her pretense of keeping their relationship casual. All she had to do was keep it up.

RANDY COULDN'T MOVE, couldn't breathe, couldn't speak. Every man had an image in his mind of the physically perfect woman, the supermodel he'd love to show off on his arm if there really were miracles. And here she was all wrapped up in the sweet, funny, difficult, confusing woman he'd slept with a couple of times, fallen in love with, then decided he couldn't love.

Who'd have guessed?

The dress was magnificent and seemed to have a transforming effect on Paris. The clear-eyed woman he'd sat across the table from this morning was now a gorgeous, sensual woman of great complexity.

But he couldn't help a slow perusal of her ivory shoulders, her slender arms and shapely legs exposed halfway up her thigh. The fabric clung to her breasts, to her narrow waist and nicely curved hips. Intoxicating beauty wasn't simply the stuff of poems. It lived.

Her eyes bored into him, waiting for him to tell her and Prue what he thought. He saw a little antagonism there, a vague defiance that made him wonder if it was the dress that had changed her, or something else he was afraid was pulling her out of his reach.

"I think she looks…stunning." The word was pale, but the best he could come up with.

"Turn around, Paris," Prue advised.

"Prue…" Paris groaned.

He arched an eyebrow to challenge her. He wasn't leaving this room until he'd seen the back of her in this dress.

Defiantly, she did a turn and leaned on one hip, her hand resting on her hipbone in classic runway style.

She did not disappoint. She had probably a shade too much flare in the hip to model professionally, but he had a personal preference for a little sway in the derriere, and she had it to perfection.

"There are no words," he finally said on a longing note he couldn't help.

Paris turned back to him, that defiance now mingled with a sadness that seemed completely out of place. He stared at her in perplexity.

"Is that it?" she asked Prue.

"Yes, I think so. Let's go home."

Paris grabbed a pair of jeans and a sweatshirt off a bench and disappeared behind a door.

Prue asked Randy if his crew could empty the trash baskets, but leave everything else alone. They could establish a more normal routine after the fashion show when she had enough time to wall off an area to keep garments under construction safe from flying dust and cleaning agents.

"How's it going with you two?" Prue asked when they'd settled their business. "She seems a little...tense."

He nodded. "I know. But I can't really explain it."

Prue sighed. "Maybe it's chocolate deprivation. I can only guess by the look of her in that dress that she's been eating carefully and working out."

"I can attest to that." He picked up a trash basket near him. "I ran into her this morning at the Barn and she was eating oatmeal. Excuse me." He carried the basket into the hall where he'd left the cleaning cart and turned it over into the thirty-gallon bag. He put a liner in the basket and returned it to the edge of her worktable.

"She's been working long hours this week to give me time to finish my line." Prue sat on the edge of the table, a measuring tape around her neck and a fat, red-fabric pincushion fastened to her arm like a bracelet. "But she pitched in with Mom and me and bought a treadmill. I may have converted her to good health habits after all.''

"Certainly didn't hurt the red dress. I'll stop in next week and we'll decide what you'd like us to do in here.''

She straightened away from the table. "Good. I heard that little boy in the accident is going to make it, after all.''

He nodded. "I heard that, too. That's a real blessing.''

"Life seems to do that to us all the time," she said. "Terrify us, then bless us. Makes it hard to keep your balance.''

He knew there was a significance in that message directed at him.

"It does.''

Paris burst out of the small room now dressed in jeans, a knit shirt and his jacket. The red dress was on a hanger, which she handed to Prue. He couldn't believe the dimensions of it.

"That's a miracle of engineering," he said to Prue as she hung it up.

"It's all in the right fabric and the right cut. And putting the right body inside it." She looked around herself. "Now, what did I do with my jacket?"

"You never put it on," Paris said, slinging her purse over her shoulder. "It's in the cab.''

"Ah." She continued to look around. "How about my purse?"

"Under the table.''

"Right." Prue reached down for a big leather pouch with fabric sticking out of it.

"Can I talk to Paris for a minute?" Randy asked when Paris would have followed her sister to the door.

"Sure." Prue waved at him. "See you later. Paris, lock the door, okay?"

"I will." Paris turned to him, an eyebrow raised in question. It was a pretense, he knew, because he could also see in those green depths that she felt the tension as much as he did. Somehow, their easy camaraderie had fled this week and they were like some star-crossed couple, angst and doom perched above them like a pair of vultures. "What is it?" she asked, trying to look calmly removed.

He didn't buy it for a minute. He could feel the waves of heat and awareness as he closed the small distance between them. The red dress had given her a powerful glamour he was surprised to see she hadn't entirely lost when she took it off.

She'd pulled her hair down and it hung like a sunshot cloud around the shoulders of his jacket and skimmed her eyebrows, making her eyes even wider, deeper.

"I have a question," he said, stopping when they were close enough to touch. "And an answer."

"Why ask me the question if you have the answer?"

"Because they're not related. The answer is to a question you asked me this morning."

She looked confused. "I don't remember asking you a question this morning."

"It was nonverbal."

She shifted her weight, a frown appearing between her eyebrows. "How can a question be nonverbal?"

He showed her.

PARIS DID NOT SEE the kiss coming. Her brain was busy dealing with the question she couldn't remember asking, so that even when he put a hand to the back of her head, she was still trying to read his eyes to figure out what he was talking about.

He'd sat in her booth at the Barn, they'd argued about her leaving a phone message, then he'd walked with her to the cash register and...

Before she could remember everything, he tipped her head back and his mouth opened over hers.

The kiss! she thought as her head spun and her ears rang. She'd kissed him that morning because she'd wanted to confuse him. He'd been the one who'd put a distance between them, then he'd been angry because he'd had difficulty reaching her for several days. Her plan had been to taunt him with all she had to offer him. She wanted him to remember what he wouldn't be able to have at his beck and call if he insisted on a casual and open relationship.

Her nonverbal question, she realized, had been, "Do you love me?" A little needy, perhaps, but sincere.

There was no denying his answer. "Yes! Yes!" It was in his plundering mouth, his exploring hands, his long body arched possessively and protectively over hers as he held her.

She responded in kind, her arms wrapped tightly around his neck, her mouth opening to him, her body pressed to his.

She had to pull away to breathe, her hands sliding to his chest.

He took a step back, his eyes still turbulent with emotion. "I do love you," he said. "I don't want you to be in doubt about that."

That was a major stride forward. She just wasn't sure he understood what it meant.

"I'm not," she said gravely. "I love you, too. But I know that things have to change, or the love between us won't be able to survive."

"Love survives everything." He looked suddenly alien to her in the dark coveralls. This was like the dark side of the man usually dressed in white.

He resisted what she was trying to tell him. He could admit to loving her but wasn't promising to do anything about it. "It can't survive neglect," she said. "Or denial."

"I just admitted that I love you."

She nodded. "I know. But you're not willing to act on it unless I can promise not to have an accident, or get sick and die on you."

He took hold of her forearms and gave her a small shake. "Paris, you're the one who's changed the rules. What happened to the way we planned all this? It was going to be fun and easy and—"

"And open-ended, I know." She shook her head,

wondering why he couldn't see the flaw in his argument. "We thought we could have that fun-and-easy thing, but I came to you when I learned about my father, and you took comfort from me after that accident. We helped each other, found comfort and strength in each other. That's not easy and fun…that's something else. That's adult and difficult. I didn't change, we changed together. You just don't know what to do about it."

He dropped his hands from her. "I said I love you."

"Those are words, not action."

"You want me to propose?" he asked. "To promise you all the small-town warm-and-fuzzy stuff that's in the air around here? I can't. I know how all the flowers and frills can be ripped apart."

She rolled her eyes. "And I don't, the child of a rape?"

"Oh, get over it." He shook his head at her. "You had every advantage ever offered anyone. A mother who let you live, a stepfather who adored you, a sister who put you in that red dress, a community that thinks you're something really special."

Paris was rattled by hurt feelings and the knowledge that he was absolutely right about her advantages. But he could stand to hear a few home truths, too.

"If you can take my problems so casually," she said, her voice tight, "maybe it's time to dismiss yours. It's very sad about Jenny, but it's over and I'm not going to stand in front of you like a shield in our 'open-ended' relationship to protect you from ever getting hurt again. You're going to love me, or I'm out of here.''

He folded his arms, looked away from her, then into her eyes. Even without understanding body language, she thought there was probably some serious withdrawal message there.

"I don't want to promise what I can't deliver."

"You don't want to promise, period!" she accused brutally. "But what you seem to be forgetting is that you stayed with Jenny to the bitter end, but you weren't married to her. You hadn't exchanged any vows. You stayed because you loved her, and in your heart, that meant something and made you stay. The big commitment you're so afraid of has nothing at all to do with it. You'd stay because that's the kind of man you are.'' She expelled a breath because her words had been hard to say. "God, you're more in the dark about who you are than I was about myself. So...goodbye.'' She tightened her grip on the strap of her bag and stormed toward the door.

"It's not goodbye!" he yelled after her.

"Yes, it is!" she shouted back.

She ran down the stairs and was almost to the cab when he caught her and spun her around. She opened her mouth to shout at him and he kissed her with that same heat, that same message of love he seemed to recognize in himself but failed to understand.

He finally freed her mouth but held her face in his hands a moment longer, his grip and his eyes intense.

"No," he said quietly. "It's not."

Then he freed her and strode back inside.

It was a minute before she could walk to the cab and climb in. She was grateful that Prue was driving.

"What was that all about?" Prue asked. "Wow. I heard shouting, then you came running down and...that kiss!"

Paris leaned her head wearily against the headrest and turned toward Prue. "Would you believe me if I told you I don't know?"

Prue smiled thinly. "Sure, I would. I've been in love."

"I thought love was supposed to make sense. You find someone you can relate to, and you promise to relate to them all the time. Why does it have to be more complicated than that?"

"Because men and women don't relate in the same way," Prue replied as she started the motor. "Women want to nurture and hold, men want to protect and understand. Only men don't like to be held too tightly, and women defy understanding. I think it's one of God's puzzles. I don't think we're destined to figure it out, just to have fun trying."

Prue drove off into the night.

"Fun?" Paris asked skeptically.

CHAPTER THIRTEEN

CAMILLE AND JEFFREY WERE dancing to a Frank Sinatra CD when Paris and Prue got home. The coffee table was littered with an empty bottle of champagne, two champagne glasses, a plate of pâté and a small basket of crackers.

They were cheek to cheek, arms wrapped around each other, Camille with her feet several inches clear of the ground as Jeffrey held her to him. Camille waved lazily at them over his shoulder, and as their dance turned them in a small circle, Jeffrey raised his head to smile at them. "Hi, girls," he said. He'd stayed last night on the sofa. "I'm staying awhile longer. I hope you don't mind."

"Of course not." Paris waved at them. "I'm off to bed. See you in the morning."

"Do you cook, Jeffrey?" Prue hesitated before she followed Paris.

"Very well, as a matter of fact," he boasted. "Quiche and fruit for breakfast?"

Paris laughed. "You're welcome to stay as long as you like."

"You can't eat until after the show," Prue reminded her with a shove toward the bedrooms. "I'll have to eat your share.'' The moment they were out of earshot, she whispered to Paris, ''Aren't they cute?''

Paris had to nod. ''But it's demoralizing that Mom's doing better with her love life than we are.''

Prue stopped in front of her room. ''And to think this all started because you called him, thinking he was your father. Good night.''

Paris ducked into her own room with a silent groan. Her search for her identity had started something else that was proceeding far less happily. She hoped Randy was right. She hoped it wasn't over. But it certainly felt like it.

ON MONDAY, PARIS AND THE CAB were both acting up. Paris experienced that same strange sound in the cab's motor and the loss of power several times over the next few days. She stopped by the garage one slow afternoon, someone looked under the hood, told her it was just a poor battery connection and repaired it.

She drove off, confident that the problem was fixed. The oil-and-gasoline smell of the garage, however, seemed to have upset her stomach and she gave up her usual stop at the Barn for a salad to go and simply drink water. She was comforted by the thought that starvation was probably good for the red dress if nothing else.

By Wednesday, the day before the show, the cab was fine, but she was beginning to believe she had a slowly developing case of the flu. Her mother had taken Jeffrey on a three-day trip into the Berkshires, though they'd be home in time for the fashion show, and Prue was at the studio day and night.

Paris kept warm 7UP and soda crackers in the cab and managed to keep driving, though nausea was with her all day long.

Starla called, needing a ride to the cemetery.

"Not working today?" Paris asked as she pulled a U-turn in the city hall parking lot and headed for Starla's.

"No. It's the first anniversary of my mom's death, so I have a pot of her favorite yellow mums to put on her grave."

"How nice. I'm on my way."

The afternoon was overcast and dreary. Combined with her physical discomfort, Paris had to struggle not to let her mood match the weather.

Starla smiled sweetly as she climbed into the back, then seemed to lose herself in a study of the rainy landscape as Paris drove in the direction of the cemetery. She was apparently having the same mood problems Paris suffered.

"How was your date with the salesman?" Paris asked, finding Starla's reflection in the rearview mirror. "Are you seeing him again?"

"He was funny, charming and really good company," Starla replied, still staring outside. The tone of her voice suggested there was more to the story. "Then his wife called on his cell phone. Oh, he tried to pretend it was something else, but between the monosyllabic answers, and the gentle voice and small words that suggested the caller had put a child on the phone, I put two and two together. I think he saw that and claimed they were separated.''

''Maybe it was true.''

''No, he looked guilty. So…'' Starla blew air noisily. ''I'm trying not to be discouraged, but I am. I'm wondering if my perception of who's honest and who isn't, who is worth pursuing a relationship with and who isn't, is antiquated or just plain faulty. I mean, I always thought I was a good judge of people.''

''I think trying to meet the right man is just difficult,'' Paris said sympathetically. ''Even if you do find the perfect soul mate, chances are he has a history that makes him reluctant to get involved, or you have your own issues that make it risky to take a chance.''

''I know.'' Starla sighed. ''I guess loving anybody is just plain risky. Children can break your heart, aging parents can cost you time and patience, and men, well…they're just mystifying. In the restaurant, I enjoy their easy camaraderie with one another, the gusto with which they enjoy their food, their laughter. But you get them alone and they brag, or get too familiar too fast, or lie to you. Why is that?''

Paris thought of Randy, and for all her grief over his reluctance to love her, he'd always been a perfect and trustworthy companion.

''I think you just haven't met the right one. I'll have to have Addy put you on her list. In fact, I'm surprised she hasn't already done it.''

Starla laughed. ''She's tried, but I've resisted. I told her I haven't been able to date most of my life because of having to care for my parents, and I wanted the experience of finding someone myself. But I'm beginning to think that was arrogance.''

Paris got another call as she turned into the cemetery.

''Berkshire Cab. Hold on, please.'' She looked into the rearview mirror. ''Where to, Starla?''

Starla reached past her to point. ''That meadow. I can walk from here. Will you come back for me in half an hour or so?''

''Sure.'' Paris pulled up to the designated spot. ''Just give me a little leeway. Wouldn't you know it. I could have just waited for you—it's been a slow afternoon. But now I've got a call.''

''It's all right. If you're delayed, I'll just sit under this tree and wait for you.'' She pointed to a giant maple, its bright crimson-and-gold leaves spreading over a large area like a giant and very colorful umbrella.

Paris looked doubtfully at the sky. ''Looks like rain.''

''That's okay. A little rain never hurt anyone.''

''Okay. See you in a bit.'' Paris backed to the last crossroad, turned and put the phone to her ear. ''Berkshire Cab,'' she said. ''Thanks for waiting.''

''Hi, Paris.'' She recognized Ashley Morrison's voice. ''Can you pick us up at school?''

''Sure,'' Paris replied. ''But this isn't your usual day, is it?''

''No. Daddy made a dentist appointment for Michael for tomorrow afternoon, so we have to go today.

I know we can't get your bargain rate, but we have to see Mom.''

"Okay. Wait right by the door."

"We will."

That was fortuitous, she thought. It would prevent Starla from having to wait for her if it did rain because she was coming right back.

When she arrived at the school, Ashley and Michael ran to the cab and climbed into the rear seat, tossing their backpacks on the floor. Michael buckled his seat belt, but Ashley reached into the front seat and handed Paris a black wax candy mustache, the kind that fitted into the mouth, then sat on the upper lip like a prop from a Gilbert and Sullivan light opera. "Our room mother brought these for us for Halloween." Ashley put on a pair of big red lips and Michael flaunted buck teeth.

"Oh boy!" Paris put her mustache on immediately and both children collapsed into giggles. She had to take it off again to speak. "Thanks, guys. I love it! How did you get an extra one?"

"Mrs. Whitcomb gave it to me. I asked her if I could have it for you. She said to tell you she wants a picture of you wearing it."

"She's the mayor, you know," Michael said importantly. "She's the boss of the city."

"Yes, I know that," Paris responded gravely, refusing to be distracted from the question on her mind. "Do you guys have permission for this trip?"

Ashley opened her mouth and Paris guessed she

was prepared to lie. But she seemed to think better of it.

"No." Ashley's eyes brimmed with tears. "But we have to talk to Mom. We *have* to."

"Are you still having trouble with the Thanksgiving play, Michael?" Paris asked.

"It's not just Michael," Ashley said. "It's me, too. Daddy wants to move to Buffalo."

"That's in New York," Michael added. "Where Grandma lives."

"He thinks it'd be better for me and Michael," Ashley explained. "We'd live with her, so we wouldn't have to go to day care after school."

"Would you like that?"

"We want to stay home," Michael said emphatically. "I like my room and our yard. I don't want to live with Grandma. She wants me to take karate lessons and Ashley to take acrobatics."

"That could be fun." Paris didn't know whose side to favor, so she tried to sound objective.

"Michael wants to raise a guide dog with Mr. Elliott, and I like to go to the library and get books to read after school." Jimmy Elliott, one of the Wonders, raised Labs and some were trained by locals to become part of the guide dogs program.

"Did you tell your dad how you feel?"

"He says we'll like it once we get there." Ashley's voice was filled with skepticism. "I like it here. And we wouldn't get to visit Mom anymore."

"Daddy found out that we visit Mom," Michael

said. "That's why he wants us to move. If we do, this'll be the last time we get to talk to her."

Oh-oh. "I should take you to the day-care center," Paris said. Big raindrops began to fall on the windshield.

"Please, Paris." There were tears in Ashley's voice. "Maybe this is the last time."

"Please," Michael added.

Paris saw the distressed dark eyes in her rearview mirror and turned and drove in the direction of the cemetery.

"I just took Starla McAffrey there," Paris said. "She's visiting her mom, too."

"I like her," Ashley said with new cheer. "She's one of the volunteers at school who helps us with our reading."

Without warning, the cab jerked slightly, the power diminished, and Paris was just beginning to groan and pull over, thinking this could be divine intervention, when it came back again as though nothing had happened.

"Sounds like a fuel-pump problem," Michael said with the sincere conviction that he knew what he was talking about.

Paris picked up speed, thinking that she was going to have some rude words for the mechanic in the morning. And she should probably stop driving early so that she didn't get stuck out in the boonies somewhere in the dark.

Paris grinned through the windshield in the direction of heaven. "I know, I know," she said under her breath. "I'll get back to the day care as soon as I can. Meanwhile, I've been patient with the little tricks you've played on me. Is it too much to expect the same consideration?"

RANDY HAD JUST SAT DOWN in a booth at the Barn when his cell phone rang. He guessed it was Baldy, calling to tell him he couldn't work tonight after all and would Randy mind covering his twenty-four-hour shift one more time.

He was tired from last week, but he was pleased for the opportunity to do something other than stare at the four walls of his apartment.

He'd gone home twenty minutes ago, intending to find something in the cupboards for dinner and have an early night, when he'd gotten a vivid image of Paris sitting on his sofa eating Chinese food, her feet in boot socks crossed on his coffee table.

It was curious how he remembered not only the physical aspects of that moment, but its emotional importance as well. He'd been happy. She'd been happy. They'd been happy together, and for that moment all the shadows had been chased from his soul and he'd felt warm and optimistic.

He had yet to recapture that moment. It had scared him, he realized. Happiness had been an alien concept for him for some time. The last time he'd been happy, Jenny had been alive and well, and that hadn't lasted nearly long enough.

His cowardice was clear enough. And he was willing to fight it, but unwilling to risk Paris's happiness if he failed.

His head aching from a puzzle without a solution, he'd decided to have dinner at the Barn.

"Hello," he said. "Baldy?"

There was a moment's hesitation, then a throat was cleared and a female voice said, "No. Randy?"

He recognized Paris's voice and felt his heart punch against his ribs. "Yeah." He tried to sound casual. *Go ahead and dismiss me, missy, and see what it gets you.* "What's up?"

Another momentary silence. "I'm stuck," she said finally.

"In what?" he asked.

He heard her sigh. "Ha, ha. Look, I didn't want to call you, but everyone else I tried doesn't answer. My mother's gone for a couple of days and all my friends are probably picking their kids up from school or whatever. Can you help me, or are you just going to do stand-up?"

He ignored her censure. "A turnstile? Mud? Traffic? Stuck in what?"

"The cab is stuck!" she enunciated loudly. "I have two children and Starla McAffrey with me, and it's raining. We'd get drenched walking home!"

He was already sliding out of the booth, waving Rita away as she came toward him with a cup and a pot of coffee.

"Where are you?" he asked, making his way out to the parking lot.

"The cemetery," she replied a little more quietly.

"The cab has absolutely no power. The battery's fairly new, so I don't think—"

"It's a fuel pump problem!" he heard a child's voice shout.

"I've been told it's something to do with the fuel pump," she repeated dutifully, "but I'm not sure how qualified—"

"Sit tight," he said. "I'll be right there. And stay inside."

"Stay inside," she repeated flatly. "How stupid do you think I am?"

"Do I have to answer that? You did tell me you thought it was over between us."

The line went dead.

He dialed another number, then chased Rita back to the counter to ask for two cups of coffee and two cups of cocoa to go.

Ten minutes later Randy followed the tow truck into the cemetery. Clete Morrison had sounded a little reluctant about the call, though he admitted that he was available. "Cemetery's just not my favorite place to go, you know?"

Randy could understand that, but when he explained that Paris had two children with her, he heard a pithy oath on the other end of the line. Then Morrison said he was leaving immediately.

The tow truck stopped abruptly at a junction in the road where Paris and her companions stood under a large maple. A little boy cried his heart out while Paris, Starla and a little girl tried to calm him. Randy thought he recognized the two children as Morrison's.

He knew them from the "Dial 911" classes he'd helped teach at the grade school.

Randy pulled over and parked to give Clete sufficient room to turn around.

Clete backed up carefully to Paris's old cab, then leapt down from the truck, anger in every aspect of his being as he headed for the little group.

Confused, Randy hurried after him. Paris, he noted, looking a little pale, stood protectively in front of the children, her arms held out to shield them.

From Clete? Randy couldn't believe that; he knew him. He'd hauled the ambulance back when a pickup slid into it on the ice last winter—without a patient in the back, mercifully. But he'd been friendly and considerate, and given Randy and Chilly coffee out of his thermos on the ride back to town.

"I can explain," Paris said, standing firm as Clete stopped within two inches of her.

Randy had no idea what was going on, only that he had to intervene. He got between Paris and Clete and put a hand against Clete's chest. "What's going on?" he asked. "What's the matter with you?"

"These are my children!" Clete bellowed at him, trying to push him out of his way.

Randy pushed back. "I know that. So, why are you scaring them?"

"Because they're supposed to go to day care after school, they're not supposed to be here!"

"Please understand, Mr. Morrison," Paris said from behind him. "They come here to talk to their mother, not to ignore your wishes. We were waiting for you in the cab, then Michael insisted on saying goodbye to his mother one more time on the chance that you do move and he doesn't get to come back."

"Their mother," Clete said darkly, "is gone. There is no one here to talk to!"

"Well," Paris said after a moment's hesitation, "there's apparently no one at home to talk to, either, and that's why they come here."

Clete's shoulder went slack under Randy's hand, a look of raw pain on his face. "Talking," he said, that same pain in his voice, "won't bring her back."

"The children know that. But they still feel very connected to her, and since you've distanced yourself from her death and their need to understand it, they're trying to…to get it from her."

The children peered at their father from around Paris's body, the boy sniffling.

"It's my fault, Daddy," Ashley said, coming around to face her father. Randy moved out of the way. "We don't want to move and we thought Mom would have some ideas about how to make you stay."

"If you were with Grandma," Clete said, obviously struggling against anger and sadness to try to be reasonable, "you wouldn't be stuck in the rain in a cemetery."

"We don't feel like we're stuck," Ashley said, smiling slightly. "Mom's here."

Clete shook his head. "Mom's…Mom's in heaven."

"This is their way to reach her, Mr. Morrison." Starla stepped forward and placed a hand on Ashley's shoulder. "Ashley and I were just talking about that because I come here to see my parents. We know we can't touch them, but we can talk to them here. The stones have their names on them, and we can put the flowers we bring into the vases near their stones, and somehow that brings us together. Michael says he always picked flowers for his mother, and remembers that she'd hug him and put them in a water glass on the table."

Michael came to take Starla's hand. "I know she comes here when she sees me with the flowers," he said, his eyes pleading with his father to understand. "Want to come and see? I bet you can tell she's here, too."

Clete initially resisted, but with a child pulling on each of his hands, he was forced to follow. Michael, still holding on to Starla, brought her with them.

Randy turned to Paris, forgetting that they were angry with each other. "How do they know Starla?"

"She's a reading aid at the school," she replied. "But I brought her here earlier, then got the call from the kids to pick them up. I was going to bring them all home together when the cab wouldn't start."

"It didn't occur to you," he asked judiciously, "that these kids were supposed to be someplace else?"

"They were safe with me," she said, "and I thought it was brave that they were trying to face their loss and find a way through it. Unlike some adults I know." That last was added with a significant jut of her chin in his direction.

Her chin, he noticed, was trembling, and his jacket and her jeans were soaked through. He went back to the truck and pulled one of the cups of coffee out of the carry tray he'd placed in his passenger seat and handed it to her.

"So, one minute you call me to rescue you, and the next you're bad-mouthing me?"

She was frozen in surprise for several seconds, then took the cup from him with a look of reluctant gratitude. "Thanks. For the coffee and for coming to get us. Though I wasn't expecting you to bring the tow truck."

"I was supposed to push the cab all the way back to town?"

She rolled her eyes. "Of course not. I just thought...you know. Guys know all about cars. I expected you to have some brilliant solution."

"If there had been a medical emergency," he said, "I might have been able to help. But, your faith in me notwithstanding, I don't know that much about cars. I can add oil and change a bulb if it isn't halogen. Otherwise, you know as much as I do. And, anyway..." He looked a small distance across the garden of headstones to the grave over which Clete Morrison was huddled with his children. He was crying and they were all holding one another. Starla, her hand still clutched in Michael's, patted Clete's shoulder with her free hand. "It looks as though I made a good move, however inadvertently. Clete needed to come here."

Paris nodded. "I think so." Then she looked at him

with concern. "Are you all right? Is it hard for you to be here?"

It took him a moment to realize what she meant. And to realize that there truly was no pain in him at the moment—at least not for himself. "No. It's not. Jenny wanted to be cremated, and her parents and I sprinkled her ashes in a little cove near Carmel where we used to fish."

She blinked at him. "I didn't know you liked to fish."

"I don't," he replied. "She did. She loved everything, and it was hard not to get caught up in her enthusiasm. Even for something as simple and quiet as fishing."

GREAT, PARIS THOUGHT. Jenny apparently had her life together and was not at all the neurotic Paris was turning out to be since she'd found out about her father.

Her father.

She looked around herself to get her bearings and scanned the area for that spot on the knoll with its view of Maple Hill where Jasper was buried. She started out for it.

"Paris?" Randy asked.

She reached a hand out for him and pulled him after her. "I want you to meet someone," she said.

Out of the shelter of the trees, the rain beat on them mercilessly. Randy took off his jacket and held it over them as she stopped at the simple stone that marked Jasper O'Hara's grave.

"This is my father," she said to Randy, kneeling down to pull weeds away from the stone. The little vase provided was empty.

Randy knelt beside her, still holding the jacket over her.

"I forget to come here," she said, a clear image of the man who'd always loved and supported her dreams unconditionally swelling her heart with love. "I guess I thought like Clete did, that I wouldn't get anything from coming, but it isn't true." She rubbed a hand over her heart where she felt his presence. "I can feel him." She laughed lightly, but tears welled in her eyes. "He was always so steady, so practical, and in a house filled with my mother and sister, I was grateful for him. I think I allied myself with him because I knew I wasn't beautiful like Prue and Mom. I liked thinking that I took after him."

"Maybe you do," Randy said quietly. "I don't think all our heredity comes to us by blood. A lot of things come to us because we love someone and learn from them."

She put a hand on the stone. "Because I went looking for my natural father," she said, needing desperately to communicate what was on her mind, "please don't think I loved you any less. You'll always be my dad."

Randy finally placed the jacket over her head and pulled her to her feet. "Come on," he said. "We have to get you and those kids home before everybody catches pneumonia."

The sound of machinery greeted them as they made

their way carefully down the wet hill. Clete was hooking up the station wagon to the back of the truck. Starla and the children were sitting inside.

Randy opened the passenger door of his car, retrieved the carry tray of cups and urged Paris inside. ''I'll be right back,'' he said. He handed her the keys. ''Turn the heat on.''

She did as he said and watched as he handed the cups into the cab of the truck, then closed the door and pulled the Berkshire Cab magnetic sign off the station wagon. He walked around the car to do the same on the other side. He stopped to exchange a few words with Clete.

Paris leaned out the window to shout, ''Would you bring the log, too, please?''

Randy held up the clipboard that was always on the front passenger seat.

''That's it,'' she said.

The car in place, Clete shook hands with Randy and exchanged a few words. Clete's coveralls were also soaked through, and Paris couldn't help but wonder if he was angry with her over what had happened this afternoon.

She had her answer when he followed Randy to the car. Paris lowered the window.

''Thank you for helping my children,'' he said. His eyes were a little stunned, as though he wasn't sure what had happened today. ''I'm sorry I frightened you.''

Paris shook her head. ''You had every right to be

upset. I was just caught in a difficult situation and they…seemed to need someone to understand.''

He nodded.

"Are you taking Starla home?''

He shrugged a shoulder, a little light in his eyes in the midst of his confusion. "Actually, she's invited us to join her for dinner at the Barn as soon as we change out of our wet things.''

A loud hallelujah! was on the tip of Paris's tongue, but she swallowed it and smiled politely. "That's nice.'' She glanced at her watch. "I'll just call the garage in the morning?''

He nodded. "I called and told him I think you have a fuel pump problem. I'll just leave it in the side lot.''

She couldn't help a grin. "Michael knew what was wrong.''

"That's my kid,'' he said, grudging pride all mixed up with the day's emotional challenges

"Thank you, Mr. Morrison.''

He grinned. "If you're going to tell me hard truths about myself, you may as well call me Clete.''

She patted his hand on the open window. "Thank you, Clete.''

Randy waited for the truck to pass him on its way to the highway, then turned and headed for town. As he pulled up at the stop sign, Paris's cell phone rang.

In her momentary confusion over the events of the afternoon, she answered with a simple "Hello?''

"Paris?''

"Yes.''

"Hi, it's Addy. I need a lift to the bingo game at St. Anthony's."

"Addy, the cab just fainted on me. I think you'll have to—"

"I'll pick her up while you're changing your clothes," Randy said quietly, holding up one of the magnetic signs he'd rescued. "Where does she want to go?"

"Bingo at St. Anthony's."

"Okay. I'll deliver her, then I'll come back to your place and you can take over."

Paris stared at him a moment, astonished that he'd be willing to help her again considering their continuing argument.

"Addy," she finally said into the phone. "You'll have a new driver, but you'll be picked up in about fifteen minutes. Is that okay?"

"You mean Prue?"

"No. I mean Randy."

There was cheerful laughter on the other end of the line. "Well, I thought you two were quits. Rita said she heard the two of you arguing at the Barn the other day."

"We are quits," Paris insisted with a firm glance in Randy's direction. "He's just being a...a friend."

He made a scornful sound, but he kept driving.

Paris noted the call on the log, then turned off the phone.

"What was that for?" she asked. "You're not being a friend?"

"I'm being the man who loves you," he corrected her.

She thought about his efforts to push her away, then his continuous kindness and eagerness to help at every turn. What on earth did it all mean?

"Actually, you're being the man who confuses me." She was starting to shiver and the last few words came out with a little tremor in her voice. And she became aware suddenly and rather forcefully of the flu that had plagued her most of the afternoon. Now that the car-and-children crisis was over, she was aware of herself again. She thought longingly of the pop and crackers she'd forgotten in the car.

"Well, that's appropriate," he countered. "I haven't been able to make sense of you since the day I met you."

"Yet you claim to love me. Why would you want to do that?" she challenged.

He turned the wipers up a notch. "It's not a case of wanting. It just seems to be."

"Well, stop it, because I'm not loving you back."

"Liar," he accused quietly.

"Okay." She turned to glower at him. "It's not a case of wanting to for me, either. Still, it does just seem to be. But you're one of the things in my life that I've decided doesn't have to affect me. It doesn't matter that I'm not the beauty my mother and sister are, it doesn't matter that I'm the product of a rape and it doesn't matter that you can't commit to me, because I'm just beginning to understand what I'm worth despite the strikes against me. I'm going to be just fine, anyway.''

He raised an eyebrow and gave her a surprisingly congratulatory smile. ''Bravo. It's about time, at least on the first two counts. But don't dismiss me so easily. We could be very happy together.''

Now she made the scornful sound. ''As physical friends? That didn't work, remember? You fell in love, then tried to push me away because you didn't like it. Or maybe because you were afraid of it. Anyway, it didn't work.''

But, was *her* plan working? She stifled the excitement she felt and studiously maintained her frown of annoyance.

''Maybe we should try it again,'' he suggested.

''Nothing's changed.''

''How do you know unless we try it again?''

She sighed as he turned onto Lake Road. ''I don't. But right now my mind's consumed with being wet and cold and having to be ready for Prue's show.''

''All right, then. We'll talk about it after the show.''

He pulled into her mother's driveway and stopped the car.

''Thank you for coming to get us,'' she said, grabbing her purse. She handed him the cell phone. ''And thank you for picking up Addy. I'll be ready to take over when you get back.''

He got out of the car to walk her to the door.

''Randy, this isn't a date,'' she said, mildly annoyed by his thoughtfulness. That made no sense, she realized, but then, what did? "You don't have to…"

He caught a fistful of her hair and ignoring the purse and the cup of coffee, wrapped his other arm around her to silence her with a kiss. It was hot and firm and vaguely angry.

"We'd get along better," he said, "if you'd stop telling me what I should and shouldn't do. Go get changed. I'll be back in half an hour."

Paris peeled her clothes off and hurried into a hot shower, praying that she'd be able to stave off the full impact of the flu until after the fashion show.

CHAPTER FOURTEEN

ADDY HAD FAILED TO MENTION when she called Paris that she was taking much of the lineup of Wonder Women with her to St. Anthony's. The women married to Whitcomb's Wonders were so called because of their active roles in the community.

Addy, Haley and Jackie climbed into the back of the LeBaron while Mariah and Beazie piled into the front. The car was suddenly filled with the rustle of fabric, the fragrance of mingled perfumes and the sound of laughter. Randy smiled to himself at the thought that this was every single man's dream—if he wasn't friends with their husbands and if he didn't care if he reached his next birthday.

"Do your husbands know you're going to gamble?" he asked as he turned in the direction of the church.

"It's a social function to support the church," Beazie disputed.

"By gambling."

"Right." Mariah, sitting next to him, elbowed him in the ribs. "We're hoping to make enough to go to the Jersey shore next weekend where they really know how to gamble."

Her companions erupted into laughter. It was catchy.

"Where are all your cars tonight?" Randy asked.

"They're home," Jackie replied. "We just wanted to see Paris and find out what's going on with the two of you and this seemed like a good excuse. But it seems we got the 'new driver.'" Her voice teasingly emphasized the title Paris had given him. "What's going on?"

Without going into detail, he explained about Paris's cab breaking down on a trip, and his having to rescue her with the tow truck. "She's using my car again until hers is fixed. She's going to take over again as soon as she's changed into dry clothes."

"All right, then." That was Jackie again. "So, I guess we'll just have to ask you. How's it going?"

"I heard you two had a fight at the Barn," Addy said before he could answer.

"And I heard you kissed her at the Barn," Haley added. "So, which is true? You can confide in the press."

"Both reports are true. We're enjoying each other, but we're having a little trouble getting along."

There was a general murmur of agreement in the cab. Even a consensus.

"We've all been there," Mariah said. "The important thing is not to give up. Sometimes making love work hurts a lot, but it's always worth it."

Another consensus—this one more shouted than murmured.

"I imagine we'll see you at the fashion show?" Addy asked.

"Of course," he replied.

"She been staying off the chocolate?" Mariah asked.

"Wait until you see her in the red dress."

"Is it wonderful?"

"It's wonderful."

"Are we each going to need one?"

"I think so."

Money was pushed at him as the Wonder Women piled out of the car in the church parking lot.

"Don't tip me!" he protested, "I'm just the—"

"We're tipping Berkshire Cab." Jackie kissed his cheek before climbing out. "You take good care of that girl, you hear me?" she whispered. "We know what happened to her mother. You'll be good for those women."

Addy pinched his ear on her way out. "This could have been so simple if you'd just listened to me months ago when I wanted to fix you up. But I guess all's well that ends well. You keep working at making it end well, Randy."

Randy intended to take her advice, though he doubted seriously that anything with Paris could have been simple, months ago or today.

Randy took a call from the Lightfoot sisters at the Maple Hill Manor School, who were also coming in for bingo. He picked them up, and while they cheerfully bent his ear about ongoing building projects at the school, he noticed Clete Morrison and Starla walking into the Barn, Ashley and Michael skipping along behind them. They were laughing as Clete opened the door for Starla and Randy found himself hoping this would lead to a promising relationship.

He understood Clete's grief, though he and Jenny had had no children. He imagined it would be painful to look into two little faces that resembled a lost loved one and be reminded every time of that pain.

He dropped the Lightfoot sisters off, logged the trips as Paris always did, then was heading back to her house when he got another call. This one was a pickup at the Yankee Inn, heading for the airport.

He was getting into this, he thought, stopping at a light. And Paris was going to need her rest if she was going to look beautiful tomorrow night. He'd drive tonight, and Balducci had promised to work a couple of his days whenever he asked. If he could collect for tomorrow, Paris could have all the time off until the show.

He dialed Baldy's number, made the arrangements, then dialed Paris as he drove toward the inn.

"I'll drive until ten tonight," he said, "and I got someone to cover for me tomorrow so I can keep driving. All you have to do is rest so you can make that red dress look sensational. Warn Prue that she'll probably have four orders for it." He told her about Addy having the Wonder Women with her.

He'd expected her to put up an argument, and was a little surprised when she offered only token resistance to the plan.

"Are you sure? You'll get tired. Do you know where all the streets are?"

"I've got your maps. I'm keeping the log. I think I'm going to be fine. Get some rest."

A gusty little sigh suggested that she needed it. "This is very nice of you," she said.

"I know," he teased smugly.

"It doesn't change anything."

"Sure it does. How can you resist a man who makes it possible for you to get your beauty sleep?"

"Thank you, Randy."

That wasn't exactly the gushy reply he'd hoped for, but there had been something special in the way she'd said his name.

"I've got a ticket for the front row," he said. "I'll see you tomorrow night. And after that, you can have all the chocolate you want."

She giggled. It was a nice sound. "Good night."

PARIS AWOKE FEELING FRESH and rejuvenated, if very hungry. Bright sunlight filled her room and she sat up with a sense of urgency. She was late! Then she remembered that Randy was driving for her this morning. She reached for the telephone and called the cab's number.

"Berkshire Cab," he answered in a cheerful voice. The sound of it seemed to coat her with comfort— like warm chocolate. She let herself enjoy that image for a moment. It was wonderful on several levels.

"Hi," she said. "How's it going?"

"Good," he replied. "I haven't been lost yet,

though I had to check your map for Bloombury Landing.''

"Oh, yeah. On the other side of the lake and into the woods. Used to be the Ericksons' summer home."

"I didn't even know it was there."

"You wouldn't, unless you were here a couple of years ago when the family was big stuff. Real estate, construction. Hal Erickson headed up an industrial growth team. Anyway, their fortunes have waned and now I think that summer house is the only property they have left."

"Well, the woman who owns the bridal shop downtown lives there. She gave me some stuff to take to Prue."

"Right. That's Rosie DeMarco, who owns Happily Ever After. She's the Ericksons' oldest daughter."

"Okay." He didn't seem to find that genealogy as fascinating as she did. "So, what do I do with this? Prue isn't at the studio. I imagine this has something to do with the wedding dress you're wearing tonight. Is she still home? Does she want me to take it there?"

"Ah…hold on. I'll check." Paris peered into Prue's bedroom and, finding it empty, headed for the kitchen. She could hear the commotion before she got there. A quiet male voice mingled with lively female conversation.

Her mother and Jeffrey had apparently gotten home during the night and were trying to calm Prue, who looked pale and harried and on the brink of hysteria.

"I have a flared skirt to hem," Prue was saying in a panicky voice. She sat on one of the stools at the work station while Camille rubbed her shoulders. "Pick up shoes and bags, borrow jewelry, give everything one last try to make sure there are no surprises…" Then her face crumpled and she covered it with both hands.

Paris looked to her mother for an explanation.

Her mother leaned close to her to whisper, "Today was Prue and Gideon's anniversary."

"Here you go." Jeffrey put a steaming mug in front of Prue. "Coffee with brandy in it. Best thing in the world to warm you up from the inside out. Come on. Drink."

Prue swiped her hands across her eyes, then dropped them to the mug, struggling valiantly to pull herself together.

Paris hated to add to her stress level by putting yet another decision in her path.

"I'm going to the studio with you and I'll try on everything while you're hemming or whatever you have to do. I'll do a turn for your approval, and you won't have to stop working unless you see something wrong. And I'm sure Mom and Jeffrey will help with errands." They nodded dutifully.

Her mother suddenly frowned at her. "Why aren't you driving this morning?"

"Randy's driving for me," Paris said. "It's a long story that I'll tell you later. In the meantime, Prue, Rosie DeMarco gave him a package to deliver to you and he wants to know if you want it brought here."

"That's right!" Prue tried to stand, but Paris and her mother held her to the chair.

"I can have him pick me up and take me to the studio with it, if that's where you want it. Or he can deliver it here."

"It's the most wonderful hat," Prue said, looking on the verge of tears again. She took a quick sip of coffee. "It should go right to the studio. I should have stayed last night, but the sofa's lumpy and I couldn't get any rest."

"Tell him to take it to the studio," Jeffrey suggested, "and I'll drive you there to meet him. Then I'll come back for Prue and your mother."

Everyone nodded at his solution. Paris gave him a quick hug, reminded of Jasper's easy influence on the sometimes frantic goings-on in the household. She picked up the kitchen telephone.

She could hear women's laughter in the background. "Where are you now?" she asked.

"On my way to the bakery. Seems there's a major shopping expedition under way that's convening over doughnuts and mochas."

"Do I hear Addy?"

"Yes. Since I started driving, she's given up on her undependable car and is going with Berkshire Cab."

There was cheering in the background and high, feminine laughter.

"Apparently they prefer me to you," he said.

There was more cheering.

"Paris, I'm scared," he said, pretended terror in his voice.

The women erupted into laughter again.

"After you deliver them," Paris said, smiling over Addy's antics, "take the package to the studio whenever you can. Jeffrey's going to drive me there right now."

"You're sure you don't want me to pick you up?"

"Thanks, but if you get another call, you won't have to worry about coming for me. Thanks, Randy."

"You're welcome. See you soon."

Paris directed Jeffrey to the Chandler Mill building on the other side of town. As he drove, he told her how beautiful he thought the Berkshires were and how much he and her mother enjoyed their time together.

"I'd like your mother to come with me to Florida next week and meet my boys and their families," he said. "It's beautiful there, too, but in a very different way."

"Is something serious happening here, Jeffrey?" Paris asked directly. She had a feeling he was trying to tell her something, but was dancing around the issue instead, unsure of her reaction.

He smiled at the road. "You get that in-your-face honesty from her."

"Yes, I think so."

"Something serious has happened," he said, "even though time's been short. We loved each other years ago and settled for a comfortable friendship because I was married and she was focused on a career. Now the time's right for both of us. We're hoping you and Prue will be happy for us."

Paris touched his shoulder. "I am, and I know Prue

will be once she's in her right mind again after the show.''

''I wish I *was* your father,'' he said with an emotional glance in her direction.

''I'm adopting you,'' she said, very happy to have him in her life. ''My natural father doesn't count, and Jasper would have liked you and approved of you.''

It occurred to her in a rare moment of clarity that she had everything a woman could want. Her widowed mother had found happiness with a man who was honored at the prospect of playing father to her family. The sister she'd sometimes had difficulty understanding had become her friend and was about to launch a successful career in fashion design, and the man with whom Paris had an on-again off-again romance wanted it on again and she was ready.

Over the past month she'd evolved into a different woman from the one who'd been so concerned about who she was rather than what she intended to become. Now she had dreams for the future with the shadows of the past safely dealt with and tucked away.

She wasn't sure what to do with the future, but she thought maybe Randy's plans for it might help her decide.

If he wanted to go back to medical school, she'd keep driving cab and support him until he was finished. If he didn't, she'd like to keep Berkshire Cab going. Law school seemed too confining for the woman she'd become.

Excitement ran up her spine. It was so enervating to have a plan. A little wave of nausea threatened her, but she swallowed it down, too focused on other things to give it time.

Jeffrey dropped Paris off, then drove back home. Paris took the elevator up to the second floor studio and let herself in, taking in the smell of fabrics she was just beginning to appreciate. She stood in the middle of the room littered with trimmed fabric, thread, the occasional button and pin, and liked knowing that Prue's dreams had come true despite the supreme disappointment of her private life.

Paris was convinced that Gideon should have his say, but it was Prue's life, not hers, and she was barely able to keep her own in order.

And yet, she felt the energy for it today. It was as though it flowed through her, giving her fingers, her legs, even her brain flexibility. It was all in knowing who she was, she thought with a rush of happiness, and that she was loved.

She heard a car pull into the driveway, went to the window and saw the LeBaron with her Berkshire Cab signs on it. She got into the elevator and went downstairs.

The doors opened on Randy, waiting to get into the elevator. She flew into his arms, laughter on her lips.

Unprepared, he fell back a few steps until he was able to catch himself and hold her to him. He took her kiss with all the fervor with which she offered it, then gave one back with the same intensity.

Happiness bubbled so high in her that she laughed again when they pulled apart. He was watching her in surprise, clearly mystified by her behavior.

"Okay, what is this?" he asked, only half smiling. "Have you come to your senses or have I lost mine?"

She wrapped her arms around his neck and just held on. "I'm sure I'm not in a position to say. I'm just happy to see you."

He held her close for a moment, then drew her away again to look into her eyes. "Have you been into the chocolate?"

"I've been in the love," she replied, certain her eyes brimmed with all she felt for him. "I'm sure it contains even more serotonin than chocolate. I've been thinking about how generous it was of you to drive for me so that I could rest. About how many kindnesses you've offered me." She grew sober as she remembered the night she'd learned the truth from her mother. "How lucky I am that you're the one I ran to when I found out about my father. I love you, Randy. We…have to talk after the show."

He caught her face in his hands and kissed her soundly. "What's wrong with now?"

Even as he posed the question, the cab's cell phone rang. He pulled a face but answered it in that same cheerful tone. "Berkshire Cab." He jotted an address down in the palm of his hand. "Ten minutes," he promised. "Right. Goodbye."

"That's what's wrong with now," she said in amusement, her world so sunny and hopeful, its entire future written in the handsome, symmetrical lines of his face. "It's a scientific fact that the moment the cab driver puts food in her mouth, has a personal errand to run or a conversation to finish, a client will need a ride.''

''Ah. As long as it's science.'' He cupped her head in his hand. ''Until tonight, then. I love you, too.'' He kissed her soundly, then ran out to the cab.

It wasn't until Paris was upstairs again in the studio that she realized he'd handed her a box of a dozen doughnuts along with the package from Rosie De-Marco.

CHAPTER FIFTEEN

THE WONDER WOMEN HAD transformed the high school auditorium into a gazebo that looked as though it was being rained on by maple leaves. They were everywhere—on the walls, attached to the half-open curtains on the stage, hanging on strings from the ceiling, pinned to the shirts of the high school seniors who served as ushers.

The room was filled when Randy arrived, but a seat was saved for him in the middle of the Wonders and their families.

He'd had a hell of a day. He'd been busy, criss-crossing all over town, to the airport and back, and once to Springfield, so that he hadn't had time to think about the way Paris had greeted him that morning, and her promise that they had to talk.

Chilly had volunteered to drive tonight, and Randy picked him up just before five. His partner had a Maple Hill map stretched out on the seat beside him. "I'd have brought Beth with me," he said, "because she never gets lost, but she didn't want to miss the fashion show. So, what do I do?"

Randy gave him brief instructions, then glanced at his map in concern. "You do know your way around?

I mean, I usually drive the rig, so it didn't occur to me—''

"Of course I know my way around," Chilly assured him with a roll of his eyes. "This is just for security. Where's the meter?"

"There is no meter. This is my car standing in for the cab, remember? You just have to watch the time and calculate."

Chilly frowned. "Calculate?"

Randy remembered that he also always figured dosages. He reached into the glove box where he kept a small calculator and handed it to him. "You sure you're going to be okay?"

"I'll be fine. Have a good time."

Before Randy could close the door, the telephone rang. "Berkshire Cab," Chilly replied. He wrote an address on the log and said he'd be there in five minutes. He smiled at Randy as he turned off the phone. "Easy start," he said. "That's the Lightfoot sisters going to the fashion show. I got it covered. Don't worry."

Randy tried not to but found it hard when Chilly took off in the wrong direction.

But he felt himself relax as he took a seat between Evan Braga and Bart Megrath. Seats were saved next to them, presumably for their wives, who were probably helping Mariah with last-minute details. Camille and Jeffrey arrived shortly after and sat behind him.

The buzz of conversation in the auditorium was loud enough that even those sitting side by side had to shout at each other to be heard.

"You'll notice you haven't even made it to Halloween," Bart Megrath said, grinning at him. "I hear you drove cab for Paris last night so she could get her beauty sleep. Sounds like love to me."

"You're absolutely right." Randy took pleasure in admitting that. Particularly when Bart and Evan looked at each other in laughing surprise.

Hank and Cam joined them, sitting at the opposite end of the row, their wives undoubtedly pressed into service, too. They came to see what the laughter was all about.

"He's one of us," Bart said, indicating Randy. "They're getting married."

Hank frowned at Randy. "I thought you were determined not to get married."

"So did I," Randy conceded. "But...you know. It's hard to hold out against all that..." He didn't have a word for what it was about her that wouldn't free him. He finally settled for "All that spirit."

"Spirit," Cam repeated with a grin at his companions. "Now it's spirit. When you've been married awhile it's stubborn single-mindedness."

Hank laughed. In his role of looking out for everyone who worked for him, he studied Randy closely. "You're sure? You were so determined."

"I'm sure," he said, surprised at the depth of his own conviction. "Loss always makes you so sure you'll never put yourself in the position to feel it again, then life heals you somehow and you're willing to forget the risk to be in the game again." He grinned. "Maybe that's maturity."

Evan groaned. "Please don't set a maturity prece-
dent the rest of us will have to adopt. I'm not ready."

Hank cast him a dry glance. "You put your life on
the line for Beazie. I think your maturity's secure."
He punched Randy in the shoulder and straightened
up. "But don't let this maturity thing get around. The
girls forgive us for acting like idiots because they insist we're nothing but big kids. We like that. Don't
scotch it for us."

"You can count on me."

"We already do."

The lights flickered. Everyone took his seat and the
noise level was cut in half. Then Mariah Trent
stepped up to the podium. Conversation quieted completely as she smiled at the audience and welcomed
them to the Friends of the Maple Hill Library Fall
Fashion Fund-raiser.

She talked for a few minutes about how important
the library was to the community, how necessary it
was to update its store of knowledge, and that that
required a new wing, new shelves, new books.

"The librarian and his staff have managed hero-
ically to keep us as current as possible without the
funds to work with. Many in the community have
donated books and magazine subscriptions, but now
we need you to dig a little deeper. If you see anything
tonight that you like, you can place your order with
me or with Mayor Whitcomb at that table."

She pointed to the back of the room where Jackie
waved from behind a library table.

"Prue Hale," Mariah went on, "the designer

who's made this evening possible, is the CEO of Prudent Designs. She promises delivery in a month, and that half the proceeds will go to the library fund.''

There were cheers and applause.

''Thank you! Now, sit back and relax, and see what the Maple Hill woman will be wearing this fall and winter. She is represented in the person of Paris O'Hara, Ms. Hale's sister, and the CEO of Berkshire Cab.''

There were loud cheers from the front row, and from Camille and Jeffrey.

Quiet music began and the curtain opened on Paris wearing a fitted green wool dress Mariah said would be appropriate for the office or for a luncheon. The dress was high-necked, long-sleeved, and fitted snugly to just above the knee. She wore it with dark shoes and a small bag slung over her shoulder. Her hair was gathered up, giving her a long, lean look that highlighted all the sacrifices she'd made for this night.

Then she began to walk, with a graceful, slightly imperious glance at her friends gathered near the runway. Randy heard the audience's collective gasp.

To everyone who knew the young woman who drove cab from early morning until late at night with a kind word for everyone and no pretensions, this aspect of her was a revelation. She looked comfortable, confident and drop-dead gorgeous.

Paris walked to the end of the runway, graced the crowd with a half smile, then turned on her heel and walked back toward the stage, her walk almost balletic, her hips trim but with just enough sway to make every man in the audience hold his breath.

She disappeared behind the curtain.

"My God!" Evan exclaimed under his voice. "What happened to her?"

Beazie laughed and whispered back, "Randy."

There was another dress appropriate to the office, a pantsuit, then caramel-colored slacks paired with a man's long-sleeved white shirt and a knitted vest. Several women applauded. Randy liked it, too. The simple lines were perfect for her long body, and the sharpness of the color and the knife-pleated pants made her delicate face look even more feminine.

There were casual clothes, capped by a jewel-green suit with a very short top that was fringed and beaded and caused a sensation when she walked down the runway. The fringe bobbed and swung and caught the light, accentuating her slenderness and the minuscule bit of bare flesh playing hide-and-seek with the audience. Everyone applauded it.

He could see that she was enjoying herself. Something had changed in her that he wasn't sure he understood. He wasn't vain enough to think that loving him had given her this new, wild freedom that allowed her to strut down the runway as though she'd been doing it for years, to scan the audience with confidence, and wink at her friends and her mother.

It was the turns at the end of the runway that Randy found amazing. She did them with a seductive over-the-shoulder glance, then a toss of her head and a spirited walk back to the stage as though she was turning her back on them, or on her old self, or on…something. He wasn't sure what.

In fact, she was so unlike the woman he'd known that she was beginning to make him nervous even while he applauded her modest, though obvious delight in everyone's admiration.

Her mother was crying.

Then Paris came out wearing the dark blue hooded cloak and a hush fell over the murmuring audience. The garment's drama lent her an air of mystery that turned her into a heroine on the run and the auditorium into the dark English moor she'd imagined herself in that afternoon he'd surprised her.

She walked to the end of the runway and back again, the lights picking up the silver trim on the sleeves and hem. At the stage again, she turned back to the audience instead of disappearing backstage. Mariah said something about turning a woman of the past into a fearless explorer of the future and Paris unbuttoned and dropped the cloak, dragging it behind her in one hand as she strutted down the runway once again—this time in the notorious red dress.

The women in the audience were on their feet. The men were too mesmerized to move. It occurred to Randy that he'd run out of superlatives to describe how Paris O'Hara looked tonight.

She'd looked magnificent in this dress several nights ago, but her confidence drove her powerful impression up a notch as she struck a pose at the end of the runway, showing the audience what could happen to a woman who'd found herself. They thought she'd found herself in the red dress, but he knew differently.

He noticed the instant her confidence wavered. It came as a complete surprise to him, considering the way she'd swaggered for an hour, a gorgeous clothes horse with the audience in the palm of her hand.

He was leaning slightly forward along with everyone else watching her artful pose. She had one leg braced forward, knee tipped slightly to the side, a fist on her hip, a smile in her eyes that reminded him of her mother. Then it changed.

The gesture was so subtle he doubted anyone else noticed—at least anyone who didn't know her intimately. Her eyes registered some kind of mild shock that dimmed the smile, though she struggled to maintain it.

Her knee straightened and she drew a breath, both gestures looking completely natural, though he wondered if she'd moved to conceal a pain or strain for breath.

His concern grew when she turned, still smiling, and started back toward the stage. The audience going wild over the red dress didn't notice the sudden tightening of her jaw, or her grip on the cloak as she walked back.

She turned to give the audience one more look at the dress, and though she continued to smile, he saw something troubling in her eyes.

Camille leaned over his shoulder and whispered, ''Something's wrong with her!''

He patted her hand and, ducking low, made his way

down the aisle to the side door and into the hallway. From there it was just a few feet to the door that led backstage.

Jackie grabbed him the moment he pushed the door open. "Randy, thank goodness! Talk about the man for the moment. Cam just got called away. A plumbing crisis at the care center. You have to wear the tux and walk Paris down the runway!"

In his concern over Paris, he hadn't noticed Cam leaving.

"What? No, I..."

But she wasn't listening to him. She pulled him over and around obstacles until he could see Paris in a silky, form-fitting wedding dress, Prue fitting a close beaded cap on her hair, veiling erupting all around it. Paris's eyes were unfocused, a stunned look on her pale face.

Prue stepped back to look at her, then reached forward to pinch her cheeks.

There was something wrong with Paris that had come on suddenly and taken complete control of her. He couldn't believe that Prue and Jackie didn't see that, but they were apparently in the zone that had gotten them through all the quick changes and probably several crises, and at that point in time Paris was simply a hanger for the clothes.

He drew a deep breath as Jackie handed him a tux and pointed him behind a screen. At least if Paris was leaning on him, she wouldn't collapse as she looked as though she might do.

IDIOT! IDIOT! Paris called herself silently as she stood by helplessly while Prue and Jackie pulled off the red dress and dropped the wedding dress on her like a hat.

She let her arms and her body be manipulated to fit into the embroidered silk lace concoction while she called herself all kinds of an idiot again. Of course! Where was her brain? She'd gone for several days feeling sick to her stomach and listless, putting those symptoms down to the flu and the long hours she'd driven so that Prue could concentrate on her designs.

Then she'd awakened this morning to a vibrant sense of well-being and attributed it to a good night's rest and Randy's help driving cab. And as the show had approached, a strange sort of near ecstasy had filled her—almost as though she was on drugs. She felt alive and invincible. She'd thought love had done that to her.

She'd looked at herself in Prue's clothes, seen what the weeks of careful eating and exercise had done to her body, and what loving Randy had done to her face, and thought herself the luckiest woman alive. She'd strutted down the runway with a confidence completely new to her. And she'd seen in the faces of her family and friends a love and approval that made all her concerns disappear.

She'd intended to tell Randy tonight that they should set a wedding date.

But she'd pranced down the runway in that red dress and smiled proudly at her audience, absorbing their admiration and applause—and then she felt the twinge in her lower abdomen and it was as if someone had lit a candle in a dark room. She suddenly realized why she'd felt sick and tired one moment, then as though she were plugged into an electrical outlet the next.

She thought back to the swimming party she and her mother had planned for Prue's birthday and the emergency run for tampons Paris had had to make that morning. That had been early September. This was the middle of October. And she hadn't used the tampons since.

She was pregnant. Trust her to find the one percent of the time when dependable protection failed.

Heartbreak and panic experienced simultaneously were not conducive to taking in air. As Prue and Jackie fluttered around her, she told herself firmly that she had to keep it together for ten more minutes. She had to make it down the runway and back, and then she could have an emotional collapse at the realization of what this would do to her relationship with Randy.

She tried to push the thought back as she rubbed her fingertips across her forehead. Prue took her hand and pulled it down.

''Don't do that, you're crushing your bangs.''

Completely unaware that Paris was on the brink of falling apart, Prue fluffed the veiling on her hat and took a step back to judge its effect. She didn't notice. Of course she wouldn't. She was having the night of her life, she was riding the tail of her personal comet.

From the stage, Paris could hear Mariah's voice reading the line of patter Prue had written about the clothes. She reminded the audience that orders could be placed with Jackie or Prue after the show, and that Prudent Designs' new studio was now located in the Chandler Mill building. She gave them the number.

Then Paris heard her cue. "June's always been thought to be the romantic month for brides, but in Maple Hill, it's the winter bride that turns heads and captures hearts."

She reminded herself that she was doing this for her sister and her own personal crisis could wait ten minutes. She took the bouquet of white roses Jackie handed her, squared her shoulders and forced herself back into character.

"Where's my groom?" she asked, looking around. Then Randy stepped from behind a dressing screen and Prue gestured him to hurry. He loped to Paris's side.

Her heart thudded.

"Cam had to leave," Jackie whispered while Prue fluffed her skirt, then her veil. "So Randy's taking his place."

He was handsome in the formal clothes, the black and white lending him a dangerous quality completely at odds with the whites he wore on duty, or the casual earth colors he preferred when he was off.

His gaze went to the headpiece, the fluffy veil, then settled on her eyes. There was concern in his. He knew! she thought in alarm. Then she realized that was ridiculous. He couldn't possibly. Maybe it was the sight of the wedding dress that caused him concern. Maybe seeing her in it made him realize he wasn't as ready to make promises as he'd thought he was.

Well, that was probably best. It was looking like everything was going to change, anyway, and it was better that he was frightened off before learning the truth activated some misguided sense of duty and made him assume a role he really wanted nothing to do with.

He tucked her arm in his and put a hand over hers. "Are you all right?" he asked worriedly.

She drew a breath—or tried to. Her lungs seemed to need more than she'd taken in.

Prue was making a shooing motion with her hands, urging them to hurry out. Paris started walking, giving Randy little choice but to accompany her. She was very grateful for his strong arm to lean on when the audience seemed suddenly larger, louder, closer to the runway.

And what had begun as a mild discomfort in her abdomen seemed to be tightening, increasing—not pain, precisely, but a pressure that was starting to worry her. Five more minutes, she told herself as they reached the end of the runway and paused to let the audience take in the drama of the wedding dress. Just five more minutes.

She tightened her grip on Randy, taking these few minutes out of time to let herself believe this was real, that they were standing in front of a minister rather than an audience, and that they were about to promise to love each other forever rather than go their separate ways.

The audience probably missed the little sob that came out of her when she tried to breathe again. But Randy must have heard it because he turned to her, looking worried.

She came very close to losing it. This five minutes was an eternity. She struggled against the tears and the panic, trying to remember that they were standing in front of hundreds of people whose donations were counted on to support the library, and whose patronage would launch her sister's career.

But for just one moment, she felt selfish. Why couldn't this be her reality? Why couldn't she have Randy and a baby? Because he didn't want a baby, she reminded herself.

His frown deepening, Randy took the hem of her veil in his fingers and swept it back, looking into her face and probably trying to assess what on earth was wrong with her.

She willed him to see just the love in her eyes, and not the goodbye.

Without warning or regard for the hundreds of people watching them, he put an arm around her waist and lowered his head to kiss her. Her arms slipped up to his shoulders and held on, needing his support as the minuscule amount of air in her lungs abandoned her in one last breath.

She was aware of the audience cheering and applauding, and of the continued concern in his eyes as all the stiffening seemed to leave her body. An itchy blanket of heat and darkness inched up from her chest to enshroud her. She fought it until the last instant and collapsed in Randy's arms.

RANDY HAD AN AWFUL, terrifyingly familiar sense of déjà vu as Paris fainted. A few people in the audience stood, but most simply watched, probably wondering if this was just part of the little bridal drama.

Prue and Jackie were already running toward him. He felt Paris's breath against his cheek, and her heartbeat as he lifted her and carried her backstage.

"What happened?" Prue demanded, pointing him toward a small sofa. "Is she all right?"

"I don't know," he said, kneeling beside Paris, checking her throat for a pulse. It was a little fast, but steady. She was breathing. So what was wrong with her? "Jackie, call 911."

"I'm way ahead of you," she replied, already on the phone.

"Did she eat today?" he asked Prue as he pulled the confining hat off Paris's head.

Prue shrugged, taking one of Paris's hands and rubbing it. "I don't know. I didn't pay much attention. She was helping me, running errands."

Camille and Jeffrey were suddenly crowded around them, as were half the staff of Whitcomb's Wonders and their wives and girlfriends.

"She hasn't eaten in days," Camille said, fanning her with the night's program. "She was so intent on looking good for Prue in that red dress. I think she overdid it."

"I never meant for her to starve," Prue said, on the verge of tears.

Jeffrey patted her shoulder. "Of course you didn't. Your mother wasn't blaming you. Paris just got a little carried away wanting to help you."

Randy heard the conversations going on around him even as he tried to tune them out so that he could focus on her symptoms and figure out what had happened. If she hadn't eaten, it was entirely possible her sugar level had fallen dangerously low and the evening's excitement had further challenged it to completely deplete her and cause her to collapse.

But something had happened to her before she'd fainted. Something had alarmed or hurt her; he was sure of it. And when he'd taken Cam's place as her groom, he'd have sworn she was in misery even while love for him shone in her eyes. What did that mean?

A real panic was trying to take control of him. This was different from, yet alarmingly similar to, the way he'd felt when Jenny had been sick. He'd been helpless to do anything despite a considerable store of medical knowledge.

This time, he had no idea what the problem was, but he'd bet it was as much emotional as physical. She was breathing, her heart was beating fast but steadily, so whatever had caused her to collapse wasn't life threatening. But what was it, and why had it caused her such anguish?

The ambulance arrived and Paul Balducci took over.

"Vitals are good," he said to Randy. "Too much excitement tonight?"

"I hope that's all it is," he said. "I'm coming with you. Camille, you want to come, too?"

"Of course," she said. "Jeffrey, can you meet us at the hospital?"

"I'll bring Prue," he said.

"You go ahead," Mariah insisted. "I'll go tell the audience what's going on, and Jackie and I will stay behind to take orders as long as you promise to let us know how Paris is."

"I will, I promise." Prue hugged Jackie and then Mariah and left with Jeffrey even as Baldy was putting Paris on a gurney.

"She was always such a healthy child," Camille said as Randy put an arm around her and led her out the back door to the ambulance.

"It's been a rough month for her," he said, lifting her up into the passenger seat.

She thanked him with a wry smile. "She thought the truth would clarify everything for her, but sometimes it just muddies things up. The real truth is that she was always loved, even when I didn't understand her."

He nodded. "She knows that. Try not to worry." He closed her in, then climbed into the back.

"Are you two getting married?" she asked candidly, looking over her shoulder at him.

He remembered Paris's look of sadness and misery and wondered if something had happened to make her change her mind about that since this morning. Then he remembered also the look of love in her eyes, and though he couldn't begin to fathom how the two emotions converged in her at the same time, he knew the only emotion prevailing in him was love for her.

"Absolutely," he replied, leaning down to help pull the gurney into the ambulance.

CHAPTER SIXTEEN

PARIS AWOKE TO THE SIGHT of a mature female face with small wire-rimmed glasses over bright brown eyes. The eyes were aimed at Paris but unfocused as the woman apparently concentrated on a black cuff that was cutting off the circulation in Paris's arm.

Paris closed then opened her eyes again, wondering if she was hallucinating. The woman was completely unfamiliar to her.

Where was she, anyway? She opened her eyes again and looked around at the pale green walls, the overhead television, the strange things attached to the walls. A hospital?

She'd collapsed. Oh, God, the fashion show!

She remembered looking into Randy's eyes, kissing him and feeling as if he'd taken all her air. Then…nothing.

She also puzzled over the terrible emotional misery of that moment and tried to remember what had brought that about. She'd been so happy that morning, so excited all afternoon, so in charge when she'd stepped out on the runway.

Then she recalled that telling moment when she'd stood in the red dress while people applauded and she'd felt as though she had everything. Then she'd felt that telling twinge.

The woman smiled at her as she removed the stethoscope from her ears and draped it around her neck.

"Hi," she said. "I'm Emily Dawson. How do you feel?" She removed the annoying blood pressure cuff and tucked it into a basket on the wall.

Paris pushed up against her pillows, trying to get some leverage on the situation.

"Hi," Paris replied. Her voice was barely there. She cleared her throat to answer the question. "A little woozy, but okay."

"You fainted at the fashion show."

"Yes. I remember."

"You know you're pregnant?" the doctor asked.

Yes. Pregnant. There was something exciting about hearing her suspicions confirmed, even though it meant heartache on another level. Paris nodded. "I was…just coming to that conclusion. But…is everything all right? I had a little lower abdomen pain."

"Your tests are great," the doctor answered. "I'd say you're only a couple of weeks along. Sometimes when the cells settle into the uterine wall, there's a little pressure, a little spotting. Add that to the pressure of walking down a runway in front of hundreds of people and I'm sure pain is magnified considerably."

The woman seemed to be looking for something in Paris's face. "You're going to have to take better care of yourself if you and the baby are going to make it through eight and a half more months of pregnancy.''

''I know.'' Paris sat up and the doctor reached behind her to straighten her pillow. ''I was modeling my sister's first line of clothing, and I was really focused on trying to sell it to the audience. I was trying to eat less and exercise more. And there was so much excitement today, I think I forgot to eat at all.''

The doctor nodded. ''Well, I've ordered you a tray of food, and I'd like you to eat it before you leave.''

''Okay.''

''You feel ready to see your mother and sister?''

Against all that was appropriate at the moment, she wanted to laugh. At her healthiest, there were times when she wasn't ready to see her mother and sister.

Then she felt a curious softening inside her as she realized what they'd been through together and how that somewhat testy dynamic had mellowed into a comforting friendship.

But the doctor hadn't mentioned Randy. Paris had a vague memory of having come to in the ambulance and seeing Randy leaning over her, holding her hand.

''Randy's here,'' the doctor said, ''but he ran to the pharmacy to get your mother some aspirin. She's pretty worried about you.''

Paris was a little surprised to hear her call Randy by his first name. Then she remembered that the emergency room worked with EMTs all the time. Dr. Dawson probably knew Randy very well.

Paris brushed her hair out of her face and drew a fortifying breath. It was time to take control of the situation. "No one knows I'm pregnant?" she asked, folding back her blankets.

"That's right." The doctor watched her measuringly. "That's your news to tell."

"Well. I'd like to keep it to myself awhile longer. So...I'd appreciate it if you didn't congratulate my mother on being a grandmother, or anything."

"Of course."

"Thank you."

Despite the doctor's agreement, Paris saw instantly that she thought Paris was making a mistake. She smiled apologetically. "It's a complicated situation."

"Life always is. But the truth doesn't change just because you keep it to yourself."

Yes. If anyone knew that, it was her.

The doctor left, and a moment later, Camille and Prue pushed into the room, filling it with scent, worried exclamations and a zest Paris had finally learned to appreciate.

"I can't believe you forgot to eat!" her mother scolded, sitting on one side of the bed. "How old are you, anyway? Do I have to remind you to wear your snow boots and take your vitamins, too?"

"Now, don't pick on her," Prue said, coming to Paris's defense, then pouring her a glass of water from the pitcher on the stand by the bed. "Jackie just called to see how you were," Prue told Paris with a grin, "and she said they've taken a couple of thousand dollars' worth of orders and people are still lined up at the table. You made my show, Paris. You were absolutely electric tonight. You made Elle McPherson look like just a pretty girl.''

Paris soaked up the praise, happy that her sister was happy, happy that life was budding inside her. She would be a contented single mother, she thought bracingly, though she'd have to move away.

"I'm so glad it went well.'' She patted the other side of her bed for Prue to sit. "I'm sorry I ended it with such dramatics, but it sounds like it might be helping you get some pity orders.''

A nurse arrived with a tray filled with chicken in a light gravy, mashed potatoes, green beans, a dish of fruit and cookies in a fluted paper cup. "You have to eat all of this,'' she told Paris, "before Dr. Dawson will release you.''

The moment she was out the door, Camille frowned over the tray. "That doesn't look like the nutritionally correct meal you'd expect to see in a hospital.''

"I'm sure if they fed everyone melba toast and grapefruit, the patients would riot.'' Prue took the fruit bowl in hand, speared a slice of strawberry and tried to feed it to Paris. "This is good for you. Vitamin C.''

Paris took the fork out of her hand. "Thank you. I can manage. You two will have to help me with the chicken and mashed potatoes.''

"No, you need protein,'' her mother insisted.

"Then eat some of the potatoes. I can't eat it all, and we have to make it disappear.'' A plan was forming in her mind, and it seemed like a good time to lay the groundwork for it. She was reminded suddenly of another plan, and hoped that this one was more successful. She smiled as she pretended enthusiasm for the strawberries. "I've been thinking about going back to law school," she said.

The announcement was greeted with complete silence and looks of hurt surprise. She might have said, "I've been thinking of having you both arrested," judging by their reactions.

"Well…that's nice, honey," Camille said finally, a stiff smile in place. She looked across the bed at Prue, her firm gaze determined to force a positive response from her as well.

"Ah…sure," Prue said. She'd been about to help herself to a cookie but put it back. "I mean…it's been great to finally connect and have fun putting on the show and making it work. I'd even been thinking that…maybe you could be my business manager and my rep, or something. But…of course you have your own interests. I can't expect you to work with me just because…it's fun."

Paris put a hand to her arm. "I think this would be good for me," she lied. "I came home originally because I needed answers. Now that I have them, I have to get on with my life." She caught her mother's hand on the bedcover. "But I wouldn't trade this time we've had together for anything. And…" She squeezed her mother's hand. "I'm very grateful that you were such a brave young woman, Mom."

Camille leaned forward to wrap her arms around

her. "Paris, are you sure about this? I mean, what about Randy? I thought you two were serious."

Paris looked her mother in the eye, hoping her direct gaze would suggest honesty as she lied to her.

"We had this open-ended agreement, remember?" she said with an easy smile. "He explained it to you."

Her mother looked back at her. Paris had to force herself not to flinch. With this new connection they had, she was afraid she'd become more readable than she used to be.

But her mother simply frowned.

The plan was beginning to grow and feel doable. She was going to move to Boston as soon as possible, keep the baby a secret from her mother and her sister until she was settled. And maybe she would register at school for the winter term. If she was going to support a baby, she'd have to do something besides drive a cab.

Yes. She could get things together in a couple of days. The sooner the better.

A light rap sounded on the door. When Camille pulled the door open, Randy handed her a bottle of aspirin. "How's she doing?" he asked.

Paris caught his eye as he moved her mother gently aside and walked into the room.

Prue got to her feet. "See for yourself," she said, her expression more stressed than her cheerful voice suggested. "Mom and I are going to find a cup of coffee and let you two have some privacy."

"Jeff's in the cafeteria." Randy pointed down the

hallway. "Just follow the arrows." Then he came to sit on the edge of the bed and took Paris's hand. As she looked into his eyes, she remembered the moment when he'd looked into hers on the runway, then kissed her. He'd known something was wrong. That kiss had been comfort, reassurance. "How do you feel?" he asked now.

She smiled widely. "I'm good. I forgot to eat today." She handed him the tray with its half-eaten contents. "Can you put that on the sink, please, so we don't have to talk over it."

He did as she asked, then came back to the bed. She was tempted to put both hands under the covers so that he couldn't touch her, thinking that it might make this easier. But it might not, and this might be the last time she got to hold his hand.

"So, what's wrong?" he asked, linking his fingers with hers again. "I saw something change in your face toward the end of the show. Was it pain? Is something wrong?"

She was pale, and the wide smile on her mouth was completely at odds with a strange darkness in her eyes and a tension about her that was really beginning to worry him. When the doctor had told her family and him that Paris was fine and that she'd fainted because she hadn't eaten, he'd expected her to be her old self again—difficult but cheerful and open.

She wasn't. She kept smiling, but it was a movement of muscles, not an expression of happiness.

"It wasn't pain," she said, taking on an animation that was as phony as her smile. Her eyes widened and she spread her free arm, hoping, he guessed, that she would distract him from the look in her eyes. "It was power."

What did that mean? Maybe he had to stop analyzing her movements and concentrate on her words. "Power?" he asked.

"Yes!" She spoke emphatically, gestured with that arm again. "For the first time in my life, I had complete control of hundreds of people. They were watching *me*."

That vanity was unlike her, and probably another tool for whatever purpose she'd undertaken, like her smile and her expressions. "You're very beautiful," he concurred, biding his time, "but tonight you were magic."

He felt the tension in the hand he held.

"I was standing there," she said, "and I thought to myself, imagine if this was a courtroom, and I had a jury in the palm of my hand."

He was beginning to see where she was going with this, and thought that maybe he'd been worried for nothing. He'd like to see her return to school if that was what she wanted.

"You're ready to go back to school?" he asked.

"Yes." There was no hesitation about it, no attempt to break it to him. That was all right. He liked a woman who knew her own mind and had challenging goals.

Then she went on. "And I was thinking how lucky I was that you'd insisted on a physical friendship instead of love. It makes it so much easier now."

His heart dropped like an elevator car with a broken cable. She wanted to go back to school and leave him behind.

He studied her face for those phony expressions, but everything about her now was suddenly unreadable, carefully removed from him as if she were a reporter in some remote telecast and he had difficulty tuning in his television.

"I'm moving to Boston," she said. "It seems pointless to try to maintain a relationship when I'll only be coming back for holidays." She forced a smile that trembled. "If you depend on me for physical companionship, you'll die a frustrated old man."

He wasn't sure if he couldn't believe it, or if he simply didn't want to. But something about her dispassionate explanation of her plans didn't ring true.

"Paris, come on," he said, looking for a chink in that careful distance she'd placed between them. "What happened today? This morning you flew into my arms and told me you loved me and that you wanted to talk tonight. And now, a mere twelve hours later, you're telling me it's over?"

She maintained a look of wide-eyed innocence and neutrality. Considering her previous passion on anything and everything they discussed, it sharpened his growing panic. "I explained that. I'm moving."

"Boston's only half a day away. I'm capable of getting there."

"I'll be studying."

"Every minute?"

"I have a lot to catch up on."

He wanted to shake her out of this cloak of nonchalance. "So, you're writing off your mother and sister, Jeffrey, all your friends and Berkshire Cab?"

He saw the look then—the look from the end of the runway. But she merely shrugged with a sort of "Oh, well" gesture and said, "I'm starting over. I'll see my family when I can, but I'm putting my life here behind me."

"And that includes me."

"That's the way we planned it, Randy," she reminded him good-naturedly.

Had she shot him in the heart at close range, the bullet could not have been more deadly than those words.

He wanted to shout and shake her, but he knew that would accomplish nothing. He had to understand this before he could react to it.

He got to his feet and smiled at her with the same easy manner she displayed. "Okay, then," he said. "It's been fun. Good luck in law school."

"You should consider going back to medical school." Her voice sounded strangled but she appeared unconcerned.

"Maple Hill's my town now. And I like being an EMT with the occasional foray into janitorial services. Keeps me balanced." He pulled the door open and blew her a kiss. "I suppose we'll run into each other over Christmas."

"Yes."

"Oh. What about your chocolate?"

She looked as though her composure had grown brittle. "You can have it," she said.

He nodded. "Okay. Then you can have my jacket. Fair trade. Goodbye."

She smiled and waved.

He stepped out into the hall and closed the door on her—for the moment, at least.

PARIS WAS SICK AS A DOG. When Jeffrey drove her, Camille and Prue home from the hospital, she pleaded weariness and they left her alone. Her mother tucked her in as though she were four, then turned out the light and closed her bedroom door.

Paris cried into her pillow until she finally fell asleep. The alarm woke her at 5:00 a.m. She was surprised to collide with her sister as she made her foggy way to the bathroom.

"What are you doing up?" she asked.

Prue was disheveled and in a nightshirt, but wielding a cup of coffee. "I'm driving for you today," she said, gesturing with the cup. "You go back to bed."

"You're not driving for me," Paris argued. "After all the orders you got last night, you'll have to work day and night to fill them even—"

She intended to add "even with help," but the sharp aroma of the strong, French roast coffee filled her nostrils, smelled wonderful for half a second, then hit her stomach and turned it upside down. She reached the john just in time. She flushed and straightened.

Prue put a wet washcloth to her face. "Are you

pregnant?'' she asked on a surprised whisper, then answered her own question with an exclamation. ''You're bugging out because you're pregnant!''

Paris pushed her out of the bathroom and closed the door. She was not surprised to find her mother standing beside Prue when she opened the door again, showered and dressed in jeans and a plain gray sweatshirt.

''Paris.'' Her mother wore a wildly colored silk robe that did nothing for warmth but looked gorgeous. She seemed worried and frightened. ''What are you doing?''

Paris tried to push her way between them, but they pushed back, and then all three of them were suddenly in the tight confines of the small bathroom.

She decided she would make one attempt to be reasonable. ''I'm making a decision about my life,'' she said calmly, ''as I am entitled to do. Yes, I'm pregnant. And, yes, I'm leaving because I think that's the smartest thing to do. I'm going back to law school in Boston, and I'm going to be just fine. I'll keep in touch, don't worry. Now, if you'll excuse—''

''What about Randy?'' her mother interrupted.

Paris sighed. ''He doesn't want to raise a baby, Mom. He barely wanted to marry me, except that I made him see what life would be like without me, so that he'd want to change his mind. I manipulated him and it worked. But I can't manipulate this.''

''Have you told him?'' Prue asked.

Paris leaned back against the wall, a hand to her churning stomach. ''To what purpose? To make him feel guilty and hate me his whole life for making him do what he didn't want to do?''

''I remember a time when you didn't want to be a mother,'' Camille said. ''And you seem to have changed your mind.''

Paris touched her arm. ''I have a different take on mothers now. But I won't make him do this—or feel like he has to.''

''You just said,'' Prue reminded her, ''that you're entitled to make your life decisions yourself. Isn't he entitled to the same privilege?''

''Not about this. Now, please. I appreciate your love and concern, but I've got to get ready for work.''

''What are you going to do about the cab company?''

''I don't know yet. I'll just keep driving until I'm ready to go.'' She pushed Prue gently aside and opened the door. Then she looked firmly at her mother and her sister. ''If anyone breathes a word to him, I'll be very upset.''

She went to her bedroom for the baseball jacket she wasn't giving up under any circumstances, then went to the kitchen for a bottle of 7UP and the box of crackers.

She ran out to Randy's LeBaron and thought as she climbed in behind the wheel that she was going to the garage the moment it opened, find out what was wrong with the wagon, and either reclaim it today or find something used to buy so that she could give Randy back his car.

She had a million things to do this week to prepare

to leave, but a reliable vehicle had to be at the top of her list.

Randy. Now that her decision was made, she was hoping she'd be strong enough to follow it through. The very thought of him made her second-guess herself, wish things could be different, wonder if she told him, would he have a change of heart.

But he wouldn't. He might feel responsible and force himself to play the role he'd sworn he didn't want, but that wouldn't be good for anyone.

No. She turned the key in the ignition. She had to work her plan. She could do this. It would be horrible and she'd feel hopeless, and nothing would ever be the same, but she could do it.

And she was going to be a mother. That was a good thing. She backed out of the driveway, reminding herself that, thanks to the baby, the effects of loving Randy would last as long as the effects of losing him.

RANDY CALLED IN SICK.

"You don't sound sick," Kitty disputed.

"I need the day off," he said. "Will you see if you can get my shift covered? If you can't, I've got my cell phone. Call me and I'll come in."

"What's wrong? Want me to call Chilly?"

"No. It's just some personal stuff I have to take care of."

"Okay. I'll see what I can do."

"Thanks, Kitty."

He was showered and dressed by 8:00 a.m. and at the hospital ten minutes later. He'd stared at the ceiling most of the night, reaching the conclusion that something serious was wrong with Paris. He couldn't imagine what else would account for her behavior.

She wasn't selfish or frivolous, or the kind of woman who'd change her mind about a relationship in a matter of hours. She must have experienced some pain on the runway that frightened her, weakened her. Then Dawson had checked her out in the ER and given her bad news she didn't want to share because of his issues over Jenny.

He didn't know whether to hope that that was the answer or not. It would be a comfort to know that she hadn't simply stopped loving him, but the thought of her being ill was a whole new and horrible possibility for him strangely disconnected from loving Jenny. He wasn't reminded of how awful losing Jenny had been, but was feeling just the hideousness of having to live without Paris. Despite all his careful attempts to keep their relationship on a level he could easily walk away from, he'd learned to love more selflessly, appreciated her for who and what she was to her family as well as to him, and still his heart had become woven with hers so that it would be impossible to lose her without part of him dying.

Well. There was little point in speculating until he had facts.

He went to Dr. Dawson's office and found it empty. The staff was involved at the moment with several victims of an automobile accident that couldn't have been much more than a fender-bender by the looks of them, but it meant he had to wait.

He wandered into the tiny office and scanned the

desktop in the vague hope that paperwork from yesterday's cases might still be unfinished and he could glance at Paris's test results and figure out what was wrong. But Dawson was damnably efficient.

Julie, an ER nurse he'd known since he'd come to Maple Hill, hurried by and waved at him. On her way past again, he stuck his head out of the office. "You were on yesterday with Dr. Dawson," he said, preparing to ask his questions in such a way that she wouldn't feel she was revealing private information. That turned out to be unnecessary.

"Right," she said with a smile. "You're talking about the pregnant girl you brought in that had fainted in that killer wedding dress?"

That had been easier—and infinitely more astonishing—than he'd anticipated.

His heart jolted, smacked against his ribs. He stared at Julie, unable to believe that hadn't occurred to him.

After a moment of shock, he felt a sense of euphoria. Pregnant? Pregnant! She wasn't dying, she was pregnant!

And she intended to simply move to Boston with his baby and never tell him the truth?

"What did you want to know?" Julie prompted.

"Ah...nothing," he said after a moment. "I'll just wait and talk to Dr. Dawson."

As he stormed out of the hospital to his truck, it occurred to him that some misguided sense of letting him off the hook might be behind this, but rage had taken over from the euphoria and he didn't consider that a valid excuse.

He dialed the number for Berkshire Cab.

CHAPTER SEVENTEEN

PARIS PULLED UP IN FRONT of Maple Hill Airport's small terminal, thinking that it really was getting a lot of action lately. Leaf peepers were all over the place in the Berkshires, leaving their urban Boston and New York lives for a glimpse of the colorful countryside when fall leaves were at their most beautiful. The air had a bite to it now, the smell of wood smoke somehow a portent of holidays and winter fun.

Painful regret churned inside her at the thought of leaving this beautiful place, leaving her mother and her sister when they'd just all learned to appreciate one another, leaving Jeffrey when he was just beginning to become a part of their lives. She couldn't even think about leaving Randy anymore. It all became overwhelming when she did, so she'd spent her last few hours driving, trying to organize in her mind what she would do when she got to Boston.

Find a job, find an apartment, locate an obstetrician. She'd have to keep herself busy until the winter term started, and she could do that by...

Every thought in her head fled when she saw a man carrying two suitcases walk out of the small terminal building and wave at her to indicate he was her fare.

He was tall and dark-featured in what had to be a cashmere overcoat. He was impeccably groomed, heartbreakingly handsome—and her brother-in-law, Gideon Hale.

She popped the trunk and jumped out of the cab, enjoying the stunned look on his face when he saw her coming toward him.

"Paris?" he asked in smiling disbelief.

She should hate him for everything Prue had told her about his betrayal, but she couldn't quite believe it. Her sister was mercurial and often illogical, and Paris knew Prue had left him after the intern incident without ever talking it out with him. Paris remembered a loving, caring man, and was sure he had to have an explanation.

He wrapped his arms around her and lifted her off the ground. "God, it's good to see you!" he exclaimed. "How are you?"

She wasn't sure why she burst into tears. Because she'd always liked Gideon? Because he didn't know anything about her situation and couldn't judge? Because she was starting to think she was making a horrible mistake and didn't know if that was good sense taking over or cowardice kicking in?

"What?" he asked in concern. "Something wrong with Mom?"

Camille had always been Mom to him even though his own mother was very much alive.

"No," she denied quickly. "She's great. Has a boyfriend."

"All right." Then he asked a little stiffly, as though it was hard to do, "Is it Prue?"

She shook her head, drawing him toward the LeBaron's open trunk. "No, she's great, too. She had a fashion show last night and made a big, big hit."

He nodded a little grimly as he put his suitcases inside. "Good. That's what she's always wanted." He closed the trunk, then frowned at her. "Then, what are you crying about?"

She drew a ragged breath. "Just…life. I have a few things I have to straighten out, but I'm not sure what to do. And I hate the indecision."

"I can relate to that," he said.

"But, more important," she said, pushing her problems to the back of her mind to deal with the surprise of her brother-in-law's presence, "what are you *doing* here?"

"A friend's invited me into business in Alaska." He opened the passenger door in the front. She climbed in behind the wheel. "I thought I'd try one more time to reason with Prue before I accept his offer."

Paris shook her head, unhappy for him. "I'm sorry you lost the election."

He smiled wryly. "Was for the best. There was a lot about politics I didn't like."

Paris let a moment pass, occupying herself with putting the key in the ignition, writing the pickup on her log. "Was there a woman in her underwear at your cabin?" she asked.

"There was," he replied.

"Were you kissing?"

"We were."

"Gideon!" she gasped in disappointment and exasperation. "What is wrong with you? Prue adored you!"

"Mmm," he said, buckling his seat belt. "And she proved that when she ran off without even asking me what happened."

"How do you explain kissing a woman in her underwear?"

He sighed and closed his eyes a moment. When he opened them, she could see clearly that he'd been more affected by all that had happened than was visible on the surface.

"Is there somewhere we could have a cup of coffee?" he asked.

She nodded. "We'll go to the Breakfast Barn. But I warn you. Every time I sit down to eat, I get a call."

"Let's take our chances."

Paris led Gideon into a quiet corner of the Barn, dropped her purse on the seat and her phone on the table, and excused herself to run into the ladies' room. She left her brother-in-law to Rita Robidoux, the short, plump backbone of the Barn's wait staff. Her hair was piled atop her head in a curious shade of burgundy. She was handing him a menu and telling him about the breakfast special when Paris hurried off.

RANDY WAS SURPRISED when a man's voice answered the phone with a simple "Hello?"

"Is this Berkshire Cab?" he asked, thinking he'd misdialed.

"Yes," the voice replied. "Hold on. Let me find something to write on. Hold on, hold on—ah! Okay. Go ahead. You need to be picked up?"

"Who is this?" Randy asked. If Paris had hired a new driver to help her out as she prepared to leave, it didn't sound as though he was going to do much for business. Randy became aware of a lot of background noise—people talking, the clink of crockery. "Where are you?"

"Paris is taking a short break," the man said, ignoring his questions. Randy was offended by the smooth, cultured sound of the man's voice. "Where did you want to be picked up?"

Randy suddenly recognized the background sounds. The man was at the Breakfast Barn—with Paris. A whole new set of possibilities for why she was leaving crowded his brain and served to fan the anger building inside him. He turned his phone off and drove to the Barn.

He spotted the LeBaron parked near the door, and noticed absently that Hank and Bart and the other guys were here, too. But his brain was too crowded with anger and confusion to allow thoughts of anything else.

He pushed his way into the restaurant, hesitated a moment to find Paris, then spotted his baseball jacket as she walked from the rest rooms to a booth in the corner where he saw a man waiting. He got that curious, melting feeling he always got when he saw her wearing his jacket.

As she slid into the booth across the table from the man, he gave her a smile filled with affection and reached across the table to catch her hand.

Randy forgot every vow he'd ever taken about using his healing powers for good and strode toward the booth, murder on his mind.

He stopped at the edge of their table and looked from Paris, who appeared pale and surprised, to her companion, who arched an eyebrow questioningly, as though thinking he was a friend whom Paris was about to introduce to him. He looked like someone who had power and wealth.

"What are you doing here?" Paris asked Randy in a small voice. She wore that look of misery that had become so familiar.

"I want to know," he said, his anger barely contained, "if the baby is mine or his."

Hurting her gave him none of the satisfaction he'd expected. There wasn't even an instant's thrill, just immediate guilt and the wish that he could take it back. But there was this *GQ*-cover dude with an anger that didn't come close to his but looked formidable, anyway, so the last thing he could do was show remorse.

The guy slid out of the booth and pointed him to the door. "I don't know who you are, buddy," he said, "but nobody talks to Paris…"

"Well, I *thought* I was the father of her baby," Randy said, staring him down, "because she was moving to Boston without even telling me about it. But, now that I see her sitting here with you…''

The guy's anger turned to confusion. ''What are you talking about? She's not…'' He seemed to check himself and looked down at Paris. ''You're not moving, are you?''

Which didn't seem like the pertinent question if he had any concerns about the baby being his.

Randy spread his arms in exasperation—and his fist collided with Evan Braga's shoulder. The rest of the Wonders sat at a table nearby, watching the goings-on. Randy realized Evan was preparing to provide backup, and the rest of his friends were ready to weigh in if necessary.

''I can handle this,'' he said quietly to Evan.

Evan looked doubtful. ''You run well, but I'm not all that impressed with your muscle.'' He pointed to Paris's companion. ''He's got a couple of pounds on you.''

''Yes, but right is on my side,'' Randy said. ''Go sit down.''

Paris suddenly pushed her way into the middle of the three of them. ''Will you all please stop making a scene!'' she demanded in a whisper. She put a hand to her companion's shoulder and said to Randy with tear-filled eyes, ''This is my brother-in-law, Gideon Hale! Gideon, I am pregnant and this is my baby's father, Randy Sanford! And now that you've met him you can understand why I'm moving!'' She grabbed her purse and her phone and stormed off.

Randy had to think quickly. He extended his hand

to Hale with an apologetic grin. "Sorry about that. Gideon, this is my good friend, Evan Braga. Evan, will you guys see that this man has breakfast while I try to talk sense into Paris?"

"Sure." Evan clapped Gideon on the shoulder and pushed him toward the Wonders' table. "Good luck, pal," he added to Randy.

Randy ran the length of the restaurant, around curious diners and out into the parking lot, catching the door of the LeBaron just as Paris was turning the key in the ignition. He yanked it open, took the key from her and pulled her out of the car. She was sobbing.

"Don't do this!" she pleaded with him, slapping at his hand.

"Do what?" he asked, turning her away from him and holding her arms to her with his. "Claim my baby? Make you tell me the truth?"

"You don't want a baby, remember? You didn't even want me until I tricked you into missing me."

He had to laugh at that. "I don't remember a moment since the day I met you that I haven't wanted you."

He held fast as she struggled against him, "I'm talking about forever. I could deal with an open-ended relationship, but a baby changes everything."

He tightened his grip on her slightly and gave her a small shake. "Will you stop struggling? We're going to talk this through, so just give it up." He pointed across the parking lot to a small creek that ran through a grove of cottonwoods. There was an iron bench bolted to a flat rock for having a picnic or simply enjoying the view. "Let's go sit down."

"If I get a call, I have to go," she said.

"You left your phone in the car. Just forget the cab for a minute and concentrate on us."

He sat her down on the bench and sat beside her, putting an arm along the back and stretching his legs out to hem her in. She retreated into the corner, arms folded, ankles crossed and tucked under the bench.

"You're not marrying me out of some misbegotten sense of duty," she said with a dark glance at him, "so if that's what you're thinking, just put it out of your head."

"I love you and you're carrying my baby," he said reasonably. "How is that misbegotten?"

"You know what I mean."

"I almost never know what you mean. But I think I know what you feel. You love me."

She gave him that look of misery again, her eyes wide, tearful pools. She didn't deny it.

PARIS WOULD HAVE GIVEN anything to be transported to another place, to avoid having to explain what had made sense to her last night and now seemed outrageous and cruel. But he had her boxed in.

"I'd like to know," he said calmly, though there was residual anger in his eyes, "how you could love me and still do this to me."

She drew a breath and tried to push away this emotional anvil she'd carried around this morning. "I didn't want you to know," she said, her voice shaky, "because I was trying to avoid this very thing. You thinking you have to be with me when it's the last thing in the world you really want."

"And what made you think that? My helping you train to get in shape for the fashion show just so I could be with you? The times I've lent you my car so you could keep the cab company going? The fact that I didn't even close my eyes last night, thinking you'd found out you had some fatal disease because I couldn't imagine why you'd leave me otherwise?"

Guilt wrenched her already churning stomach. She'd imposed on him the very pain she'd been trying to save him from.

"I'm sorry," she whispered. "I was trying to avoid hurting you."

He looked at her as if she was insane. "By leaving me?" he demanded. "Paris, are you living in some reflected reality where everything's backward? How could hiding my baby from me protect me from pain?"

"Because you wouldn't know!" she shouted at him, that anvil hanging even more heavily around her neck. "Because I'd have gotten away clean and you could have just moved on the way we'd intended in the first place!"

To her surprise, he smiled at that. "I can't believe how stupid we were that we thought that'd work. We fell in love and it soon became clear—to me, anyway—that open-ended relationships are for vagabonds and cowards. I'm neither."

She stared at him, taking his words apart and reassembling them and still sure she'd misunderstood. "You said—"

"Can you please forget what I said," he asked urgently, "and pay attention to what I'm telling you now? Even during the night, when I thought Dawson had probably told you you were dying, I wanted to be with you. I didn't want to be safe and carefree and not have to deal with it, I wanted to be with you. It was all I could think about. But I had to know for sure so I knew what we were facing."

She didn't know what to say. She just stared at him while hearing the sounds of cars coming and going from the Barn's parking lot while the creek rushed and the wind blew. She had to be on some parallel plane where things looked the same but weren't.

"So I went to the hospital this morning, intending to make Dawson break all the rules about sharing a patient's information when Julie inadvertently spilled that you were pregnant."

Anger threatened to overtake him again, but he sighed and ran a hand over his face. "Paris, I've come to terms with my life. Losing Jenny was awful, but I'm over it. Better than that, I've accepted it and put it away."

She believed him but was still concerned that duty drove him rather than any real desire to have a family.

"Okay, look at it this way," he said gravely. "Do you want to go to law school, find somebody great, then have this baby come to you twenty-some years down the road and ask you why her blood type doesn't match her father's?"

She put both hands to her heart at that thought, as worried about him now as she was about their baby. "I want your *heart* to match the baby's heart. That's what I want, Randy."

"Paris, it's already as woven into that little life as it is into yours!" He took her hands and crushed them in his. "Please. I'm sorry for all the stupidity, the selfishness. If you want to go to school, we'll move to Boston, no problem."

"Stop," she pleaded, leaning forward to put her cheek against his. It was cool, but his hand came up to press it to him.

He meant it. This was no sense-of-duty promise, no guilt-ridden expiation of sins. He wanted to love her and their baby. The anvil was suddenly gone, replaced by a bouquet of flowers in her soul.

"I don't want to go to Boston," she said, turning her face into his hand to kiss it.

"What about law school?"

"That was just a reason to give for leaving here. And I thought if I had to raise the baby alone, I should do something responsible."

"Then, what *do* you want to do?"

"I want to stay here and drive a cab as long as I fit behind the wheel. Then when the baby comes, maybe I can find someone to buy it from me." She smiled, ecstatic enough to feel silly. "The cab, not the baby."

He rolled his eyes at her joke. "Good."

"Prue wants me to help her with sales and promotion. I think I might enjoy that. And it'd be easier to do with a baby around than law school."

He kissed her gently. "That sounds like a plan. I hope I haven't just made an enemy of your brother-in-law."

"You haven't. I always thought he was great. But, Prue…well, that's another story."

"Okay. Want to go back in and have breakfast?"

She kissed him back. "Can I tell you that I love you first?"

He pulled her into his lap. "I guess that'd be all right. But I'm feeling besieged after the events of this morning. Make it clear."

She made a valiant effort.

When they finally got to their feet and started back toward the restaurant arm in arm, she saw that half the people in it had come out to see what happened. Clearly pleased with the outcome, the crowd now hurried back inside to their food.

Her mother and sister and Jeffrey stood in a little knot near Jeffrey's car.

"I didn't know you were here," she said as they approached.

"We weren't," Camille replied, smiling at their obvious reconciliation. "Rita called Addy who called me to tell me the two of you were having it out in the parking lot. So we came down."

Paris turned to Randy in disbelief. "The beauty and the bane of life in a small town," he said, pointing to the Wonders and Gideon, who'd apparently been standing with the crowd and now came toward them.

Deliriously happy, Paris reached up for Randy's kiss, and as their lips met, she heard her sister's strangled gasp.

"Gideon!" she exclaimed.

"Hello, Prue," he said.

"Oh, oh," Paris whispered to Randy.

"What?" he asked, following the direction of her gaze.

"Confrontation. My sister and her ex-husband. He's here to talk about their breakup."

He turned her face away from them and looked into her eyes. "I'm tired of confrontation. They're adults—they'll settle it. But we're together. Can we just concentrate on that—maybe plan a future over sausage and eggs?"

When she looked doubtfully in the direction of her sister, he cajoled her with, "And you don't have to have oatmeal this morning. Fashion show's over."

A little light went on inside her. She could have real food. But her efforts at being healthy had taken root and she didn't want to abandon them completely, particularly now that another little life depended upon her.

"An egg-substitute omelette," Randy suggested, reading her mind. "With spinach and Swiss cheese?"

She wrapped her arm around the back of his waist, thinking what a harbor he was in a life that had once felt so adrift. "That would be the perfect compromise."

"Hey." He hugged her to him and started for the restaurant. "We're getting good at it."

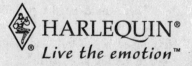

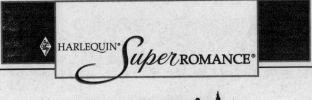

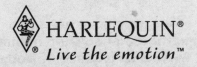

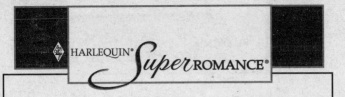

HARLEQUIN® *Super*ROMANCE®

Crystal Creek
TEXAS

If this is your first visit to the friendly ranching town located in the Texas Hill Country, get ready to meet some unforgettable people. If you've been here before, you'll recognize old friends… and make some new ones.

Home to Texas
by Bethany Campbell
(Harlequin Superromance #1181)
On sale January 2004

Tara Hastings and her young son have moved to Crystal Creek to get a fresh start. Tara is excited about renovating an old ranch, but she needs some help. She hires Grady McKinney, a man with wanderlust in his blood, and she gets more than she bargained for when he befriends her son and steals her heart.

Available wherever Harlequin Superromance books are sold.

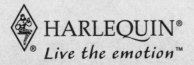

HARLEQUIN®
Live the emotion™

HARLEQUIN Super ROMANCE

The Rancher's Bride
by Barbara McMahon
(Superromance #1179)

On sale January 2004

Brianna Dawson needs to change her life. And for a Madison Avenue ad exec, life doesn't get more different than a cattle ranch in Wyoming. Which is why she gets in her car and drives for a week to accept the proposal of a cowboy she met once a long time ago. What Brianna doesn't know is that the marriage of convenience comes with a serious stipulation—a child by the end of the year.

Getting Married Again
by Melinda Curtis
(Superromance #1187)

On sale February 2004

To Lexie, Jackson's first priority has always been his job. Eight months ago, she surprised him with a divorce—and a final invitation into her bed. Now Jackson has returned from a foreign assignment fighting fires in Russia and Lexie's got a bigger surprise for him—she's pregnant. Will he be here for her this time, just when she needs him the most?

Available wherever Harlequin books are sold.

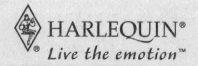

HARLEQUIN®
Live the emotion™

Visit us at www.eHarlequin.com

HSR9MLJ